ALL THE QUEENS' CURSES

Praise for *All the Queens' Curses*

'This whimsical fantasy combines a beloved lesser-known fairy tale with Scottish folklore in a beautiful celebration of sisterhood, true love, and embracing ourselves inside and out.'

Marissa Meyer, #1 *New York Times* bestselling author of *Cinder*

'Steeped in curses, magic, trickery, and featuring a very good dog, *All the Queens' Curses* has all the makings of a great fairytale. A beautiful portrayal of resilience and sisterly love.'

Ann Sei Lin, author of *Rebel Skies*

'Brimming with magic and fairytale-like wonder, *All the Queens' Curses* is a tender portrayal of disability, sisterhood, and healing ... the story was handled with thoughtfulness and discernment that truly shone through every page. I'm eager to read whatever Hollingsworth writes next!'

Kalie Reid, author of *The Sacred Space Between*

'A remarkable blend of history and fairytale. We venture into worlds that are sometimes dark and cruel, sometimes dazzling and wondrous. But the true message comes in what remains unspoken.'

Juliet Marillier, winner of the World Fantasy Award Life Achievement 2025

'Poignant, heart wrenching and healing all at once, *All the Queens' Curses* is a fairytale of finding strength and resilience in each other, of the quiet power of love and forgiveness, and the serenity of poetic justice.'

Intisar Khanani, author of *Thorn*

'A beautiful retelling of a lesser-known fairy tale about what it costs to break a curse – and who should bear that cost. Themes of abuse and trauma are handled with care, and the relationship between stepsisters is deeply touching. Bonus: there's a very good dog. Reflective, atmospheric and true.'

Joanna Ruth Meyer, author of *While the Dark Remains*

ALL THE QUEENS' CURSES

ALYSSA HOLLINGSWORTH

ROCK THE BOAT

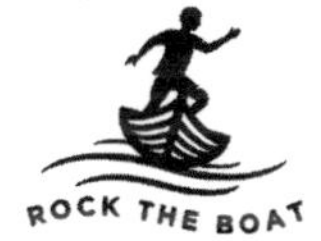

This book contains material that some readers may find distressing, including references to sexual assault as well as depictions of abuse and chronic illness.

A Rock the Boat Book

First published in the United Kingdom, Republic of Ireland and Australia by Rock the Boat, an imprint of Oneworld Publications Ltd, 2026

A CIP record for this title is available from the British Library

ISBN 978-1-83643-287-6
eISBN 978-1-83643-286-9

Typeset by Geethik Technologies
Printed and bound in Great Britain by Clays Ltd, Elcograf S.p.A

The authorised representative in the EEA is eucomply OÜ,
Pärnu mnt 139b–14, 11317 Tallinn, Estonia
(email: hello@eucompliancepartner.com / phone: +33757690241)

Oneworld Publications Ltd
10 Bloomsbury Street
London WC1B 3SR
England

For Megan –
we read, we spoke,
we trekked along the cliffs,
and posed in cloaks.
Who says research
is boring?

ONE

Kit

I open my eyes and study my hand on the pillow beside me. The skin is taut over every joint and heat runs through the muscle. I inhale carefully, concentrating on the soft cotton of the fabric against my cheek, the weight and warmth of my blankets.

Then I bend my fingers.

The joints catch in three of them, and I swear I can feel bones scraping bones. Pain explodes—but then something slides and pops and I can move freely again. Or, freer, at least. The pain recedes to an ache that hums in the back of my head, where I don't have to pay it attention.

I release my breath, and it mists in the air above me. The fire died long ago, and I've told the maids to use their time on more important rooms this morning—after all, the king and princes from the Islands of Skyare are visiting.

I hadn't considered what the cold might do to my bones. Last year, it wasn't so bad. And none of this had been a problem in the winters before my mother's second marriage. My stomach shrinks at the thought of the dark months ahead.

"Bear what must be borne," I whisper. My mother's family saying sounds empty in the frigid room. But I have no time to lie here fretting.

Setting my jaw, I dart free of my bed in a rush. The thin carpet does nothing to protect my feet from the freezing flagstones, and I'm halfway to my wardrobe when my body starts tightening in protest. My pace slows and a slithering discomfort rises up my legs. I grit through it, blindly yanking on my working outfit: chemise and stays and petticoat and, finally, a wool dress in a color somewhere between gray and green. I fumble as I tie the apron round my waist—my fingers don't want to bend with the deft ease they once did—then slide my arms into my warmest pelisse and twist my long hair into a bun at the base of my neck. I cover this with a simple bonnet and pull on my boots. I'm ready.

This early, our guests won't be up, and I can help with the chores before anyone would suspect a princess to have left her room.

I'm still not used to being a princess. I'm not sure I'll ever be.

In the hall beyond my door, the floor creaks. I freeze in the middle of tying the bonnet's ribbon under my chin. I am all listening, all hearing. I wait.

There is not another sound.

Not footsteps. Not him.

I breathe slowly. My joints pinch as I finish the bow. He hasn't come for me here before, but…

When I open my door, I keep the gap narrow. No movement outside. Phantom sounds aren't unusual in this old castle, but my body doesn't care for logic just now. I release the door and tap my fingertips against my collarbone. *I'm all right. I'm all right.* Somehow, the solidness of the beat makes my faltering heart steady. I slip into the hallway.

Catharine's door is closed across from mine. Normally she would meet me and help with the morning tasks, for all she's the one born into royalty, but today there is no sign of her. The fear still coils round my lungs and I take a step toward her door. If she is with me, he won't come.

But even though her father made me leave before our guests' arrival last night, I know Catharine stayed up late to greet them, and she'll be up late again tonight dancing. I'd rather she sleep.

I lift my chin and tap my collarbone a few more times as I walk on. It feels good to move.

Down in the kitchens, I grab grains for the chickens and a basket for eggs. The sleepy cook gives me a nod, leaning over a pot of boiling water.

"We appreciate it, Princess Kit, but you know your mother..." he starts to say, but is interrupted by an involuntary yawn.

"We need all the hands we have," I reply, pushing the door with my back. The cold wind knifes through the opening, searching out any gap in my clothes. "Besides, who *wouldn't* want to take in such glorious weather!"

Cook waves me out. "Very well, then, off with you before everything turns to ice!"

I grin and duck into the open. The wind slams the door shut behind me. I cross the wide area at the front of the castle and reach the cover of the castle walls. Immediately, the air becomes placid and calm. I rub my streaming eyes with my sleeves and say a silent prayer of thanks for thick, sturdy stone.

The chickens clatter when I reach their coop. I toss enough feed to distract them, then snatch the warm eggs from their nests. Once I've collected them all, I linger to scatter more seed.

My gaze wanders to the castle. From here, I have a good view of the back. The guest suites are above me to the right, and I'm just wondering about the princes inside when a window latch clangs and someone pushes the pane open, scattering shards of ice down the wall. Startled, I duck into the shadows.

A young man leans out into the cold, his arms resting on the casement. The first hint of dawn has begun to turn the sky a gentle velvet, and I can see him clearly: dark hair in a tangle of curls, white shirt creased, and collar undone. The tanned hue of his skin looks more gray than warm, though I think that must be due to the low light. His shoulders lift and fall with a deep breath.

Something jabs my foot and I jump, even though my boots keep it from hurting. While I was distracted, I dropped feed on my skirt's hem and the hens have come after it. I shift away, trying to keep quiet, trying not to draw the young man's attention. I back into the door of the coop, but I can't stop watching him. For all Catharine would scold me—the man's barely dressed, honestly—there is something desperate and familiar in the way he turns his face into the sharp cut of the wind.

He must be one of the princes. The older, Idris, if the descriptions I've heard are right. The one whose birthday we will celebrate later. I wonder what brought him to the window so early. A dream? A nightmare?

Or maybe they rise at this time for the tides, I tell myself practically.

While he stays, I stay. It's odd, but somehow I feel I must—I feel he should not be alone. Even if he does not know I'm here.

A dog's nose creeps up by his elbow, sniffing, and he shifts as a great beast of a hound puts its paws on the sill to stand beside him. The prince rubs his face with both hands and tousles the dog's ears before he steps back. The dog looks right at me—or at the chickens—before it hops down again. The prince pulls the window closed.

I breathe again—had I stopped? My hands are cold round the basket. My fingers, stiff. I stretch them, one by one, and shake off the inexplicable shroud that's fallen on me. I have duties to do. I don't have time for princes.

It's nearly eight by the time I dart back up to my room to change for the day. When I come to my door, it is cracked open. I tense.

If my mother is within, she'll know I was working and I'll be in for a severe scolding.

If *he* is within…

My arms shake as I touch the latch. The door swings wider and shows—Catharine. Just Catharine. Dressed in her fine white muslins and wrapped in her intricate plum shawl, she kneels on the hearth and coaxes a fire to life.

"Catharine!" I hurry in and shut my door, just in case my mother *does* come down the hall. "You'll ruin that skirt!"

Catharine looks, laughing, over her shoulder. "Ah, well. Maybe next time you won't sneak off without me."

I'm drawn to the fireside, my bones still icy, but when I offer Catharine a hand up, she tugs me to the floor beside her. The stone isn't so cold now, but I scoot closer to the heat anyway.

"You promised we would split the chores," Catharine goes on. "You're not supposed to let me sleep in."

"These are special circumstances." I unbutton my pelisse and tug off my bonnet. "You're supposed to be charming a ring out of the prince's pocket."

Catharine shakes her head. "My father dreams."

I glance at my stepsister—fresh as the world's first morning, the fire's glow bringing a healthy flush to her cheeks, dark ringlets framing pale skin—and wonder for the thousandth time how she can be so unaware of her own beauty. When we first met four years ago, I thought she only pretended to be modest. But time has taught me that there is no one more guileless. She can pretend at nothing, even if she tries.

At least, not to me. To the public, she might seem almost too well-mannered, but sitting shoulder to shoulder with her, I know she has only spoken what she believes is true.

"Well, what about our visiting royals?" I ask, thinking of the young man at the window. "Did one of them catch your eye?"

"They're both very kind," she replies. "Prince Abram was rather quiet, but I think maybe he was only tired or shy. Prince Idris has a rather…large…hound." Her lips twist a little in an attempt at a smile. Catharine has not particularly liked dogs since an incident involving the hunting hounds and her childhood pet, a rabbit. With forced cheerfulness she adds, "He's trained it to bow in greeting. Isn't that sweet?"

So I had seen Prince Idris.

Catharine shifts on the hard floor and I poke her in the arm. "Come, the room's warm enough now. Get comfortable. I need to dress."

Catharine gets to her feet and stretches. She plops into my reading chair nearby. I lean forward to add a handful of peat to the fire.

A cold draft hits my back and I turn to find my mother in the doorway. Her face is already fixed in a scowl. I see the room as she must: Here is Catharine, pampered and lovely and lounging in my chair, and me still plain as a servant and knelt over the fire.

"Mother!" My voice comes out more startled and guilty than I'd like. I scramble to my feet.

Catharine rises, too, though with considerably more grace. She drops a curtsy. "Your Majesty."

My mother's look could pierce armor. "Catharine, I couldn't help but notice last night that your sleeve had a tear at the shoulder. I've had the gown laid out in your room and I expect you to mend it before you come downstairs."

"Yes, Your Majesty." Catharine curtsies again, glances at me, and steps toward the hall. My mother barely moves out of the way, so Catharine has to twist to get past.

Once Catharine is gone, Mother turns her full attention to me. Her gaze softens, though her blue eyes still simmer with frustration. My mother is a beauty—skin like moonlight and hair like a raven's feathers. Unfortunately, I took after my father—prone to freckle under the dimmest sunlight, with hair somewhere between brown and blonde, and eyes a murky hazel. I'm never entirely sure if my mother pities me for this, or if she blames me.

Her eyebrows lower. "Why are you dressed like that?"

"I couldn't decide what to wear," I lie. "I asked Catharine to help me pick an outfit. I just pulled this on so I could cross the hall without being in my robe, since we have guests."

"It would be worse if they saw you like this," my mother scolds.

Worse to see me in humble clothes—the sort I might have worn any time before her marriage—than undressed? I close my mouth over the question. Perhaps I'm not one to judge, considering I watched Prince Idris when I ought to have blushed and shielded my eyes.

Mother strides to my wardrobe. She emerges with one of my better white morning gowns, with full sleeves in the latest fashion, and adds an emerald sash.

"This," she commands. "Even if you are not introduced until the ball, it doesn't hurt to look your best in case they catch a glimpse of you."

I begin to disrobe without answering. As Mother lifts my simple gown off me, she tuts and continues talking almost to herself.

"I do wish you would see the tailors when Catharine does. You don't have enough gowns to suit your status as a princess of Aberloche."

I don't answer. We both know that my stepfather, King Byrne, has a habit of sending me on errands whenever it would give Catharine an opportunity for more: more attention, more to spend, more to impress. The sash is from Catharine, in fact—she has taken to asking for clothing specifically to find it "not to her taste" and gift it to me.

"It's just as well the princes stay only a week," Mother goes on, looking back at my wardrobe. "You don't have enough to be presented much longer than that."

Mother steps nearer to ease the new dress over my head, and I remember the before times—when we lived in my father's house, and he was returning from some court case or another, and we helped each other dress in our finest. The way Mother used to let me braid her hair, even though it would fall out by the time he walked through the door. Not that he minded. His smile was always wide, and when he embraced me, I felt nothing but joy.

"I wish you would do your best with the princes," Mother says as she ties the back of my dress. "This is not an opportunity for Catharine only."

"I don't know that anyone will notice me," I reply honestly.

Mother's tone becomes sharp. "There are two princes. Why shouldn't one of them favor you?"

"Why *should* they?" I ask

My right pointer finger aches and I massage the swollen joint. I think of the twisted hands of old women, the creak and click of my bones even on a good day. I think of the way even footsteps in the hallway can make me freeze with fear. Who would want that for a bride?

Mother moves in front of me and cups my hands with surprising gentleness, as if I were a frail bird. My throat tightens unexpectedly.

Almost to herself, she whispers, "I must get you free of this."

My voice comes too sudden, too alarmed. "Free of what?"

She does not answer immediately, her lips compressed in consideration. At last, she says, "The women of our family carry a curse, of sorts." She closes my hand between her two perfect ones. "When we are hurt, we become ill."

My heart slows. She does not ask if I have been hurt. I do not say.

I wonder how long she has known. How she discovered it. Whether I revealed it in my fear or whether King Byrne's gloating gave it away. Why she hasn't done anything about it.

But then, what can anyone do against a king?

But I do not ask. She does not say.

"My mother suffered as you do."

I glance up. I knew my father's mother: She taught me to gather from the fields and tend fevers and tap away my fears. But I never met my mother's mother, never heard a single story about her.

"Well, not exactly," Mother amends. "But her sister was endlessly cruel—tormenting her with impossible tasks, keeping food and drink from her when she could not finish them. Beating her, even. And your grandmother became ill with a wasting sickness."

A tremble runs through me. Am I wasting? Are my hands the first signs?

"Later in her life, after everyone considered her a spinster, my mother escaped through her marriage," Mother says softly. "She escaped and had me, and for a time she seemed stronger. But the wasting returned, and even with all the food and water and love Father could give her, she became no more than skin stretched over bone."

I swallow on a dry throat. I had not considered that the pain in my hands, the weakness in my fingers, might be the first sign of something permanent. Something worse.

"She thirsted. Always. No matter how much she drank." My mother's voice grows pained. "Eventually, she did not rise from her bed. Never did again." Her grip on me tightens, and her tone grows stony. "It was her sister's doing. Though years had passed, her sister's cruelty killed her."

I had not thought that my pain might never end, that it would only grow worse until it claimed me. Tears prick my eyes, but I wrap my heart in numbness before they fall.

I don't know, I tell myself firmly. *I don't know if that will be my fate.*

"Her *sister* should have been the one to bear it," my mother whispers.

In her eyes is the anger I saw when she opened the door, when she saw me kneeling before the fireplace while Catharine sat comfortable in my chair.

"Catharine has never harmed me," I interject, pushing away my distress. "She would never."

"But you reap pain." Mother's voice hardens. "She reaps fortune."

I jerk my hands away. "This isn't her fault."

I do not say whose fault it is. My mother does not ask.

"All I want is for you to be safe." Her lips tremble. "If you can get out sooner than my mother, you might not share the same fate."

My heart tears, fear on one side and a stinging love on the other. I want to curl into my mother's arms, shrink to the size of a child and curl myself onto her lap. I want her to stroke my hair and run her fingertips down my back, to murmur comfort until all of this fades to a dream. I wonder what she would do if I asked for comfort—I wonder if she would welcome or chide me. I hope she would cover me, protect me, keep me. But if I fold now, I'm not sure I'll ever be able to stand again.

There is a blackness in me that needs to be carved by freezing winds, that needs to lean into the gale of sunrise, the way the prince did this morning. And maybe if it cut sharp enough, deep enough, all this terror would drain out.

My thoughts have tangled, and I cast wildly for a way to pull myself back into this room, this moment. My fingers find my collarbone and I tap a few times.

"I have thought of an idea," my mother whispers. "But the hedgewitch wasn't powerful enough."

Hedgewitch? I think she must mean the strange woman at the edge of the next village who soothes children's colds with herbs and claims to read a woman's fertility in bone dice. If my practical mother has gone so far as seeking aid from a folk healer, she must truly be desperate.

"Well, if we are reaching for magic, maybe I *will* marry one of the princes," I say in a fragile jovial tone. "Get out the way my grandmother did, and sooner."

I mean it as a joke, but Mother steps close and presses a firm kiss on my forehead.

"Yes," she says. "I *will* see you married and cared for. I swear it."

There is a vow in her voice—a fervent promise that considers no cost too great.

But somehow it only makes my fear grow.

TWO

Idris

No one could contest it: King Byrne's ballroom is far grander than our own.

Three hours into my eighteenth-birthday celebration, I still cannot stop gawking at the number of windows and the vibrant color of the tapestries. Even the wine is a better quality than at home. I've sampled thoroughly just to be certain.

"You might want to try some of this, brother," says a voice at my elbow. Abram holds a glass of water under my nose. "It's not even midnight yet."

I roll my eyes but take the glass. Somehow I've ended up on the edge of the room, without a partner or a delegate to engage me. In the unexpected pause, an image rises in my mind: vivid darkness and the hot bite of iron. I've worked hard all day to put aside the nightmare that woke me early this morning, but it returns every time I am still. It keeps coming, and each time heavier, even though the details of the dream have become muddled.

Trying to chase the dread away, I gulp the water. It tastes like fresh snowmelt—crisp and cold. How is even their water better than ours?

"I take back all my complaining," I say, drinking more. "Father was absolutely right to drag us to another country for my eighteenth."

"I guess we've solved the mystery of why a foreign king would go to all this trouble." Abram nods toward the king's daughter, currently joining hands with a man who stares so openly that he trips over his feet.

I keep my thoughts to myself. I've never been troubled about why King Byrne would be quick to host us—he's been angling for a match between me and Princess Catharine since I attended his second wedding four years ago. His people have ruled this region for a thousand years, though mine only came to power a few centuries back. We were humble fishermen while his grandsires waged wars. But though he has the finer palace, the better lineage, we have the trade routes—connections to every ship crossing the Terallic Sea. With land traders opting for roads farther south, he will soon find this sort of extravagant living far beyond his reach. Unless he can make an alliance.

No, I'd never been particularly curious as to why *he* would want us here. What always confused me was how fast Father agreed—almost the moment the offer was out of the messenger's mouth.

I glance over the ballroom, wondering where my old man has gone. He's on the far side, head turned toward a modern brass-and-walnut clock, and then he looks around—apparently for me, because once our gazes meet across the room he starts walking my way.

The music ends and King Byrne steps into the circle of revelers to take his daughter's hand. He, too, searches the crowd, sees me, and makes his way over. He's closer than my father.

"Well, that's my exit," Abram says.

I gulp the last of the water and give him my glass. "Please don't go and sit with the old men, *little* brother. You could easily be dancing yourself."

"No, thank you!" He slaps me on the shoulder and grins. "I'd much rather be talking with the dusty councilmen."

He melts into the crowd before I can argue. I exhale. Abram can never stand too much merriment. To those who don't know him, he might easily be mistaken for dull and humorless. But I've seen him make ridiculous costumes for my dog from discarded clothes, rally the staff's children into a fierce snowball fight, and more than once I've opened my notes in council to find he's left cartoonish doodles of the members.

Of course, everyone thinks all that was me. *Idris, please stop dressing up your dog like your father. Idris, you shouldn't excite the children. Idris, it's disrespectful to draw caricatures of the nobles.*

And every time I nod and apologize. Abram shrinks under even the hint of disapproval, and if he had to bear the price of his pranks—small as it is—he might truly turn into a dusty old gentleman overnight. The scolding I receive is hardly anything, and in return I have a brother who comes alive, if only around me.

"I hope you are enjoying yourself, prince."

I pull my thoughts back and find that King Byrne is already in front of me, Princess Catharine on his arm.

"Immensely." I take the hint of expectation in his look and tilt my head toward Catharine. "I hope this means you have no partner for the next dance?"

She opens her mouth, but her father answers for her. "She would be honored."

Catharine smiles uncertainly and offers her hand. I take it and lead her out, where we assume our positions on opposing lines of the dance—me with the men, she with the women. Though we've spent dances, conversation, and even a formal dinner together, the sight of her is almost as bewildering as her family's aged wine. Her hair is an impossible black, startling against the sea-foam white of her skin. Her eyes, when she glances at me shyly, are a silver brighter than the simple circlet on her head. A silver like... fish scales.

Fish scales? I try to shake my thoughts into order. *Abram was right, I need to keep a closer count of my cups.*

The music starts and we pay honors in a bow and a curtsy, respectively. We step together and turn a full circle. I take the opportunity to ask, "Did you really not have another partner?"

"My father is a bit...over-keen for, ah..." She doesn't finish with the words *a match between us*, but her blush betrays her thoughts.

"Don't worry—mine is a little *over keen* about everything," I say, and she smiles.

We move down the line of the dance, me teasing and her with an ever-present smile. Her every movement is graceful but almost timid. Sweet and friendly but cautious. She strikes me as someone born for political friendships, but whose heart would not be easily touched.

The dance brings us sometimes together, sometimes apart, and as I wait for my next chance to take her hand I glance idly behind her. My father stands farther back in the crowd, being talked at by one of the nobles, but he stares at me and then glances at the clock again. His jaw tightens.

Perhaps he's annoyed I'm not making more of this opportunity? Catharine would be a good match for many reasons, and I don't plan to object to an arrangement. Yet she seems to me untouchable. I'd like to surprise that polite smile into an unguarded grin. I wonder if she snorts when she laughs, or if she ever gets food stuck in her teeth. She must sometimes, I suppose, since she's human, but it's hard to remember that when her wrist turns like an ethereal willow branch and her eyes shine like silver as she faces me.

We join hands again and step close, looking at each other through the window of our arms. The serenity of this dance certainly shows her to advantage, but I wonder…

"Do you like jigs?" I blurt.

She blinks and pauses, as if trying to find the answer I want in my face. "I like all dances."

"I prefer the faster stuff," I admit. "There's nothing like the energy of it—you should end a dance breathless and dizzy. I wonder if the next one will be livelier."

As if on cue, our current tune ends. Catharine looks toward the musicians in their booth. "Well, let's see."

Movement snags my attention—my father coming to the edge of the dancers but not quite stepping out. His expression is hard to read. Expectant? Nervous? Likely hoping I won't waste this chance to take a turn with Catharine again.

Sure enough, the rapid notes from a fiddle and quickened tempo of a drum marks the start of "St. Ramble and the Hidden Folk."

"There you have it," Catharine says, smiling at me.

I lift her hand between us. "Can I steal you for one more, then?"

She lowers her voice conspiratorially. "I'm sure my father expects no less."

As it turns out, Catharine is very good at a jig—though rather too precise in her steps, maybe. She smiles, but her eyebrows are knit with concentration. She is more well-schooled than wild. Which is a pity, but perhaps something I could tease out with time.

But these observations take me only the first rotation to make—and after that, I am lost to the music. My blood pumps to the beat. The turn and turn of it spins the room delightfully and my feet barely seem to touch the floor. When the fiddle reaches its fastest, I am all impulse and motion like a river, a bolt of lightning, a gale. A laugh bursts out of me. I can't quite stop once it starts and I'm wonderfully breathless when the musicians hit their last note.

Then I am back in the ballroom, surrounded by civilized people who seem remarkably calm and held together. Catharine gives me a refined smile and sweeps a deep curtsy. I manage to bow in return. Unlike the dance, this movement feels stiff and formal. My spirit settles back into my body, and for a moment I wish I didn't have to go back to playing prince.

I begin to thank Catharine, but before I can finish someone lays a hand on my arm. I turn to find my father beside me.

"Come, I need you for a few minutes," he says. His face is strangely pale. When he nods an apology to Catharine, the gesture is tight with unease.

I excuse myself and let him lead me away, wondering if I've done something to upset him. I talked to Catharine and danced with her twice, so surely it isn't that? Or maybe Father caught word that I'd been complaining about coming here in the first place, though I've only really expressed my frustration to Abram.

Father takes me down the hall and ducks into a side room. Books line the walls floor to ceiling. A library. Abram would like it. A large wooden clock is tucked by the door, and the thud of its second hand dominates the space. The fire has been lit, but the air feels much cooler than in the ballroom. I shiver despite my formal coat.

"To what do I owe the pleasure of a conference?" I ask cheerily. Music for the next dance echoes down the hallway. Not a jig, but there might be another after this one.

Father clasps his hands behind his back and studies the floor, his jaw tight. Something in his seriousness makes me shiver again.

"Has something happened?" I swallow. When had I last seen Abram? Not for nearly half an hour now. He isn't one to get into scrapes, but… "Is Abram all right?"

"What? Yes." Father waves aside the question. "Do you remember when I told you there would be an…event on your eighteenth birthday?"

I cock my head and glance toward the door. "Er, yes? We…are at it?"

"No, not a party." Father scratches his beard like he does when he's irritated with me. "Something else. I wanted to tell you more but…"

His gaze strays to the clock behind me. I look over my shoulder. Five minutes to midnight.

"I thought," Father continues, "perhaps, coming this far—you might be spared. However, I don't know what kind of distance they will travel. But if you're asked, I want you to say no."

I blink, my attention back on him. "Huh?"

He shakes his head. He won't look at me now. "I can't reveal more. But it has been this way for a long time now. Simply say 'no' and return to the party."

"I don't…"

The second hand thrums behind me. Has it grown louder? Father nudges me toward a door that leads outside.

"Go for a walk," he says. "If they have come this far, they will find you. They won't harm you if you say no. Return as soon as it's done."

I take a slow step toward the door. "I don't understand. Who—"

"It's better to wait outside." He nudges me again. "If you are in the ballroom, they will make a spectacle of it."

His prodding is now nearly a push, so I step outside. The temperature drops perilously.

"I hope you meet no one tonight," Father says, his hand on the door's latch, "but if you must—I won't have it be in front of all these people."

He shuts the door before I can speak. I'm in the gardens, though I know it more by the smell of leaves than the shadowy shapes of bushes. Candles in glass jars have been placed along a paved path, but they barely do anything against the night.

Out here, only fragments of the loudest or highest notes of music drift through the dark. I hesitate, perplexed, then reach toward the door. I'm not prone to fevers, but even I know better than to stand in a frosted garden with sweat still drying on my back.

The clock inside the library begins to strike midnight, and my hand stops just above the latch. An unexpected dread holds me there. Each clang of the bell thuds in beat with my heart, louder and louder. *Ten…eleven…twelve…*

"Oh, he brought you out here," says a voice behind me. "Pity."

I turn. The air has grown thick and heavy, so that I can only move with effort. A young man stands behind me. He is exactly my height, with youthful features—perhaps only fifteen. In the faint candlelight and against his dark skin, his eyes shine unnaturally bright, the glowing orange of a harvest moon.

"Um," is my astute reply.

"Yes, quite." He sighs and waves away his disappointment. "Well, I see the promise has been kept: You have been warned but given no details. Your father plays close to the breaking of his word. However, I will not hold this to his account." His uncanny eyes flick over me, becoming calculating and curious. "Or, rather, yours."

"You know my father?" I ask, crossing my arms for warmth. My breath mists in the air.

"I've known all the men of your family, back to your great-great-grandfather."

The young man's words make no cloud. He smiles with gleaming teeth.

I open and close my mouth. Not a single wrinkle mars his face, but the telling tilt of his chin makes me suddenly feel I am a boy standing before a mountain. This man isn't young—he is *ageless.* My mind runs through the shanties, folktales, pub gossip. Stories of magical beings. They stretch back even farther than the times of my great-great-grandfather Mervyn and his impossible tasks.

There is a very slight point to the tip of this stranger's ears. His clothes have a scaly glimmer to them in the faint light. When a gust of wind hits us, the salt-sweet tang of the North Sea rolls off him as if I stood now on its jagged shores.

The sea-dwellers. Tide-walkers. Hidden Folk.

"You're catching on now. Good." The man—the Hidden One—places one hand over his chest. "You may call me Speir. I have come with a tale and a question. You must listen to both and give an answer."

I open my mouth to speak, but Speir reaches toward my lips. Rather than touch me, he gathers the frozen mist of my breath from the air. It wisps after his fingers like spiderweb, and he paints it into a circle between us. My frozen breath turns solid. A mirror. Frost shoots across the surface, reflecting my face in a thousand splintered duplicates.

Then my image fades, and instead there is a man with the same dark and curling hair as me turning from a forge.

Red light cuts his features into sharp angles, but I recognize the arc of his nose and the line of his jaw. He looks like my father. Like Abram.

Like me.

Part of me wants to pull back, to turn my gaze away from the magic, but curiosity holds me in place. How do I know this man in the vision—and how does Speir?

In the image before me, the man lifts something from the fire and strikes it with a hammer. The sudden sparks and crash make me flinch. I feel the sound deep inside me, behind my eyes, as if I were remembering rather than hearing. The scene seems to surround me and the heat of the fire raises the hairs on my arms.

"You'll not change your mind?" the man says over his shoulder.

A woman's voice answers, "You have a bonny face but a rancid soul, Mervyn Walker."

A bolt of cold surprise goes through me. Mervyn Walker—my great-great-grandfather.

She hisses, "You will rue this day."

"Oh?" He adjusts his lump of blazing iron. "And when will I rue it, little dancer?"

"In the time of your sons, and their sons." I cannot see her, but it's as if we're the same person, inhabiting the same space.

"That doesn't seem like my problem." Mervyn examines his work. The iron lump pulses golden-white with heat. He holds it with long tongs. "My problem is much more immediate, and you've set me behind."

"I have only said 'no,'" she replies. Though her voice stays even, I feel her pounding heart in my chest.

Something pricks through the air. I think it is the heat of the furnace turning everything to fire. "Perhaps the next time you need a wife in a hurry, you will not begin with violence."

"I have harmed no one." With his spare hand, he lifts a silver seal skin from the ground and shakes it in front of her. Her pulse in mine quickens with a longing so strong it sears. "I took what you left unguarded, and *you* are the one who does not honor the old ways."

"The old ways?" she hisses between gritted teeth. She draws herself up, straightening like a queen on the rickety board. "Let us see whom the old ways honor. I curse you, you and every son you sire, and every son he sires. All you do to me will be etched in their blood. One day the cost will be paid and I will claim my dancing days back."

Mervyn's expression is unconcerned as she speaks. But with her last word, a gust of wind hits the forge with such force the building shakes. A window shatters and the cold, salty air floods in like a riptide, stealing all light and warmth from the room. Mervyn falters, his face white. It strikes me that he is young—only twenty, maybe.

Her life stretches centuries, back before the first man set foot on her islands. Mervyn is a child to her. A dangerous, cruel child.

"Selfish fool," she sneers. "But see here, I will give your children something you haven't given me. Not because you deserve mercy, but because *I* am not a filthy thief." She spits on the ground. "They will have a choice."

Mervyn's expression hardens. In the pale light, he looks nearly corpselike.

"Give me back my skin," she says. "Save your descendants."

"As I said before—" Mervyn tosses the skin onto the dirty floor—"that doesn't sound like my problem."

She whispers a word even I cannot hear. White mist swirls around Mervyn. He steps back, closer to the forge, but she sees him involuntarily inhale, and she knows. The curse has set. A moment later, the red glow of the fire returns. The room is a normal forge again, albeit colder for the broken window.

Mervyn shakes his shoulders the way a dog might shrug off rain. With a final look over his work, he pulls it from the fire. Heat ripples in the air around the lump of iron. He kneels, and I see her feet—bare and small—her legs bound at the knee.

"I made my claim fairly," he says. "For all you say men take, do note that *I* am not forcing your hand."

She says nothing. The twinge of discomfort has morphed into a radiating pain, like sparks sizzling across her skin. It isn't from the heat, I realize. It's from the iron.

The Hidden Folk cannot stand the touch of iron.

Mervyn watches her closely. "Very well. Don't marry me, then. But you won't be going back under the sea either."

The metal has cooled to a livid orange and he takes it with a gloved hand. It isn't just a lump. It's a boot.

Horror sweats down my back and I try to pull my consciousness free. I don't want to see anymore. But I'm tied to the woman as true as she's tied to the table. "*Let me go,*" I try to say, but her voice shouts it.

He slips the glowing boot over her left foot. She screams, and I scream, and our foot chars and the skin peels and the pain blisters and pops and—

And there is something in her lost now, something that pulled like the tides and roared in her blood like the sea. There is too much hurt to name it.

"*Let me go!*" I try to shout, choking on my raw throat, but her cries drown out my voice.

The scene shimmers, agony-edged, and then I see Mervyn move another iron boot into the fire. He takes nails and a hammer from the table. I cannot pull myself out of this vision. He positions the first nail against the sole of her foot. He strikes.

She—I?—we want to pass out. We want to gnaw our own legs off.

But it doesn't end. Pain beyond pain, burn beyond burn. And we are conscious every moment. The ocean in us recedes, farther and farther, and we are no longer starlight and moon-pull and magic. We are thin skin and broken bones.

My thoughts are soupy and hot when they come back to me. Her tears are salty on my lips. I am looking through her eyes. I am seeing as she sees. Two iron boots nailed into her feet.

"Now your dancing days are done," Mervyn says. "I would have given you a kingdom, but you'd rather drown. So be it."

Frost gathers across the image, and suddenly I am in my own body—my own mind—again. I'm staring at the dark beyond Speir's shoulder. Cold tendrils slink through my clothes and freeze my bones. They sting my lungs after the warmth of the forge. When I exhale, there is only the smallest cloud to testify I still live.

"This is your heritage, prince," Speir says. "The tie that has bound your family to mine. And now that you've seen, I have a question."

My arms shake and my stomach heaves. I press my hand to my abdomen and swallow bile. Echoes of pain still race up from my feet and my knees nearly knock together. I can hardly pay attention to Speir's words.

"This question has been posed to every father and uncle before you, all along the direct line to Mervyn himself." Speir studies me with mild curiosity, as if he anticipates my answer and is already bored by it. "Will you pay the price of the crime?"

My father's order comes back to me and I wet my lips. *No.*

But her screams ring in my head. Her pain howls like a hole in my own chest.

"What happens if I say no?" I ask, breathless.

Speir lifts a hand toward the ballroom windows. "I will ask your brother, come his eighteenth. And then I will ask your son, come his. And one day, the price will be due a hundred times over, and no choice will be given."

Abram. I remember a golden day at the beach. My mother, Abram, and I were trying to dig a hole in the sand so deep we could visit her country on the other side of the globe. "Once we arrive, Idris," she said, blowing hair out of her face and grinning, "I expect you to take care of your brother. The world is wild and strange, and little Abram needs looking after." And though it was all play at the time, her command went straight to my heart. She died soon after, and the command morphed into a sacred vow. I have done everything to shield him from harm. I have given everything so that he could be safe. If he saw this, faced this choice, he would be changed forever. He would become tainted by everything wrong.

Mervyn's words ring in my head: *That doesn't seem like my problem.*

My father believes that. He told me to say no.

But if my mother were alive, and knew what had been asked, and what the cost would be, she would have told me to answer differently.

"What happens if I say yes?" I whisper.

A smile tugs at the corner of Speir's mouth. "You will pay the price of my queen's loss with your life."

My heart thumps, muffled. "I'll die, you mean?"

"No. Well, not as such." He rocks back on his heels. "But you will live out her dancing days, and mortal days are short."

A lumpy weight gathers in the base of my throat. Perhaps it is *no.* But my mouth stays closed.

You always have a choice, my mother says in my mind. I see her as she was when she spoke the words: cuddling a tiny crying Abram to her chest, her dark hair neatly braided against her tanned neck. She waves a stuffed whale toy—one of my old favorites—in front of Abram's face, and his crying calms to coos. *Look how your choice matters.*

Mervyn chose as he did, even knowing others would pay—both his victim and his own family. The choice has come back again and again, and my family has said *no.*

My grandfather, with his stern eyes always turned to the horizon, and my father, who held me as I learned to swim. They said *no* and allowed the crime to bleed across the years.

Hadn't I had a nightmare this morning? A nightmare about heat and hammers?

But it wasn't a nightmare. I see that now. It was a memory. I knew this queen, this Hidden One, in my blood, even before I knew who or what she was to me.

If I say no, I become part of this—this cruelty stretched through generations. I pass it down to Abram.

If I say yes…

"What happens to my family?" I ask.

"The curse would stop with you."

"But if I die," I press on, "what assurance do I have that they'll be safe? That the harm will stay with me?"

Speir touches a hand to his chest. "I give my word, on behalf of my people: You alone would bear the punishment. We have no interest in vengeance, only in justice."

So my family would be protected. And my death—or absence, or whatever would happen—wouldn't leave the throne vulnerable. Abram could make a good king. I wouldn't be betraying my responsibilities; I would only be moving myself out of the way. The cost may be great for me, but I could pay it alone. I could spare everyone following behind me.

Once, many years ago, my father was given this choice. And he chose to give it to me.

But I refuse to give it to Abram.

An undercurrent runs beneath these thoughts, sticky and dark. It is more feeling than phrase, more instinct than language. But I do not want to taste it, whatever it is.

I am done with thinking about it.

"My answer is yes," I say. My voice comes out stronger than I expected. "I'll take the punishment."

Speir stares at me, eyebrows lifted. Then he smiles, teeth white in the darkness. "*Interesting.* Very well. I will return to collect your dues."

"W-when?" I stutter, all my bravado draining away.

"Oh, I would not want to ruin the surprise." He gives me a short bow. "Happy birthday, prince."

"Wait—what about—?" My mind is sluggish and cold. "Aren't you going to forbid me from speaking of it or something?"

Speir laughs, the brief humoring laugh one might give a child when they suggest something ridiculous. "Oh, tell whomever you like. I even release your father from his promise of secrecy. Announce it to everyone you meet. You will find no help."

Then he turns and simply walks away. Doesn't vanish, doesn't drop into the ground. Just strolls into the darkness of the garden.

My legs shake. Iron shoes and screams. A debt to be paid— how, and when, I have no idea. I stumble into the library. The clock ticks—only a minute has passed. Impossible.

The door opens and Abram looks in. "Oh! I didn't expect you to be hiding in here—"

My voice wheezes out of me. I reach for a chair, my legs almost giving way.

"What—Idris!" Abram hurries forward and catches my arm, his eyes wide behind his glasses. "Here—sit, sit. What's wrong? Should I get Father?"

"No," I manage. "Just—some water?"

He grabs a glass and pours from the pitcher left on the writing desk. I drink slowly, using the time to collect my thoughts. If Abram knew everything, he'd carry it, sure as if I'd passed the curse to him. He'd feel it was his fault that I am... whatever I am now. And whatever the inevitable outcome, he'd blame himself. There's no point in telling him. Speir himself said there's no helping me. I chose to bear this—so I'll bear it.

"You all right?" Abram asks, watching me anxiously. "Maybe you should call it a night."

I shake my head. "I'll be fine in a moment. Just got overheated."

"Overheated?" He frowns and touches my forehead. "You're cold as ice."

I knock his hand away gently. "I promise I'm fine, Abe."

The door swings silently open. Father looks in. A prick of concern crosses his face when he sees Abram, but he enters. "Idris?"

I hear the other question in his voice: *Is it done?* And beyond that, my ears still ring with the Hidden One's screams. Father chose pretending, chose ignoring, chose ease at a price he gambled on us. My muscles tense and I stand, though a moment before I didn't think I could. I move between him and Abram.

"I'm fine," I answer, not ready to give him the sign he wants. I'm not sure he deserves to know. It's as if he's an entirely different person to me now—a stranger.

His gaze darts to Abram. He won't ask directly with my brother here.

I put the empty glass aside and throw an arm round Abram's shoulder, pulling him toward the hallway. "Come, brother, the night is still young! I would see you dance."

He grimaces. "I danced earlier."

"What, three times?" I shake my head.

"Are you sure you're feeling well?" He tries to get a look at my face and I force myself to grin harder. "You seem—"

"Of course I'm well. It's my birthday! And you need to put a bit more effort into having fun. Look, I'll introduce you to the prettiest girl here."

Abram groans. "Please don't."

We enter the ballroom, where the party continues as if nothing's happened. To them, I must have been gone only ten minutes or so. The movement and color and voices and music grate against my head, against the image of the iron shoes that flashes in my mind every time I blink. I press on, trying not to remember, and search the faces.

"There." I pull Abram toward Princess Catharine.

He stutters an objection, all but digging in his heels. When she lifts her silver eyes to us, his protests cut abruptly into a stunned silence. I smile and this time it isn't an effort.

"Princess." I bow. "You remember my younger brother, Abram."

She drops an elegant curtsy, almost a dance all its own. When she straightens, she tilts her head to look up at him and her dark curls fall over her nearly bare shoulder. The curve to her mouth is both gracious and kind. "Yes, of course."

"It—yes—you—good evening." Abram makes a too-fast bow. His cheeks darken and he shoots a glare at me.

I cough into my fist. "*Ask.*"

Abram fixes a tight smile on his face and his desire to kick me radiates between us. But he manages, "Princess Catharine, I would—would you—that is, are you free for this next dance?"

"I am, actually." Her gaze flits to me in something like amusement—this time, she is not being stolen away. She lifts her hand, indicating to someone beside her. But my eyes fix on her silver bracelet. As she moves her hand into a shadow, the metal goes dull and plain. Like a chain of iron.

I feel the heat of the furnace all over again. The spark of iron before it even touches my skin. Hear the hammer pound. The screams. My family did that. *My family.*

Princess Catharine is speaking. Something about her sister. The screams swell in my head and I can't breathe. The gaiety around me is too close, too bright, too *wrong* for a world where my own great-great-grandfather nailed shoes into someone's feet. I tear my eyes away from the princess, looking desperately for a way out.

An empty chair. It's on the edge of the older men's card tables. One man lifts his hand to me in greeting, and that's all I need.

"I'm afraid I'm called elsewhere," I say to Catharine and her sister both. "I hope you'll excuse me."

Unsteady in my rush, I make my escape. Dimly, I hear Abram saying something about his friend Jay. Perhaps suggesting him as a partner. It doesn't matter. If I don't sit, I will collapse.

I reach the chair and sink down. The man—I can't place his name—chuckles and claps me on the back, almost spilling me onto the floor.

"Too much to drink, aye?" he says merrily. "Poor bairn. Best let up on the hard stuff or you'll regret it in the morning."

I nod and murmur in agreement. I want to curl over, but I don't. I cover my face with my hands, making myself breathe deeply.

Has the curse started? I can't tell. Perhaps it's only just taking root. Nothing feels right anymore.

THREE

Kit

"Princess." Prince Idris makes a flourishing bow to my stepsister. "You remember my younger brother, Abram."

Catharine replies graciously, and while pleasantries are exchanged I take the chance to study the brothers. I'm surprised to find Abram, the younger, is actually the taller of the two. Prince Idris carries himself with the air of the tallest in the room, but it turns out he's dwarfed next to his quiet brother.

I've lost track of the conversation.

"If I am to dance," Catharine is saying, "I hope my sister could have a partner as well. Prince Idris, are you unengaged?"

I glance aside at Catharine, grateful for her tact. But Idris stares off past both of us. A strange tightness comes into the set of his jaw. It makes me think of this morning and his face turned into the sharp cut of the wind.

"I'm afraid I'm called elsewhere," he says with a sudden exuberance. "I hope you'll excuse me."

Before any of us can react, he takes off toward the far side of the room. He weaves between others in a pitching, unsteady way.

My cheeks flush and I try desperately to school my expression. Such an outright rejection, after he'd clearly been happy with Catharine—it shouldn't surprise me, shouldn't sting, but somehow I still manage to feel hurt.

"Oh," says Catharine softly.

"I have a friend!" Abram interjects. "I mean—I have—several friends, but—I have one named Jay—" He stops and closes his eyes. For a moment, my own mortification eases in light of his. With determined effort, he finishes, "I have a friend named Jay who is probably free right now and would be delighted to dance with you, Princess Kit. I'll just—find him."

Then Abram's gone, too, in another direction. I glance the way Idris went. He's sitting now at a table by the card players, his head in his hands. Maybe he's had too much to drink.

"What a rude thing to do," Catharine whispers to me. "I'm so sorry, Kit. I thought he was nicer than that."

"I think he might be feeling poorly," I reply.

"Well, my father noticed." Catharine lifts her chin to indicate. "He will note the insult."

A coil of unease winds round my lungs. A glance in the direction Catharine motioned is all it takes for me to spot King Byrne, standing with some courtiers, watching us. Watching me? All evening I've felt followed, every step marked. Maybe I've only imagined it—maybe he pays me no more attention than any other guest.

He *is* watching me now, though. And he doesn't look insulted. He looks pleased.

My hands throb and I realize I've clenched them into fists. I pull my gaze away, stretching my fingers one by one. The king has been eager to secure a match between Catharine and Prince Idris. But I wonder for the first time: Is he *not* eager to secure a match for me? Does he intend to keep me here…?

Regardless. Even if *he* doesn't feel an insult in the prince's actions, my mother will. I take a quick look around the ballroom, dread pooling in my stomach. If she saw that Prince Idris wouldn't dance with me, after multiple times with Catharine, I'm not sure what she will do.

But I can't see her anywhere. I don't think she's here at all.

Then where—?

"Here, this is him," says Abram, suddenly returned. "Jay. Um, Mr. Berd."

"Jay Berd?" I blurt, caught by the name.

"My parents have a sense of humor." The young man smiles, apparently unbothered by my lack of poise. Introductions are made. I leave Catharine to Abram and join the dance with my new acquaintance.

Mr. Berd starts a polite conversation, but I can't follow the simple niceties. With every turn, I search the faces for my mother. She certainly isn't here. I can't imagine why she would leave in the middle of such an important event—especially after our conversation earlier. She seemed almost determined to have me proposed to by the end of the evening.

Without her present, I feel King Byrne's gaze more heavily as I dance. The gown that seemed flattering hours ago now hangs too low, the fabric too thin. My shoulders tighten, making the turns awkward and difficult.

Sometimes I spot Prince Idris, still sitting with the old men, now staring into space like he's lost in a dream.

The end of the dance arrives. I realize, too late, that Mr. Berd stopped trying to talk to me some time ago. I muster a smile that doesn't want to come, thank him, and turn to a new partner. I dance again. My mother still has not returned.

Nearly a half an hour from the time I realized she had gone, I see Mother emerge from the west side of the room—the side that leads to the gardens. She smiles a strange, satisfied smile to herself, and when her eyes meet mine it only grows wider. My latest dance ended, I excuse myself from a courtier and go to her.

When I am within reach, Mother places her hands on my shoulders and kisses my forehead. "You look radiant, my dear."

"Where were you?" I ask, and cringe at the childish wobble of my voice. I try again with a more assured tone. "It is too cold to go outside."

"Never mind that." Mother nods toward the dance floor. "I see your stepsister has exchanged one prince for another. She seems determined to flirt with both boys."

I follow her gaze. Catharine still dances with Prince Abram. They seem caught up in a deep conversation. I wonder if Idris will mind, but when I check, he is no longer at the side table. Some partners shift on the floor and I spot him leading a lady through a turn.

Dancing again.

I could be the size of a thimble, for how small I feel. It seems he wasn't ill. Just, perhaps, uninterested in dancing with me.

"He is shallow, like any man," my mother says in my ear. "But we can ensnare him all the same."

I start to ask what she means.

But a distinct pine scent warns me King Byrne is close before he speaks. "How are you tonight, my dear?"

King Byrne touches my mother's arm and I try to breathe. He isn't speaking to me. It feels as if he's staring at me, but I cannot lift my eyes to check.

"Well enough," Mother answers, formal.

Somewhere, a bell tolls a quarter-hour to one o'clock. The current dance ends and the musicians pause to arrange their music. The piece performed on the hour is considered special, and King Byrne has participated in each one—the first with my mother, and then with other honored guests. He chose the briefest earlier in the night to take with Catharine, so she would not be kept from eligible men for long.

As the dancers begin to assemble, King Byrne moves nearer to me. I feel it without turning my head. My bones go cold and I struggle to stutter an excuse to get away, to escape.

"Why don't you have a dance with me, stepdaughter?" he says casually before my incoherent sounds can form a word. "Let's celebrate the new day together."

Mother stiffens. "I think Kit should rest. She has over-exerted herself already."

A spark of hope begins to thaw the ice in me.

"Nonsense." King Byrne takes my hand. Despite his frequent hunts, his skin is smooth. "Kit has had a break while talking to you. I'm sure she's fresh as ever now."

My mind goes blank and quiet, a quiet that lines my insides like a smothering coat. I do not hear if my mother responds. I cannot move my own mouth. I want to flail and scream and bite, but numbness spreads from his touch. The only part of me that lives is my heart, beating louder and louder every moment. My hand looks small and coarse and callused in his. My feet follow his lead without me deciding anything. My body exists very far away.

I am standing opposite him on the dance floor. He has been talking, I think, and I make myself nod. The music begins—at a great distance, almost the next room it seems. A slow piece. A long one. Sweat drips between my shoulder blades. But my muscles move to the rhythm, taking me toward him, lifting my arm and turning me.

"Now, Kit," King Byrne says, his breath on my neck, "a princess should acknowledge a compliment."

I do not remember him giving one. But I fight against the fog in my mind. I must stay alert. "Oh. Thank you."

I retreat to my side of the dancing line again, waiting as he exchanges steps with the girl beside me. My lungs resist when I try to breathe. I must concentrate to expand them, to fill them even halfway. People swirl around me, nearly brushing my arms or skirt. Witnesses. So many eyes. My mother, watching us—she must be, though I cannot lift my head to look. I inhale, slow and deep. *One, two, three, four...* and exhale. I can afford to stay sharp this time.

"What do you think of Catharine and the prince?" King Byrne asks, tone almost gloating, as he returns to me.

I ought to fawn and assure him a proposal from Prince Idris is round the corner. I ought to gush about how he has orchestrated the match perfectly.

But something rises in me. It is much more sick than strength, but it loosens my tongue all the same. "Catharine and *Prince Abram* seem to enjoy each other's company greatly."

King Byrne's jaw tightens just for a moment. I do not lift my eyes higher, but I can imagine his eyebrows drawn into one of his severe frowns.

Then he shakes his head. "She is destined for better than second," he says. "She'll have the heir."

"I don't know whether Catharine favors Prince Idris," I persist, a little curious as to whether Catharine's feelings will move her father. "She seemed displeased with him earlier. She thought him rude."

"To you?" King Byrne's tone lifts. "My dear, one can hardly fault a man for refusing to dance with you, particularly in a room full of such delights."

It doesn't sting, I tell myself, willing it to be true. His words do not sting because they are not true. I know they are not true. Prince Idris was ill. Or, even if he wasn't, there are a thousand other reasons he might be unwilling or unable to dance with me. And, even if there weren't, it wouldn't matter because I don't need a prince as a partner to validate my own worth.

It doesn't sting. It doesn't.

King Byrne crosses with other dancers and I mirror him, weaving between the line of people. His voice carries over the music—pleasant compliments, polite exchanges. I can't seem to say anything. I wish one of the dancers I pass would sense something, would know somehow, would whisper, *Are you all right?*

I focus on their sleeves—the embroidery of the cuff or shirt, the color of the fabric. Green with copper thread. Blue and white.

Am I real? I want to ask them. *Do you see me?*

Then I am back with my stepfather, and I wish I wasn't real or seen or existing at all.

"I know you'll be sorry to lose Catharine," he continues as if we had been in the middle of a friendly conversation. "You two are so close; it's almost as if you were truly kin."

"Not all kin are tied by blood." I draw strength from the crowd of people around me. I lift my chin, but I still can't meet his eyes. "She is my sister more than you are my father."

He tilts his head, stepping near as we turn together. The smell of evergreen nearly overwhelms me.

He says, quietly, "I would not have you for a daughter."

"You won't have me forever," I hiss. I'm shocked at my own words, and then furious with myself for the flood of fear that rushes through me.

"Don't make it a challenge, my dear." His grip tightens on my hand, pressing into the swollen joints, as he lifts my arm. The final turn of the dance. I am so eager to have it over, I follow the steps.

Pain shoots from my wrist, a bolt of burning that goes up to my fingertips and down to my elbow. I bite my lip to stifle a gasp. His grip is too tight—I can't twist the way I'm meant to.

But I'm so near freedom. I push through. My wrist strains, throbs, cracks. He does not lower his arm until I have completed the turn and face him again. His thumb still presses firmly into my palm.

"Perhaps your mother was right," he murmurs. He squeezes my hand and pain needles through my pinched joints. "Perhaps you should rest."

I can't hide my wince. He waits, watching, until I drop a curtsy. Then he finally releases me.

I don't wait for whatever he would say next—I escape.

The crowd crushes round me, as indifferent as a hedge of thorns. Catharine—I search for her among the bodies. She's far away, on the other side of the room, talking with Prince Abram. I move to go to her. I want to bask in her kindness and innocence and I know, I *know*, he won't follow me there. But more people cross between us and there isn't a way through.

That gives me enough pause to find my reason. I've never told Catharine about her father. She loves him, and I did not want to take that away. But even more, I did not want to see if she would choose him.

My breath shudders in my chest. If I go to Catharine now, she will know something is wrong. She would ask, and I wouldn't be able to answer. Especially not here.

A couple on their way to the next dance knock into me, and I stumble aside with a mumbled apology. I can't seem to fix on a destination. The edge of the room? He might follow me. Conversation somewhere? I might suffocate.

An arm slips through mine and Mother is there, guiding me toward an empty space near the grand fireplace. I all but collapse against her.

When we are safely out of the crush, she turns me toward her and tucks back the hair that has fallen behind my ears.

"Let me have a look at you," she says, taking my arm.

When she traces my wrist with careful fingers, I nearly gasp. It pulses with an ache from the joint, right in the center.

"That *damn…*" She closes her lips, tightly. Her face flushes with fury and a storm of curses fills her eyes. She cannot risk being heard. For all Byrne is her husband, he is also the king. And no one sullies a king's name without paying a price.

"It isn't so bad," I find myself saying. I want to cool her anger, contain it.

Mother huffs and searches the crowd. "Where are those blasted servants when you need them?"

We barely had enough staff to cover this ball and no coin in the coffers to give to hired hands. Most of the servants are scattered around the wine and food, assisting guests. Nowhere near us.

"Never mind," Mother goes on briskly. "I'll get some ice myself. Stay here."

My heart quickens.

It must show, because Mother adds, "Byrne is speaking with King Hugh. He won't bother you."

She plants a firm kiss on my forehead and marches off. I swallow and look down at my wrist. Nothing about it seems out of the ordinary from the outside. If I hold still, it only aches dully. I experiment, angling my hand back and curling it forward. The pain snaps into sharp focus and I cradle my arm to my chest.

I should have just answered him the way he wanted. Deferred to him and praised him. He always finds a way to punish any sign of opposition.

It's probably no more than a sprain and will sort itself out in a few days. But my mind still jumps to the conversation I had with Mother this morning. The pain in my wrist isn't so different from the way my fingers feel regularly now.

Has even this small interaction with Byrne made the wasting spread?

"Are you all right?"

I jump at the unexpected voice, sheltering my arm against my chest. Prince Idris stands in front of me, a glass of water in one hand. His gaze drops to my arm.

"A dancing injury?" he asks.

"My…my partner held too tightly," I stutter. We had been formally introduced at the beginning of the evening, but it had felt like being presented to a distracted puppy. And then there was our second meeting only a short while ago, when he seemed to barely see me. With his full attention on me now, I am strangely discomposed. "It isn't bad."

"Not bad?" Prince Idris makes a face. "I sprained my wrist a couple of months ago. Riding accident." He tries to meet my eyes, but I don't raise my gaze quite high enough. Still, I can read his deadly serious expression, as if the next thing he says will be the gravest secret. "It was, without exaggeration, the darkest, most terrible moment in the history of humankind."

I snort, startled, and immediately slap my other hand over my mouth.

His serious expression breaks into a grin. "No, but honestly, it was not good." He tilts his head. "Even though you seem to be more adept at coping with pain, I'd be happy to help if you'd like some relief."

"My mother has gone to get ice," I say.

"Excellent idea. But I know something that can help now."

I am curious despite myself. "Very well."

"The trick is to put pressure on it before the swelling gets bad." He sets the glass of water on a nearby chair. To my surprise, he reaches up to the cravat under his chin and has the knot undone with a twist of his hands. "My friend showed me how to do this so I would be more comfortable riding with the sprain."

He holds out his hand to me. I blink, too startled to speak. I'm struck that he doesn't just grab me.

Hesitantly, I extend my arm. I don't quite touch his palm.

Prince Idris wraps the cloth in a series of crisscrosses round my wrist, up over my palm and thumb, then back round again. The stark, perfect whiteness of the silk contrasts dramatically with the brown skin of his hands. I try not to notice that the cloth still radiates his warmth. My stomach swoops with an emotion I don't recognize. We are close enough that I can smell salt and sweat on him. The ballroom, full of boisterous sound and swirling color, fades to a distant scene. We are our own clearing in the forest—the prince, me, and my fragile bones. When he finishes, the makeshift brace holds me tight and steady.

"How's that?" he asks, poised over the final knot. "Still feel your fingers?"

"I—yes." My face burns. We are back in public. Our fleeting moment might have been something I only imagined.

"Excellent." He finishes the knot and moves back. "Give it a test."

I lift my arm and turn it carefully. I can't move my wrist very much, but it feels more settled. The pain dims.

"There's another benefit, too," he adds, his ever-ready smile flashing again. "Everyone will notice the brace and be extra careful while you wear it. When I was in mine, people would barely shake my hand for fear I'd just fall apart!"

"That could be because you're a prince," I point out, letting my arm drop.

"Maybe. We are liable to break." He smiles, a little tighter than before.

He doesn't point out that I'm a princess, and I remember my own status too late. A princess probably would not consent to wearing a man's cravat as a brace. But then, a prince probably shouldn't offer such an intimate piece of clothing to a woman.

I realize suddenly that he hasn't addressed me like a princess. No bows or formality. Perhaps in his distracted state this evening, he has failed to remember who I am.

It is almost nice, though. Nice that he has spent his kindness on a stranger who could be anybody. Not worthwhile because of her title or her stepsister.

"Well, do you think you'll dance more tonight?" He glances toward the guests. The pale uncertainty of him earlier, when he went to sit with the old men, has faded. He seems just like any boy on the cusp of manhood. Apparently, his state of undress gives him no concern.

A small thrill of pleasure warms me. He's going to ask, I think. But I run my fingers over his makeshift brace and still feel the tender throb in the joint. I shouldn't test my luck. And if I went out with the honored guest of the evening, I would be the center of everyone's attention. I don't want to be watched, just now. I don't want Byrne to notice me.

"I think I shouldn't," I admit.

A pinch of awkwardness twinges between us. I could invite him to sit with me and maybe we could make ourselves a clearing again. Something new flutters in my chest at the thought.

But instead of asking him, I blurt, "It would be a shame for you to sit out on your birthday. Please don't let me keep you. I'll go and busy myself with…the gossip." I want to wince at my inelegance, but the prince doesn't seem to notice it.

"Ha!" He points at my wrist. "You will dominate the conversation now."

"With my injury?" I ask, a flare of panic rising up my throat. Will there be rumors? If anyone suspects Byrne, he will be angry with me—or my mother.

"A prince's cravat," Idris corrects, lifting his eyebrows and giving me an exaggerated wink. "Think of all the stories you could spin!"

The fear melts away and my skin burns. I can't help a surprised laugh. "Wouldn't that be risking both our reputations?"

He snorts. "I can't speak for you, but personally I'd trade my reputation for a great story any day." His gaze catches on something—someone—and I follow his look. Catharine has a new partner now, and she's spinning through the end of a reel with all the grace of a sunbeam across water.

I glance back at Prince Idris. He's at attention, focused and alert.

"Go on, then," I urge, striving to sound light. "Maybe she'll have the next with you."

He shoots me a smile that makes my rib cage feel too small for my heart. Pointing at my wrist, he says, "Keep that elevated tonight, and you'll be good as new in a few days."

Then he's off to my stepsister like an arrow from a bow. As I watch him join her, I wonder if King Byrne is right. Would anyone choose me over Catharine?

FOUR

Idris

The morning after the ball, I sleep late. Abram starts stirring at some point and finally tiptoes out, carrying his shoes, apparently unaware he's already woken me up. I keep my eyes closed and wait to doze off again. My hound, True, lies at the foot of my bed with his head resting on my tired ankles.

But my groggy thoughts turn to the garden, and the memory, and the curse that must be on me by now.

All you do to me will be etched in their blood, she had told Mervyn.

Mortal days are short, Speir had said.

I shake myself and roll out of bed. My father will be on me the moment I emerge. He shadowed me almost all evening, trying to get a moment alone. I would have retired earlier, but I knew he'd be on my heels asking questions I didn't want to answer, so I stayed up and danced until a few hours before dawn, long after he had gone to bed.

True flops to his full length, now that he has the bed to himself, and nearly takes up the entire thing. I pull on my clothes for the day. If I can put off getting caught alone, I might be able to avoid any unpleasant conversations until we're home again. I doubt Father will bring up our family's past in front of our hosts, and I certainly don't intend to.

I don't know what to think of my father, of my entire family. And I know he'll be furious that I said yes. I anticipate raised voices and vigorous scolding. My head aches from the late night and drink. Any kind of confrontation should be avoided at all costs.

"True." I snap my fingers to get his attention.

My Goliath of a dog heaves a sigh and leaves the blankets, trotting after me as I move into the hallway. No one in sight. Good.

I take the hall toward the only exit I've seen, wishing I knew the secret passageways that doubtlessly line these walls. I slow as I come to a place where the hallway joins the Great Hall, motioning with a finger for True to sit. He obeys, ears erect and alert.

My father's voice drifts from inside—his, and King Byrne's. They're talking about the shipment of timber from Byrne's land to ours. Skyare always has a great need for ships and a distinct shortage of trees. I'm well versed in Father's rants about imports and taxes and transportation delays, and from the sound of it he's only about a quarter into explaining the difficulties to King Byrne. Good, that will keep him absorbed for a while. An excellent chance for me to slip by unseen.

I take a breath and hurry past the open door. Their conversation continues, uninterrupted. I look back and realize True, the good dog that he is, has maintained his *sit* command. I open my palm to wordlessly signal he can move, and he trots across to me. The click of his claws on the flagstones seems loud as a trumpet to me. But there is no lull in my father's lecture.

We hurry the rest of the way to the courtyard, which is sheltered by massive stone walls, and then through the grand gate into the open land. Penkirk Castle sits on the edge of an immense brackish loch, surrounded by cloud-cloaked mountains. The ship that we took to get here sits at anchor.

I pull my greatcoat closer and set off in a random direction. The more space between me and my father, the better. The gravel path crunches under my boots.

In the distance, a woman stands on a dock. The still water around her acts like a mirror, reflecting the endless silver of the sky. She wears a dark coat, the only thing that sets her apart from the landscape. From here, I can't tell what she's looking at. The loch dissolves into a curling fog only a few feet beyond her. I find my steps carrying me toward the dock, curious if she can see something I don't. Do the lochs down here hold monsters? Or kelpies? Our lochs only have otters

True lopes ahead, barking in greeting. The woman turns, smiles, and offers her hand to him. The hand she holds out is bound in a cloth brace.

The young woman from last night! I quicken my pace. We never exchanged names. I forgot to introduce myself, though she obviously knew who I was. When I came across her yesterday, standing alone and colorless with anxiety, it hadn't occurred to me to act out the formalities of making an acquaintance. I had only wanted to find a way to help.

"Hello," I call as I step onto the dock.

"Good afternoon," the woman says. From under her bonnet she glances toward me—not quite *at* me—just long enough for me to get an impression of her eye color. Something between green and gray and brown. Freckles spatter her face, like sprinkles of cinnamon. Her hair has come out of its tidy bun in rebellious, frizzy strands. Droplets shimmer along the curling tips.

"Is it afternoon already?" I ask, stopping a proper distance away and slipping my hands into my pockets for warmth.

"Only just." She has a bouquet of wild flowers in one hand. She shifts it into her bound one and kneels to rub True's neck under his collar. He's nearly taller than her like this and leans all his weight into her scratching. Her smile grows wide, unguarded, and I find myself smiling with her.

"How's your wrist?" I ask.

"Well enough." She tilts her head back so she can see me better. A simple brown ribbon secures her bonnet, framing her cheeks and hanging in a loose knot under her chin. "Thank you for your help, by the way."

I shrug. I saw the turn at the end of the dance, and her wince when King Byrne held her hand too tightly. He should have noticed his mistake and done something himself. But I suppose he was too distracted to even realize it had happened, and of course this girl wouldn't have wanted to point out the accident to a king.

"Let me give you your cravat back," she adds, her cheeks coloring. She reaches to undo the knot.

"Keep it," I say with a wink.

Her whole face turns red now. I can't help grinning. She's easy to fluster.

She shakes her head and whispers to True, "Your owner is a flirt."

True's only response is to sniff at the dock. I let her statement lie.

"Can I ask what you were doing out here?" I say. "It's a bit cold for standing around on the water."

"I wanted to think." She takes her flowers and prepares to stand, not looking at me. I offer my hand and she hesitates, then takes it and lets me help her rise. Her fingers are curiously callused, though I'd taken her for a lady at the ball. Southern kings, in my limited experience, tend to put undue emphasis on social class, so it surprises me a little that King Byrne had been magnanimous enough to not just invite commoners but dance with one. I open my mouth to ask her name, as I should have done last night.

"Idris," calls a voice behind me.

I stiffen and glance back. Father is nearly at the dock. He raises his arm, motioning me to come his way. Perhaps standing out on the water with a strange girl wasn't the best place to lie low, even with the fog for cover.

"If you'll excuse me," I say reluctantly. I can't outright refuse to go to him.

The young woman dips a shallow curtsy. I'm still holding her hand, somehow, but let go now and start toward the shore. True trots behind me.

"Good day, Father!" I call with as much levity as I can muster. "And how are you?"

He frowns and steers me away from the water. "I take it you are feeling more at peace today?"

I shrug. "What is there to be upset about?"

He scrutinizes me a moment before he seems to catch on to the anger that still simmers just under my skin. "I felt the same way you do, once," he says. "But it is for the best, Idris. There is nothing we can do to help what happened long ago."

He still thinks I've said no. I don't correct him. Let him think he knows. Let him think we are the same. I want to savor how wrong he is about me.

"There's no need to look to the past now," Father goes on. "You're at the beginning of your life. And I have cheering news."

"Oh?" I hold out my hand so True will bop his nose against it. He obliges, and the simple normality of it cools some of my temper.

Father nods. "You know, of course, that part of the reason we came here was to visit Princess Catharine."

"It would have been hard to miss," I answer dryly. True wanders off to sniff at the grass.

"Yes, well, it seemed to me that the two of you got along well last night. King Byrne thought so too." He smiles at me. "This morning, he agreed to an arrangement between you two. All you need to do is propose."

I stop walking and stare at the ground. Before today, when I had pictured my inevitable arranged marriage, I had imagined I would be pleased. Nervous, of course, but excited. So the sudden flood of dread—and something else that's dark and coiling and hot—takes me by surprise.

"Does Catharine know about this?" I ask, buying time. My mouth tastes bitter. Does she know our fathers arranged for her to be given to me, like a birthday present?

My father waves this away. "She has expressed her willingness before."

Willingness, I think, remembering her polite friendliness yesterday. Imagining a life with a willing, quiet, compliant wife. Always a little formal, a little guarded, a little shielded. *Willing* but never wanting. Poised but never passionate. I don't even know her well enough to imagine if she'd be as miserable with that life as I would be.

"If you speak to her before we leave, we can have it all settled in a few months," Father goes on. He searches my face. "Don't let the past swallow your happiness, Idris. You have a future."

"Do you think this erases what happened last night?" I demand. The strange tangle in me burns into fury. "That you can give me a wife and a family and expect I'll just fall into line with all I know now?"

He seems surprised. "There is nothing you can do about what happened before. You can only look forward."

"Fine! Let's look forward. What about my sons, if I have any?" I shake his hand off my arm. "Before even that, what about *Abram*? Sometime, somewhere, the debt will come due."

"Not for a century or more, with any luck," my father says. "You can't think like that."

"Maybe *you* can't."

"I'm sorry you have been brought into this," Father says, measuring his words.

I wave aside his caution. "Speir says we can speak freely now. You aren't held to whatever promise you made him about keeping it all a secret."

My father frowns. A new suspicion enters his eyes. "Regardless, you have no reason to be ashamed. You won't always feel it so keenly."

"Maybe that's the problem—no one seems to feel it enough!"

"For God's sake, Idris," Father snaps, his patience breaking. "You are in this now, whether you want it or not, and there's no use fussing about it. You said no, and Abram will say no, and it will go on. There's no point being upset."

I clench my jaw and meet his eyes.

Father pauses. "You said no, correct?"

"I'm not like you," I almost spit. My voice cuts my own throat. "I would not leave my brother to this fate."

Father's eyes widen. He takes a step back and runs a hand through his hair. "Tell me you said no, Idris."

I don't answer. True returns, sensing the tension, and cautiously sits between me and my father.

I don't expect the sudden redness in my father's eyes, the gloss to them. "What did he say? What did he tell you would happen?"

I spread my hands. "That I'll fulfill her dancing days."

"What does that mean?"

"I'm not sure," I admit. "He said mortal days are short."

"Damn it, Idris!" Father throws up his hands. "You didn't even gather details about the terms you were agreeing to? Did you give this any thought at all?"

"Of course I did!" But as I say it, I feel like a child, petulant and whining.

"How could you do this?" Father demands. "I told you to say no!"

"What, the way you did? Grandfather, Uncle Matthias, all of them? You would have me pass this on to Abram and my sons in their turn?" I shake my head. "Maybe you could live with that, but I can't."

"I have lived with that. I've lived with many things, Idris, so that *you* can thrive. If I had said yes, all those years back, you wouldn't be here. Neither would your brother." He steps closer again and True tenses at my feet. "Do you think you've done something noble? Something heroic? You've only played into their games."

"I've done what's right. I've stopped the cycle."

"You've stopped *nothing*." Father rubs his eyes. "The Hidden Folk might not be hunting our family from now on, might not come asking their simple question, but you've done *nothing* to stop the cycle of grief—you've only made it fresh. Do you think that by sacrificing yourself, you've spared any of us from pain?"

"It is on us to make amends. We are the ones who committed the original crime. One of us has to pay the price."

Father shakes his head. "None of us can restore that—woman. She suffered enormously. And that is regrettable. But her suffering will not be eased by yours, or by ours. Nothing that we can do now will atone for what's already done and finished."

"It isn't finished," I point out. "And I will not leave this burden for someone else to carry."

"You have only surrendered what they might never have taken! Who's to say that you would have a son? Who's to say that you and Abram wouldn't both have daughters who would have lived without this ridiculous curse? The magic in our land is fading. The Folk draw deeper into the sea. In another generation they may not have the strength to even impose this curse. If you had just followed my orders!"

I had imagined my father being frustrated, of course, that I disobeyed him, displeased that whatever was going to happen would happen to me now. But I did not expect this anger, this thing that is almost disdain.

"Did you not teach me, as a prince, that my duty is to right wrongs?" I ask him. "Isn't that the entire point of our whole family—to seek and distribute justice, even when we are the party at fault?"

He rakes a hand through his hair and his voice rises, almost to a shout. "You are not bringing justice! Mervyn is dead, and when he died the crime died with him. If the Folk cannot move beyond this, it is not our responsibility to offer our blood to satisfy *their* need for vengeance."

"But it didn't die," I say through my teeth, "and they aren't after vengeance. She's still suffering."

"What did he say? That you will dance? How is that to help her?" Father holds up his hand. "We will argue this no more. But make no mistake, Idris. Your foolish decision will echo through the family just as loudly as Mervyn's did."

I am too shocked to speak. And in the moment of silence the flame in me cools to a simmering resentment. Father is right about one thing: We will never agree about this.

"We need to go home," he says, gazing back at the castle. "Perhaps one of the wise women can help you get out of your poorly made agreement."

I shake my head, but Father is already marching back to the castle double-quick. I jog to catch up. My anger has shifted into something more confusing, and I find an apology on my lips. I don't know what I want to apologize for, though. For doing the right thing? Because surely this is right.

Abram sits in the Great Hall with Princess Catharine, talking to her while she spins wool. He straightens when we come in, glancing from Father to me. The smile of greeting fades from his face. I suspect he can sense the tension between us hotter than the hearth's fire.

"We need to return to Skyare at once," Father says. He smooths his voice as he addresses Catharine. "We're sorry to be so abrupt, princess, but urgent news calls us home."

Catharine rises and makes a deep curtsy. "I will let my father know."

"I will speak to him myself," Father says. "Abram, please see to our preparations."

Abram glances at me, bewildered, but goes to let our servants know. He gives True a pat on his way out, and then True trots over to Princess Catharine. She stiffens uneasily.

"Idris." Father turns to me. He looks steely, but there's still a flicker of panic in his eyes. "Why don't you rest here while we put everything together?"

I'm not sure if he thinks I'm already dying and too frail to pack a bag, or if he thinks leaving me alone with Princess Catharine will lead to a proposal after all.

Perhaps he's hoping for a grandchild before I perish. He'd have better luck rearranging the engagement to replace me with Abram.

Nonetheless, I nod. Anything else would be obstinate. Father leaves as soon as he sees that I mean to stay.

"Can I get you any tea, Prince Idris?" Catharine asks. True takes a sniff at her hem and she edges away from him.

My stomach remembers suddenly that I haven't had any breakfast. "Yes, if you don't mind."

Catharine steps out of the room to speak to a servant. She returns almost immediately with a tray of tea things and a plate of the dense cookies popular in this part of the mainland. True lifts his head in interest and begins wagging his tail pleadingly, but I take Abram's seat by the spinning wheel and tell True, "Down."

With a sigh, my dog obeys. Princess Catharine gives a wan smile and begins to pour the tea. Her every move is measured, cool, and controlled. I think of the young woman on the dock and her sudden unguarded laugh. The way she buried her hands into True's fur with a grin.

"I hope you've found your visit enjoyable," Catharine says.

I give the required compliments. She converses about the weather I might expect as I travel home. I make some observations about our horses. Soon we're into a conversation so polite, romance wouldn't be possible even if I did hope to propose. King Byrne and Queen Mari join us before too long, the king self-assured and pleased and the queen her cool and quiet self. Her gaze tracks Catharine the way a hound might watch a rabbit.

Abram and Father return, and the farewells begin. The queen keeps glancing impatiently toward the door. I'm not sure if she wishes us gone, but then someone comes hurrying inside. It's the girl from the dock, wearing her plain pale-brown dress and her dark jacket. She's taken off her bonnet and her hair frizzes free of its braided bun. A maid trails behind her and slides into the hallway.

The girl flushes and comes forward.

King Byrne chuckles. "Just in time. Tell our guests goodbye, Princess Katherine."

Princess Katherine—*Kit*—the stepsister. I feel like a fool for not realizing it sooner. But then, she hadn't been at the dinner when we arrived. I'm not sure she was ever formally introduced to me, which seems odd. Or—perhaps we were, when we were surrounded by noise and movement? As the guests were coming in last night, maybe?

Kit silently crosses in front of the king to reach her mother. If the queen watched Catharine like prey, the king's lingering gaze on Kit is more like a gambler gloating over his winnings. Kit seems to shrink in front of him.

"We hope you have calm seas and a strong wind," King Byrne continues, as if he hadn't just invited Kit to speak. "And we eagerly await our next meeting."

"You and your family are welcome to the Islands of Skyare any time," Father says in a distracted tone. "We would be honored to return your hospitality."

"I'm sure there will be occasion for that soon enough."

My father and Byrne continue in this way for another few minutes. I find myself watching Kit. Her carefully composed expression is so far from the genuine ease she showed when we were outside. While Catharine stands with faultless poise, there is something fragile behind Kit's carefully compressed lips and downturned eyes.

The kings finally finish their leave-taking. I kiss the queen's hand, and then Catharine's. No words were spoken between us. I wonder if Catharine is disappointed, but there's nothing but gentle politeness in her voice when we say farewell. No regret or sorrow at our parting. I feel little pain at going either. I think, in another life, we might have been friends. But I don't think it could ever have turned to romance, and now I doubt I will ever see her again.

I turn last to Kit and lift her hand to plant a parting kiss on her knuckles. Her wrist is still bound in my cravat. Quietly, releasing her, I say, "I hope you heal quickly, princess."

Her gaze darts toward the king and then drops to the floor. She has gone colorless, the way I found her last night. Almost without noticing, she lifts her bound hand and taps her collarbone with her fingertips. "You are kind to say so, prince, but there is no need for concern. I am hardly hurt."

King Byrne watches us with keen interest. Kit moves ever so slightly back, ever so slightly behind her mother. My mind flits to last night, and King Byrne dancing with his stepdaughter, and holding her hand too tight, and her alone and in pain.

Suddenly, I'm not so sure the injury was a mistake.

FIVE

Kit

Four days have passed since the princes left, and Byrne is no less determined to believe that Prince Idris and Catharine are engaged.

From what I understand, an arrangement has been made between the two kings. But according to Catharine, the prince himself said nothing that would make her believe he even cared to propose.

I scoffed at this. "Why would anyone balk about proposing to you?"

"I don't mind," Catharine added hastily. "I am only saying what I think."

But regardless of what she thought, or indeed what might be happening in the prince's head, Byrne remains no less set on having the match made official in every way. The guest suites had barely been cleaned before the king started talking about the next steps.

"We cannot expect them to return any time soon," he says to himself over dinner one evening. "We must press the advantage: Send Catharine at once. King Hugh extended an open invitation to our family to visit the Islands of Skyare whenever we pleased, and of course he meant that particularly for Catharine."

I glance across the table at my mother, wondering if she will point out how desperate this makes our whole family look. Catharine herself studies her plate with a twist to her mouth that shows her embarrassment. But my mother only watches the king quietly, her eyes bright with calculations.

"We could send Catharine by the end of the week," my stepfather goes on, caught up in his own plans. "That is plenty of time to prepare and send word. If she stays at least a fortnight, she must have a proposal by the end of it."

"Won't such travel impact your session with the council next Thursday?" my mother asks.

He dismisses this with a wave. "I cannot be spared. You will have to accompany Catharine." He glances from his daughter to my mother, then his gaze lands on me. I drop my eyes quickly, but not before I see a new idea bloom in his expression. "Kit should stay here to manage the household while you're gone."

My hands clench in my lap involuntarily, and my chest squeezes my lungs. A new brace binds my wrist, a stark reminder of what King Byrne is capable of even when we are not alone. But a fortnight with no one between me and him? No one to buffer or distract him? I can't help casting a desperate look at my mother.

To my surprise, she seems pleased. "Yes, that would be an excellent arrangement."

I stare. I cannot breathe. I cannot follow the conversation as the specifics are sorted. I hardly seem to be at the same table anymore. My hands ache as I spread them over my knees. I concentrate on the fabric of my dress—the fiber of the linen in its tight weave. I trace the small rise and fall of the threads, trying to feel out a path, trying to find a way to connect each tiny piece.

The dinner ends after an everlasting time. I murmur something about a headache and excuse myself from an evening of reading and piano in the drawing room. My mother follows me out and kisses my forehead on the pretext of checking for a fever.

"Trust me, my darling," she whispers. "I will keep you safe."

You haven't before, I want to say.

"There are greater powers than even a king's." She tucks back my hair. "It has only taken me some time to find them. You will be all right."

I want to ask how in the world she can promise that when she'll be as far north as land reaches, and I'll be here. With him. But before I can venture a question, Catharine steps out to join me. She pauses, glancing uncertainly at my mother. As always, Mother immediately turns to stone, stiff and cold as she faces her stepdaughter.

"Catharine, be of some use and help your sister to bed. You might as well retire for the evening, too, as we'll have no need for you."

Catharine dips a curtsy. I think my mother means sending Catharine to bed to be a punishment—I don't know what for, but my mother is always reprimanding her—but I am silently grateful. Catharine takes my injured arm gingerly.

I still have Prince Idris's cravat hidden in one of my trunks. It was foolish to take and more foolish to keep, but knowing that it is there… It reminds me of our moment in the ballroom, our own little clearing amidst the chaos. The shelter we shared together. His kindness to a stranger—his gentleness to *me*—still sits warm and bright in my chest. And, though it may be silly and improper, I haven't been able to give up the memento he left with me.

"Are you well, Kit?" Catharine asks as we walk. She rubs my sleeve. "You hardly ate."

I pause, unable to settle on the right words. Eventually I manage, "I'm fine. Just tired."

Catharine takes me to my room and stokes the fire while I change into my nightdress. For someone who hadn't made a fire in her life before we met, she's become skilled at it. I wrap a blanket round my shoulders and hesitate. I should let Catharine go and rest, but I can't bear to be alone.

Catharine unties her silk shoes and stands, brushing ash off her skirt. She nudges a few bricks nearer the heat. "Why don't I call for some tea? Would that help?"

"That sounds nice," I admit. The tension eases out of my shoulders. She intends to stay a while longer. I sit on my bed while she rings for the servants. My insides still feel unsettled. Cold, small. I can't decide. I only know that I can't remain here for two weeks alone. Absently, I tap my collarbone. "Could you ask your father whether I might come with you?"

"I did," she says, looking puzzled. "At dinner. Are you sure you're all right? Should I send for a doctor?"

"Oh," I murmur. "I must have—been thinking of something else. What did he say?"

"He felt that the house needed your management, and he didn't think that you would enjoy the travel."

"Could you press him?" I ask, my voice growing fainter.

"Of course." She tilts her head, concern clear across her face. She wants to ask me why this is so important, and I want to say something true. I want her to suspect. I want the secret out. But how do you tell your sister that her father makes your skin crawl? That the man who raised her is a monster?

Would she even believe me? I don't want to know.

"Is it the princes?" Catharine asks conspiratorially. She perches on the edge of my bed. "You can tell me if that's why you want to come."

It is such a simple, sunny idea compared to my reality, I almost laugh.

"You *like* one of them!" Catharine grins and pokes me in the ribs. "I knew it!"

I long to wrap myself in her world. So I shrug and say, "Believe what you will."

The servant comes with the tea, and Catharine fixes it for us. She takes the hot bricks and slides them under my blanket.

"Come on then," she says. "I'll read a bit."

I shift back against the pillows. Catharine ducks into her own room to get a book, then returns and climbs up beside me. Catharine is a great reader. I once enjoyed reading too, but after my father's death it became hard somehow. He always used to read with me, or to me, and when he was gone I just…didn't do it anymore. I was out gathering herbs and food. Or, when I was home, I was spinning wool and helping my mother balance accounts. By the time I had finished all my tasks, it was dark and the candlelight on the pages hurt my eyes. Even when I had time to read, I was always studying almanacs or housekeeping guides.

But Catharine, who grew up with servants to do most of those tasks for her, had much more leisure to read whatever she pleased. She grew fond of folktales from a young age and she constantly pulls out some book or other. I spin faster than her, so when we are left alone to do our work, she often reads while I spin for both of us.

Catharine runs her hand over the leather cover of her book. On it an embossed silver seal or selkie sits atop a rock in the middle of a troubled sea. She flips to the first page and its simple map. The very tip of our own kingdom rests at the bottom. Aberloche's highlands are noted with symbols of triangular mountains. Then there is an expanse of sea, and above that the cluster of the Islands of Skyare. Skyare, the largest, sits about in the middle. The outliers—Verron, Glett, Twinehallow—scatter out in mismatched sizes, some as small as dots.

"This is new, isn't it?" I ask, looking again at the cover. It is well-worn, obviously much read, but I have never seen this volume on her shelves.

"I wanted to read about the northern isles," she says, looking sheepish. A blush rises in her cheeks. "I mentioned it to Prince Abram and he, ah, left me this."

I lift my eyebrows. "Oh, did he?"

"He said it was just his travel copy," she adds hastily. "Nothing important. Meant to be creased and such."

"Hmm." It would be easy to tease her further, but I just tuck my cheek against her shoulder. "Go on, then."

Catharine clears her throat and begins. "*The goodman of Kelda in Twinehallow had always mistrusted women, and swore he would never marry…*"

I sip my tea, relishing the warmth against my fingers and the hot brick radiating comfort against my thigh. Catharine reads on and the story unfolds: An arrogant young man has sworn off women. He lives only to plow his fields and fish the sea. His eyes are ever to the task at hand and never on the horizon. Until one night.

The darkness is heavy and still in the height of summer, and the air smells of a storm. The goodman of Kelda readies his yole for one last try at the herring before the rain comes in. But as he is bent over his boat's knots, he hears the sudden ring of laughter. He lifts his eyes and sees movement on the rocks farther down the shore. There is more laughter, and music. He thinks of the youths in town out to cause trouble, and he sneaks across the length of beach. This is his land and his sea, and he will not abide mischief.

But when he reaches the turn in the coast and peers over the edge of a dune, he freezes in place. The women dancing on the sand are none of his kind. They are white as the crest of a wave with hair long and salt-tangled. And when the goodman of Kelda looks to the rocks where they'd scrambled in from the sea, he sees a pile of seal skins, and he knows these are selkies. He creeps to the pile, but a clumsy step gives him away. The selkie women run for their skins. He is closer and manages to snatch one first: a skin as golden-brown as the hay in his fields. The selkie maidens each take their own and, donning their skins like cloaks, vanish into the black water. All except one, left shivering and naked on the shore.

Tears fall from her big brown eyes and she begs, "Please give me back my skin. I cannot go home without it."

The goodman of Kelda takes in the sight of her, and the more he looks the more he wants. He puts the skin in his bag and turns home. Crying, she must follow.

"*He hid the skin away, and the selkie had no choice but to be his wife,*" Catharine reads. "*Soon they had seven children.*"

I pull the blanket tighter. I wait with the selkie maiden, breathless with pain, knowing how selkie stories end. Willing her to her ending.

The smallest child is near five when she and her mother are left alone in their croft. The selkie wife settles her daughter by the fire and begins a search—a search she's made every time she has a moment to herself. She checks cupboards and chests and loose stones in the floor. Her daughter watches and asks what her mother is looking for.

"A seal skin," she says, "as golden as the water in the evening."

"I've seen one such," the daughter says. "Da takes it down sometimes to gaze at."

"Where?" the mother asks, and her daughter tells her. He has hidden it in a hollow near the ceiling in the bedroom. Just as the daughter tells her, so it is. The selkie woman kisses her child, takes her skin, and flees to the sea.

The goodman of Kelda, just then rounding the headland in his yole, sees a seal golden as the hay of his field dive into the waves.

"*And he never does see his selkie wife again,*" Catharine concludes.

I smile down at my tea. Catharine—and the writer themselves—almost sound sad about this ending. But the selkie and I know it is a happy one. She is free.

"I don't think that's my favorite of the selkie stories," Catharine says thoughtfully, flipping back through the pages. "The man is kinder in the other versions."

"But doesn't he take her skin in every one?" I ask.

Catharine twists her mouth, considering. "I'm not sure. I know in the mermaid stories, there's at least one where he catches but releases the maiden and later she returns the favor."

I shift and rub my eyes, rousing myself from my thoughts. "So the islands have selkies *and* mermaids?"

"Oh, they have plenty of magical creatures." Catharine tallies them on her hand, her voice growing more animated as she goes. "Mermaids, finfolk, selkies. And then on land, there's trows and fairies and hogboons… They all get grouped together as the Hidden Folk."

I could remind her that we live in a world of carriages, tea, and whist. That if there ever was magic in our land, it died long ago. But I smile. "I hope the islands are as enchanted as you think."

"I might not be there long enough to find out." Catharine sighs at the ceiling. "I wish everyone would understand—Prince Idris doesn't *have* to propose to me. He might not want to."

I prod her arm. "Well, you'll get the chance to look, proposal or not."

Catharine tucks her book against her chest. "I just want to believe there's some magic left in the world."

"All right." I lean my head on her shoulder. "You believe in that, and I'll believe in you."

✦

Time passes faster than I thought possible, and I still do not have a plan ready the day before Catharine is meant to leave. King Byrne has not changed his mind about me staying, and I haven't made up my mind about how to escape. In some ways, I wish I were like the selkie maiden—that I could grab a skin and vanish into the water.

As I prepare to join the others for breakfast, I consider my options. I could run away and hide until my mother returns. But the weather is cold and the days are dark, and it will only become colder and darker. And even if I survived on my own, my reputation would be ruined. King Byrne could use that to his advantage.

I could go after Catharine and Mother and simply claim the king changed his mind. But one message from my stepfather and the ruse would be undone. Still, maybe between us, we could make some excuse for why I could not travel back to him? I could fall ill, or break my ankle, or…

Exhaling, I tap a rhythm onto my collarbone. If Mother would give me a sense of what she has planned, this would all be much easier. But she has refused to speak of it, no matter how often I ask.

I join Catharine in the hallway, and we link arms as we head to breakfast. Catharine talks about a book she's reading and an amusing dream she had, small nothings that help my frantic thoughts settle. Before we can get to the breakfast room, Mother steps in our way.

"I need you both to come to town with me," Mother says with a smile. "Kit, your new pelisse should be ready to be collected and Catharine could use a warm blanket for the carriage ride."

"Oh!" I exclaim, hope blooming in my chest. Perhaps this is part of her plan? "Very well."

"Of course," Catharine agrees. She glances past my mother to where her father sits with his breakfast, his eyes on a report.

Squaring her shoulders, Catharine walks to her father. She places one hand on his arm, and I flinch even though it is not me who touches him. I wonder how it is that one person can feel so strongly, so horribly about a thing, and the other be completely oblivious.

King Byrne glances up. He only ever looks kind when he faces her. "What is it, Catharine?"

"I am nervous," she says plaintively. "Nervous to go alone to the north."

"Your stepmother will be going with you." He pats her hand.

"I wish Kit could come." Catharine puts on all her charm. Her lip seems to quiver. Her eyes are downcast and begging. I wonder if she's only doing it for my sake, or if she really does need me with her. I selfishly wish that she does.

"I've told you, she must remain here," my stepfather says patiently. "You won't be with strangers—you know the princes and their father, and everyone else you meet is sure to love you. You have no reason to fear."

I wonder what it would be like: to actually fear nothing. To grow up without worrying about your father's health, or your mother's finances, or your stepfather's behavior, or your withering hands. But then, even I have it better than many. Not only do I have a roof, but I have a *castle.* I have education and skills. I have Catharine.

I know my stepsister has attempted several times now to convince her father to let me come, but this is the first time she's tried in front of me.

"Kit is vital to me," Catharine says, in the closest thing I've ever heard her come to a commanding tone. "I need her to come."

Her father smiles, indulgent. "You will be parted soon enough, my lovely. Best get used to it now." He plants a kiss on her hand—I grimace—and shoos her away. "Go and help your stepmother. Enjoy the day. Tomorrow you'll be off, and with any luck you won't be back for quite a while."

Catharine turns to me with an apology in her eyes. I dip my head, trying to show her that it is all right. I will just have to get myself out of this.

As Catharine returns to the hallway, my stomach tightens with hunger. Turning to my mother, I ask, "Should we eat before we set out?"

"We'll find something in town," Mother says lightly. "Will you be all right to wait? Have neither of you eaten since last night?"

"No, Your Majesty," Catharine says. I nod in confirmation.

My mother looks pleased. "Good."

The carriage is already in the courtyard. Catharine and I slide into one side, intertwining our arms for extra warmth. Mother sits opposite us, turning her face to the window. She has one hand clenched on her lap and her eyes are unusually bright. I frown. Mother enjoys town and shopping, especially now that we have funds, but she radiates a strange, eager energy. If I had been alone with her, I would have asked. If I had been alone with Catharine, we would have talked. But with Catharine and Mother in the same place, any familiarity with one feels like a betrayal of the other.

I tighten my hand on Catharine's arm, wondering for the first time if I am not the only one at risk if left alone with one of our parents. I am not sure what sort of harm my mother would cause—certainly not the same as the king—but she has always been estranged from my stepsister. I can't place exactly when it started, but I feel it happened around the first time I met Catharine. I remember the way Catharine grabbed my hands, laughed over our shared name, and declared us sisters with such enthusiasm that I instantly believed her. I remember grinning and looking to my mother for her approval. And I remember her frown.

The trip to town passes without incident. The pelisse fits me fine. A blanket is found for Catharine. Breakfast is never brought up. Catharine stops near a vendor with a spread of nuts and small pastries on display. It feels silly to me to spend money on what I might easily find in the fields, but I take a handful of hazelnuts and hold out a coin. Catharine reaches for one of the pastries.

"Now, girls, there's no need for that," Mother says suddenly, touching the back of my hand to signal I should release the nuts. "We'll be home in no time. I'll have Cook make you a grand midday meal."

"But you said…" I begin. My mother just taps my hand again in a short, firm pattern. I release the nuts one by one—but keep two hidden in my palm. I set down a coin as I turn away from the puzzled vendor. Catharine walks beside me as we follow Mother to the carriage.

I put my hand out and press one of the nuts to Catharine's palm. She glances at me and smiles, but doesn't take it.

"I still don't like nuts, Kit," she whispers. "Besides, I'm not hungry."

Her stomach growls right then, and she grimaces. I hold back a laugh, but I slip the nuts into my reticule and pull the drawstring to close it. If she won't eat, I can last longer.

We catch up with my mother as she places the folded blanket inside the carriage. "You know," she says, turning toward us, "the weather is remarkably fine today. Why don't we walk back?"

She's right about the weather—the sun has made a rare appearance and, though the wind is as cold as ever, in the sunlight the day feels almost balmy. But it's a good hour's walk home and my stomach tightens at the thought.

"I'd rather ride," I admit. "We could walk after lunch."

Mother gives me a disappointed look.

Catharine must see it, because she jumps in, "Kit can take the carriage and I will walk with you. It is turning into a lovely day."

Mother's expression sours even more. I feel for Catharine—she can never seem to gain my mother's approval, even if all she has done is agree with what Mother already said.

"I think you should both come," Mother says, looking at me firmly. "The walk will do you good."

I frown back at her. Perhaps she means this as part of her plan, whatever it is, that's meant to keep me safe? She's been behaving strangely all day. A fragment of hope sneaks back into my chest. Yes, that's the only reason she would be so demanding about this. My hunger can wait.

"Very well." I take Catharine's arm. "If you insist."

The carriage goes on ahead. As we walk, my new pelisse swishes against my skirt. The narrow cut keeps the wind from pulling it off, the way it does with a cloak, and I relish the protection it offers. My mother takes the lead at a brisk walk, while Catharine and I trail behind.

"What other stories have you gleaned about the far north?" I ask her.

"Oh, plenty," Catharine answers. "I finished that book and came to an author's note at the end. Apparently, the writer—named Muir—has been gathering tales for the last fifty-odd years. *But*—" she casts me a triumphant look—"not all the stories are even as old as that. Some of them happened in the last decade!"

"Hmmm." I tilt my head. "It might be in the best interests of his sales to say so."

Catharine shakes her head. "Magic still exists up there in the north. I'm sure of it."

I let myself imagine it: a place where selkies, mermaids, and goblins roam. Where one might go to church on a Sunday morning and have a chat with a fairy on a Sunday afternoon. I wonder whether the princes might have had any dealings with them. Perhaps Idris has his own tall tales. Whether true or not, I find myself wanting to hear him tell them. It would undoubtedly be entertaining.

I open my mouth to coax Catharine into a story, but my gaze catches on Mother ahead of us. We are well out of town now, on a stretch of track bordered on one side by evergreens. Mother has stopped and is speaking with an oddly dressed man. I don't recognize him. He must have come from the forest, because I would have seen his approach from a mile off on the road.

Catharine and I exchange a curious look and walk faster. The two of them turn to us as we approach. The man is younger than I expected, perhaps a little younger than me. His skin is a coppery dark, but his eyes are strangely bright, almost orange.

"These are the daughters?" he asks Mother. "The Katherines?"

His voice lilts in a musical accent, almost a song. He's dressed in an odd, old-fashioned way—a green coat that comes almost to his knees and sleeves that flare out from elbow to wrist. The fabric shimmers like fish scale when he shifts his weight.

"My daughter Katherine." Mother lifts her hand to me. She turns her hand to Catharine and her tone grows cold. "My stepdaughter Catharine."

"Good afternoon," Catharine says, dipping a curtsy. Even though she has the presence of mind to be polite, I notice her staring at the man's coat. Belatedly, I mirror her greeting.

"And they have not eaten?" he continues.

"No." Mother asks the young man, "Can you do it, Speir?"

Her use of his first name catches my attention. No formal title—*Mr.* Stranger or *Lord* Traveler—just a familiar address, as if they've known each other for a while. Or as if he doesn't have a last name at all.

His uncanny eyes fix on me. I feel as if he sees through my very skin, down to my bones. Unnerved, I tuck my warped hands behind my back. The joints ache as I link my fingers together.

"You are lucky in their names. A name shared is not so different from a soul." He smiles. "Yes, I can do it. This will be interesting."

I look to my mother, wondering if she's going to explain any of this—or even formally introduce us to this man. Her eyes are lively, her cheeks rosy. She's animated in a way I've never seen before.

"Mother?" I venture.

"The price is still acceptable?" Speir asks her.

My mother nods. "Yes. Come in five months."

Dread rises in my throat. This feels like one of Catharine's stories. Bargains made with a passerby on the road, men with strange names and mystical looks. This is all part of the plan Mother has alluded to, I'm nearly certain, but it doesn't feel right. More urgently I ask, "Mother, what is going on?"

Speir's eyes crinkle in mischief and he steps off the path, walking into the trees without a glance behind him. Mother takes my hand and follows without answering. I grab Catharine, pulling her close to me.

Catharine presses my arm and whispers excitedly into my ear. It takes a moment for her words to register.

"He's dressed like the finfolk."

One of the magic creatures of the islands.

I want to say that perhaps it's just an unusual costume. He could be a vagabond. There must be a thousand other explanations and the Islands of Skyare—the islands Idris comes from, the islands Catharine has been reading about—are far from here. What would one of their kind be doing in our highlands?

But in the tight evergreens all light goes dim and freezing water drips from the branches onto my clothes. My words stick in my mouth.

We emerge into a narrow clearing with a broken tree at the center. Either lightning or wind has snapped its trunk. Jagged wood pierces the air like spears, higher on one side than the other. It looks like a brutal throne. Speir approaches it and takes a shallow grayish bowl from—I'm not sure where from; it seems to appear out of the fold of his clothes.

Speir balances the bowl precariously on the sharp spikes of wood. He takes a canteen from his belt and pours out water. It doesn't so much as ripple when it hits the bowl. A smell rises from it, foreign to this forest. Cold and salt.

The smell reminds me of Idris.

"I told you," Catharine whispers. Her face is alight with curiosity and awe. "Magic is real. The stories are real!"

Speir's mouth quirks up. He clearly hears her, but he does not reply.

All I feel is a shroud of heaviness settling on my shoulders. I shake Mother's arm. I hardly dare speak louder than a whisper. The weight demands reverence. "Mother?"

"Trust me, love," Mother whispers back. "I said I would protect you."

Speir steps away from the bowl, apparently satisfied. He turns to Catharine and me. "Will you look?"

I do not move. I can't quite make myself believe this. My world is one of linen sheets and toast. Ledgers and pencils. And yet, here I am with someone who seems less and less human every minute.

"Go," Mother urges, releasing me and giving me a gentle push.

I do not move. My mind struggles to make sense of what I'm seeing. Even Catharine hesitates now.

Mother's excitement sours into a severe frown. She turns it on my stepsister. "Go and look in the bowl."

My hand is still clasped round Catharine's. I feel her tense, but she dips her head in submission and walks forward. I step with her, wanting to protest or plant my feet. But the instant I move, something pulls me on, as if the bowl is the eye of a storm and we are caught in the wind. The pressure does not ease even when we stand beside the tree trunk. My head fogs with it, with the need to know what is inside the water.

I knew how the selkie story would end. But how does this one go?

Catharine raises her gaze to me. Her look seems to say, *Whatever comes, I am with you.*

I nod and squeeze her hand.

We bend over the water, which shimmers with unexpected opalescent color. Not a bowl: a seashell.

Our reflections stare back at us, unnervingly clear and still—sharper than even the mirrors in the castle. I can see every blemish on my face. The darkness under my eyes. The severely critical tilt of my eyebrows. The softness of my jaw and flab under my chin. The blotchiness of my skin. I lift my hand to a crumb at the corner of my mouth—but no, it's a freckle I'd never noticed before. But my hand… In this ruthless reflection, I can see every bulge around the joints, even the joints I'd never realized were affected before. I hate every unnatural bend in my fingers, the stretch of bone against skin, the puckered wrinkles over the knuckles.

I want to claw my way out of my body, to escape this thing that is aging and dying when it hasn't even reached eighteen years. It closes round me. A trap. A noose. My breath catches with the force of my panic. My bones are too fragile. My body too breakable. I am suffocating.

I close my eyes tightly. My heart—or maybe my soul—lurches inside my chest, trying to break free. It happens again and pain blossoms across my ribs. Again, and the pain spreads to my head and my fingers and my toes. Again—

And I am tumbling through air. The cold cuts at me. I am a raw thing with no case, no protection, falling and falling and…

Something warm envelopes me.

The pain stops.

I take a trembling breath. The panic has eased, just as suddenly as it came. I open my eyes.

I am still looking into the shell. But something is wrong about the angle. I am standing on the left, but my reflection is on the right.

My hand is still against my lip—I can feel the touch of my finger—but in the reflection my hand has dropped.

Then I turn my gaze to the Catharine in the water.

And she has her finger against her lip.

"Kit…?" says my voice. I tear my gaze away from the reflection and I am looking into my own face, my own eyes. I look terrified.

But it isn't me.

I am staring at my own body. But I am not in it.

SIX

Idris

In my dreams, I dance.

Every night after we return home to Skyare, music follows me when I sleep. I am in constant motion, and the color and sound of it all burns in my head like a fever. Come morning, I wake late and feel no rest.

On the ninth day, I can't help groaning when the cathedral bells toll eight. I promised Abram I'd go with him to the holms, a series of tidal islands. Low tide is at—what, ten? I try to figure out how early we need to leave so that we reach the harbor at Stromwell and depart with time to spare. The journey time once we're in the yole will depend on the wind, and I need to account for the current being against us. Maybe we should just take horses…

But my brain hurts and I press my palms to my closed eyes. These stupid dreams have me going mad. And it doesn't help that Speir still hasn't shown up to collect on the curse. No wonder I keep dreaming of dances, with something about fulfilling her "dancing days" hanging over my head.

A big slobbery tongue licks my wrist. I nudge True away with my elbow before I open one eye to give him a look. "Thanks."

He wags his tail.

I sigh heavily and heave myself out of bed. As far as I can tell, I still have time to go with Abram. The cold sea air might do me good. Clear away the fragments of the night.

I start pulling on my clothes, hardly paying attention to what I'm grabbing. Buckskin trousers? Sure. Green-wool waistcoat? Great. Bright orange hat Abram found washed up on shore? Perfect.

As I'm grabbing my boots, I knock one over. A shimmering sort of dust spills out across the floor.

I pause, surprised. I squat—my legs protest, unexpectedly sore—and rub the stuff between my fingers. It's too fine to be sand and it isn't the right color—not the faint pink of the beaches on Varmyra to the west or the startling white of Glett to the north. This color shifts between gray-white to lavender and the softest of yellows, like dawn on a foggy morning, depending on the way I angle it in the light. The dust coats my fingertips in a thin pigment, the way I suppose a lady's rouge would.

Cautiously, I tip my other boot. More of the dust falls out.

Finally, I make myself check my feet.

My soles are covered in the stuff. Even the skin on the top of my feet has a slight shimmer.

A sinking dread settles in my chest. My gaze catches on my leather dancing shoes, dumped in a messy corner. But they look just as good as they did on my birthday—I haven't been wearing them anywhere.

My feet hurt, I realize. More than they did when I went to bed last night.

A creeping suspicion raises the hairs on my arms.

I jump to the wardrobe and throw it open. My everyday garb is the same as always, but when I push back to the formal attire I'm hit by the smell of kelp and sweat. I stick my nose close to the armpit of one jacket and, yes, I have definitely worn this very recently. The fabric is crusty with salt. I wince at the silver buttons that are already starting to tarnish from exposure to seawater. I'll have to polish them.

Polish them? It is so ridiculous I almost want to laugh. Clothes and buttons—what does it matter?

Because I haven't been dreaming.

I lower myself to my bed, taking a shaky breath. The curse has started. I'm already enchanted. And I have no memory of what's been happening to me.

True puts his big head on my knee, turning his brown eyes up to me. I rub his wiry fur between my fingers. Speir is already collecting the dancing days, but I hadn't even realized it. I've been going somewhere in my sleep.

But where? And how?

I swallow on a dry throat. My body is possessed. I have no idea what they're doing to me, aside from—apparently—making me dance.

Someone knocks lightly on my door. Abram's voice asks, "Idris?"

I spring forward and slam the wardrobe shut guiltily. I grab my wool socks and shove them on, then the boots. I kick at the dust to disperse it.

"Yes, come in!" I shout, too loud.

Abram pushes open the door and gives me a worried look. His glasses make his eyes a little too big, a little too concerned. I ignore him while I run my hands through my hair instead of a comb.

"Are you all right?" he asks, for what must be the thousandth time since our trip south. He asked that on our journey home, as soon as he got a chance to speak without my father present. And yesterday when I got so tired I tripped over a cobblestone…

Tired. I've been so, *so* tired. Of course I wasn't dreaming. I want to bang my head against a wall.

"Yes," I say, sliding my arms into my greatcoat. "Never better. Let's go and find some—what are we looking for today?"

"I want to check if the storm dredged up any more flotsam from the *Rover*," Abram says, naming a pirate ship that wrecked a few months back. "See if the winds have exposed any more of the old chapel."

"So we aren't hunting beetles and owl pellets?" I ask, relieved.

"Not today, anyway." Abram smiles, a little cautiously. "Are you sure you're up for it? You look a bit—"

"Never better." I hear myself repeat the words and see Abram's eyes narrow. Feigning indifference, I snap for True's attention and slip past Abram into the hallway. "So excited to go scrambling over beaches."

He follows me downstairs. Father sits alone in the breakfast room, examining a newspaper. He must hear us come down, but he doesn't look up. Ever since our fight, it seems he has decided to just not talk to me until he can find a way to "undo" my "horrible decision." I wonder if I should tell him that the curse has started.

"Do you want breakfast?" Abram asks me. "I think we still have time."

I *would* like breakfast, actually. But I do not relish the thought of sitting down to a cool table with a distant father and Abram looking between the two of us, trying to figure out why we're both not speaking. Instead, I take a cloth napkin and fill it with whatever I can grab from the sideboard—ham and toast. I stick an apple in my pocket as well.

"This will do." I hesitate at the table. I could send Abram ahead, get a moment alone with Father…

"Stay safe," Father says without lifting his gaze, his voice hard-edged.

My inclination vanishes. I won't confess with my tail between my legs, like the scolded dog he thinks I am. He can break our silence. After all, it is still mostly his fault.

"I am your obedient son!" I call, half jogging to the door.

Outside, a thick haar has come off the sea, enveloping the city in cold gray. Our manor house stands at the top of the hill, and on a good day we can see the distant shape of the other islands. In this weather I can barely make out the shadow of the cathedral's spire at the city's center.

"Sure you want to go treasure hunting in this?" I ask Abram, pulling my coat closer.

"It'll clear up," he says confidently, heading down the street with True at his heels. "It's off the water. We just need the wind to shift."

He doesn't have to tell me it's off the water—I can feel it in the air's cold bite. As I follow him through narrow alleys and small busy courtyards toward the harbor, I think back to the fog over the loch. And Princess Katherine—Kit—standing at the edge of the dock. She never did tell me what she had been looking at.

The houses of Stromwell are built at odd angles to keep the wind from blowing even fiercer through the alleys. It's more effective in some places than others. When we get to Kabyl Pass—named for a treacherous mountain path halfway around the world—the straightness of the way channels the full force of a gale. The haar closes around us, stinging in the wind.

"It's slick here," Abram calls over his shoulder. "Be careful."

"I know how to walk," I reply. My foot lands on polished stone and slips suddenly from under me. I curse, stumbling—but Abram catches my arm to steady me. Sighing, I add, "Thanks."

"Are you sure you're all right?" Abram asks, staying by my side as I keep making my way cautiously down the steeply paved hill. True has reached the bottom and sits to wait patiently. "You seem a bit…on edge."

I don't answer, keeping my gaze on my feet and my hand on the nearest wall for balance.

Abram shifts beside me, then takes off his glasses to rub them with a handkerchief. "Did…Princess Catharine reject your proposal?"

"No." I slide the last few feet to the main street and release a breath, grateful to be on even ground again. "I didn't ask."

The streets are already bustling, and I cut into the flow of people before Abram can pose more questions.

Carts pulled by horses labor their way toward the mills on the far side of town. Women hold out knitted goods for sale—socks and gloves and colorful hats like mine. Men pass back and forth on their way to the water or from it. I wave to Merlin Muir, a retired fisherman who spends his days exchanging stories outside our one hotel.

He tips his cap to us. "After the tide, my lads?"

"That's right," I answer, still walking. "How's the fishing?"

"Got a few good tales." He winks. "Come by when you're in less of a hurry."

I slow, curious. But Abram catches my arm. Quietly, he reminds me, "If we stop for five minutes, we'll be here for sixty."

"Right." Abram must be very keen on that potential flotsam to avoid Mr. Muir's stories. But he's correct—the tide waits for nothing, not even a good yarn. More's the pity. I lift my hand to the old fellow and continue toward the harbor.

Abram steps into the lead, taking us down a natural slope, quiet and calm after all the hurry of main street. My small yole is hauled out and beached on the grass noust, high on the slope of the land before it meets the water. *The Prospect* painted along the bow in looping script. My steps slow as Abram's quicken. This boat has been in our family for generations, back as far as Mervyn. Some storytellers claim it is his own boat from the impossible quests, though Abram hasn't been able to confirm that in any of our documents.

But what if it *was* Mervyn's boat? Does it mean something if I have inherited both his boat and his curse? Or maybe that's just my privilege as the eldest.

Abram has the lines already tossed inside and pushes the boat easily into the water. He glances back at me. "Everything all—"

"Right. Yes. Everything is all right." I try to shake off my apprehension and clamber aboard. The boat rocks, and it's strange how the comfort of that familiar motion mixes with all my sudden unease. True jumps in behind me, and when I take the forward bench he climbs over me to sit in the gap right in the bow.

Abram pushes the yole deeper and hops aboard last, settling with one of the oars. We've been doing this since we were boys, and we barely need to think as we maneuver out of the inlet and into the broader harbor. The main street might be busy, but this calm stretch of protected water is the lifeblood of Stromwell. I watch the haar swirling around the buildings, as thick as ever. I can't see our house up on the hill above town.

The water livens once we clear the sheltered harbor. We hoist the sail and Abram at the tiller turns us south. I keep my focus on the haar, preferring to stare at the gray rather than at my brother's face. I think, again, of Kit, wondering absently if she is even now gazing at the fog north of the loch, toward me, as I gaze south toward her.

"You said you didn't propose," Abram says suddenly. "I thought that was rather the purpose for going down there? What put you off?"

I shrug, trimming the sail. I could tell him. Speir didn't say I needed to keep it a secret. But I know Abram. He'd press into the story, dig out my reasons, and finding himself in the mix he'd take on the weight as surely as if I'd handed the curse to him. And while Father can't be right about looking the other way and passing the curse on down the line, a part of me wonders if it wouldn't be better to let the whole thing sink with me. End with me. If I don't tell Abram, maybe it will spare him something.

"I just…didn't think she really liked me," I say instead. It's the truth too. "She's pleasant and agreeable but something didn't fit between us."

I glance over to see if he'll accept that. Abram seems preoccupied with the tiller, rubbing a rag over a bird dropping near the handle. He doesn't look up from his task for a few minutes.

"I'm sorry for that," he says, finally lifting his gaze. There's a smile in the corner of his mouth.

I narrow my eyes. "Are you?"

His ears and neck turn so red, even the dim light can't hide it.

I laugh, surprised. "Were you…? Wait, how many times did you dance with her?" I ask, trying to think back. My memories of that evening have blurred, other than the garden confrontation. Even my conversation with Kit has shifted into flashes of moments—her eyes avoiding mine, the curl of one strand of blonde-brown hair against her freckled cheekbone, the way she hesitated before giving her hand. "Twice?"

Abram coughs. "Four times."

I jab him in the shoulder. "What scandal! My own brother!"

He's still red as a sunburn. "I wasn't—I mean—It wasn't—I was only—"

"Trying to steal a princess from under my nose?"

Abram looks genuinely horrified. "I would never do that! And anyway, it isn't anything nearly that serious. I only talked with her, and it was nice, and the dancing was nice, and she was nice." He runs a hand through his hair, then adjusts the tiller to guide us toward shore. "I only thought—if you weren't—then maybe—but it's nothing serious."

He seems sincerely worried, so I curb my teasing. In as near a serious tone as I can, I say, "It's fine, Abram. She *is* nice. And even a polite princess wouldn't spend four dances with you if she *didn't* like you."

Abram glances at me, mortified and hopeful, but quickly turns his attention back to the shore. "Help me get us in. The haar's making it hard to spot the noust."

I let the conversation drop as we locate our landing spot, a slope carved into the shoreline by some long-ago sailors. Once we've hauled the yole a safe distance from the sea, we gather our empty bags and set off for the holms.

In the spring, we can't step near this place without terns diving for our heads. But in the late autumn, it's silent and still. The first tidal island is little more than a jumble of rocks and seaweed, and then the second another jumble, and finally an even smaller holm after that.

Abram turns his attention to the tide line, searching the rocks. I make a halfhearted search myself. True slips and slides over the rocks until he reaches the grass of the first holm, and then takes off to hunt rabbits.

My luck isn't good today. There are only rocks, some bird bones, and a whole lot of kelp. The stony causeway keeps rolling under my feet, and my ankles pinch in protest. *Sore from the dances*, I think again bitterly.

When I reach the first grassy holm, I have a look at the ruined chapel while Abram catches up. The crumbled walls are almost entirely covered in grass, buried by the centuries. The storm doesn't seem to have exposed anything new, but I try pulling up a chunk of overhanging turf anyway.

"No, don't expose it," Abram says, hurrying up to me.

I try not to let out a sigh. "Why don't you just go digging, if you're so curious about it?"

Abram moves my hand away from the grass clump. "It's protected like this. I don't want to accidentally destroy anything."

I look at his lean form and then out at the churning sea. "Um, I don't think you can do more harm than *that*."

"You'd be surprised how much harm a person can do," Abram says, smiling.

My mouth tastes bitter suddenly. I don't think even Abram knows how right he is. I force a smile and move on, not about to let him in on it.

Should I, though? I wonder as I poke at some old oystercatcher nets. Is keeping it from him so different from what Father did to us?

Eventually, I plop down near to the rocky causeway that leads to the second holm. I pull a few stones closer and, like a boy, begin absently stacking them into a cairn. True comes to join me, rabbit-less, and leans his body against my back. It's almost enough to put me off balance, but I'm grateful for the added warmth against the rising wind.

I've been dancing somewhere for several nights now. But where is it? And will it always be like this—sleepwalking with only dust to show for it?

It makes me think of the one time I got really drunk. It was an accident—I hadn't had a lot of experience and I was with my student fellows and their fishermen fathers at a small pub in the city. They kept buying me drinks, or passing me drinks, and I was eager to match the rough men pint for pint. I woke up at home with a splitting headache, sick on my floor, and only the faintest impression of what had happened. I dreaded what I'd done while I was out of my senses—and I had, indeed, made a fool of myself. But, luckily for me, the fishermen are kind and once they realized I'd had too much, they got me home safe and didn't tease me *too* badly afterward for my renditions of popular ballads.

But I still remember waking up, my skin crawling with the feeling that I'd been somewhere I didn't intend to be, someone I didn't know.

I haven't drunk nearly that much since. Even at the ball I did not black out.

Now I'm out of my mind again, but I'm not surrounded by kind people. I know I've been dancing—or I guess I have—but I doubt I have friends there. I doubt they'll gently escort me home if I get in over my head.

If? I *am* in over my head.

I look across at Abram where he's pulling some rope from the rubble. He scrutinizes it before putting it into his bag. He leaves nothing to waste and always finds scraps that are miraculously useful.

Abram was there the morning after my drunken escapade. He helped peel me off the floor. When I finished washing, he showed up with several concoctions for hangovers recommended by our cook. And when I was tempted to sulk in my mortification, he was the one who distracted me with his latest doodles. He was the one who got me laughing again.

I may not have friends at the dance. But maybe I don't have to be entirely alone at home?

The bone-weary, breath-stealing tiredness washes over me again. I close my eyes against it. How much longer will I be up for an excursion like today? Perhaps Abram deserves to know that our time together is limited. Perhaps it is kinder to let him prepare.

Or perhaps it is selfish to want him to carry this with me, when he can do nothing about it. He could help with a hangover but even he can't save me from a curse. When I am gone, he'll be hurt—but he doesn't have to hurt anticipating it.

I'm still warring with my thoughts when I hear the sound of someone coming over the rocky causeway. Abram straightens, staring into the haar a moment before he calls, "Good morning, Mrs. Westness!"

"Good morn, Abram!" The old woman becomes a shadow and then a solid person. She has her arms outstretched for balance. Abram hurries to help her over the last of the rocks and onto solid ground. I get to my feet and go to join them, True staying close to my heels. Mrs. Westness is exchanging pleasantries with Abram, but when she sees me, her bushy eyebrows lift. She speaks with the heavy lilting of the old folk here. "Well, well, Idris! I wouldn't have thought you'd be out so early!"

My ears warm. "I hope I'm not known for keeping late mornings."

"Not at all!" She winks. "But I wouldn't expect you out and about after your busy night."

My heart stutters in my chest. "What?"

Mrs. Westness has turned to Abram. "And who's the fancy lass, I ask myself? Who's got our prince out on the waters after midnight?" She pats my arm and prepares to walk past. "Just be careful of the seal folk, will you? It's an enchanted hour."

Abram looks at me, confused.

"You—you saw me out last night?" I ask. True leans against my leg and I put my hand on his head. The ground doesn't feel solid anymore.

She nods. "Was waiting on my Tom's return and you sailed right up the coast. Called out to you but you must not have heard. Wind was something awful."

"You're sure it was me?"

"The moon was out bright as anything. Sure seemed like you and that hound there." Seeing my earnestness, she hesitates. "Well—maybe I was mistaken."

"I think you must be," Abram says. "Idris was home all night."

I don't contradict him. My mind is racing. Mrs. Westness lives on the southeast side of the island. For her to see me, I must have been headed toward Twinehallow Sound, one of the worst stretches of water around all the islands. It's nothing but riptides and whirlpools.

Abram is still talking with Mrs. Westness—I catch something about Tom and the mainland and fouler weather ahead—but I can't pay attention. Twinehallow Sound could lead me to many different places. It doesn't give me any more of a sense of where I've been, except that, apparently, I've sailed through waters that claim men even on the calmest days. And I've been doing it at night without my own mind.

The conversation tails off and Mrs. Westness wanders away. Abram is staring at me, frowning.

"She's wrong, isn't she?" he asks. "You haven't been going out like that alone?"

I look at him silently. I don't know what to say.

His eyes widen. "Where are you going, Idris?"

I can't keep it from him anymore. Softly, I admit, "I don't know."

SEVEN

Kit

"Kit?" says the girl who looks like me. The body that looks like mine.

I lift my hands. Unblemished. Delicate. Slim.

Catharine's hands.

I shift my gaze back to the me-who-isn't-me and whisper, "Catharine?"

She nods. I try to take a steadying breath. When I glance at the clearing, Speir is gone.

"It worked?" Mother asks, approaching me. Her eyes shine. "You have switched?"

"What have you done?" I demand. My words are strange and lilting in Catharine's mouth. They do not sound as angry as I feel.

"I've saved you." As Mother reaches for me, Catharine retreats behind me. "I promised I would protect you, and see? You're out of that wasting body. You're engaged to a prince. You're free."

"Did you know?" Catharine murmurs, her fingers grazing my sleeve. "Did you know she would do this?"

I turn to protest. Before I can, Catharine gulps a breath and runs for the forest. I start after her, but my mother catches my arm.

"Let her go," she says. "We have no need of her."

My heart pounds. "*I* need her."

I wrench away and run after Catharine. Mother calls my name, but soon I've left her behind. Catharine's trail is clear—she was never taught how to move in a forest and even my basic lessons in tracking from my grandmother are enough for me to follow her. I'm struck that my ankles don't hurt when I run. How long have my ankles been hurting?

Catharine has not gone far. I find her sitting at the base of a tree, arms round her knees, trembling. Except it's me—I'm looking at myself, small and shaking.

Have I always been so small?

How is any of this possible?

"Catharine." I drop down in front of her. "I didn't know."

She hugs her knees tighter. "Why did she do it?"

"I'm—not sure." She meant to protect me, but I don't know how to say that. I take Catharine's hand—*my* hand, twisted joints and swollen knuckles—and hold it gently. "I don't understand, but I—we'll find a way out of this. We'll make it right."

"How?" She looks up at me with wide eyes. "A deal with the Hidden Folk is almost impossible to break."

"Deal?" I echo.

"That finman said there was a price." Catharine's words almost run together in her worry. "Your mother made a deal. And we don't even know the exact words they used! The words mean everything!"

I take a moment to collect myself. Catharine is panicking, but she seems to understand what's happening better than me. She has accepted our world turning impossible more readily than I have—maybe because magic isn't impossible to her. I tap at my collarbone and breathe away my own uncertainty.

"It's a curse," I say, partly to convince myself. I lift my chin. "What happens in the folktales when there's a curse?"

Catharine's shoulders begin to steady. "The curse breaks."

"We know the person who cast it," I continue, thinking out loud. "You said he was one of the finfolk?"

"He was dressed like them." Catharine closes her eyes. "The stories say they dress in shimmering clothes like fish scales."

I cast back to the tales she's read to me. "Is it common for one of them to be so far inland?"

"He might have come down the loch, the same as the princes."

It's too much of a coincidence: two princes from the north followed by a magical being who features in northern stories. "Could he have come from the Islands of Skyare?"

Catharine nods slowly. "Yes. I've never heard of the finfolk in our own tales. Only the ones from the islands."

"Then we follow the stories," I say, seizing onto the plan as it forms in my head. "We search the places where magic is still strong and we find a way to undo this."

"It would help to have the exact terms used for the deal," Catharine says. "A bargain can't be just...broken, but sometimes there's a loophole in the wording."

That means I need to speak with my mother. We need a solution and we need it now. Catharine cannot be allowed back to the castle in my body.

Out loud, I add, “We’ll have to go north in secret.”

Catharine frowns. “My father would want to help.”

My heartbeat picks up speed at the thought. “But if he found out what’s happened, he would punish my mother.”

We look across at each other and for a moment the few feet between us seem to widen. I feel the hypocrisy of my concern. Should I even worry for my mother after what she has done?

If we return but do not reveal that Mother has switched us, Catharine will be in danger from the king. But if we tell the truth, Byrne might kill my mother.

Despite everything, I want to protect her. To protect them both.

I am at Catharine’s mercy.

At last, Catharine gives a small nod. “All right. We’ll go in secret. Once the curse is broken, we can decide how—*if* we tell him.” She brightens, just a little, and my stomach clenches at the sight of my own face showing relief as my own voice says the words, “Perhaps it will be better this way—we can arrange it so Father will worry less.”

I tap my collarbone and swallow back my nausea. That secret can wait.

✦

It is well into the afternoon by the time I return to the castle, alone. Mother is waiting outside, apparently expecting me.

She beams as soon as I come in sight and I try not to clench my jaw. I school my face into a passive expression. Perhaps it will come easier in Catharine's body, because she has so much practice in appearing polite.

"I know it's a great deal of change," Mother says as soon as I'm close. "But I swear, it's for the best. Where is your stepsister?"

"I couldn't find her."

I adjust my pelisse, not used to the way it fits so snugly. This one is tailor-made and meticulously adjusted, unlike most of my old clothes. I have a whole host of questions for my mother. I start with the one that's been burning my throat the whole walk home.

I take a steadying breath. "Would you have left Catharine here? With him?"

She frowns. Stands a little straighter. "He had no intention of letting you leave, Kit."

I feel as if I am falling. As if I am standing before a stranger. "You would have abandoned her to—" I can't say it. My voice cracks and my heart is breaking. "You know that he would—"

"Why should it matter?" she demands, suddenly angry. "If he hurts you, why should his own daughter be spared? You are his daughter, too!"

I want to sink to the ground. "Catharine could tell him the truth. If he learned about the curse, he would execute you."

"She would not dare." Mother lifts her chin. "You have a warrior heart, Kit. A clever mind. You would have done as much or more. But she—she will break under his first look and not have the courage to reveal the truth."

And I see it as Mother wished—me, in my new and beautiful body, gone to the islands to marry, have babies, and live my days in splendor. And Catharine, my sweet Catharine, the victim of her father with him never knowing he is harming his own precious child. It is perverted and sick and I hate that my mother could ever think of it. I hate that *I* can imagine her thinking of it.

"Catharine is innocent in all of this," I hiss. The emptiness, the crumbling in me turns hot.

Mother shakes her head. "And even if she *did* attempt to communicate the truth, I have some safeguards in place. Speir promised that neither of you would be able to speak of it to anyone who wasn't involved. We don't need to worry."

It is disgusting to hear how she's thought it through. I want to point out that we wouldn't need to *speak* it for anyone paying attention to recognize I am not Catharine, even if I look like her.

I grasp for another question. One that's practical and logical and not full of everything wrong in this situation. "How did you even find Speir? Isn't he one of the Hidden Folk?"

Mother looks a little surprised. "I see you've been listening to Catharine's stories. Yes, he is. And I found him—of all places!—in our garden on the night of Prince Idris's birthday. They had been speaking, the prince and he, and I followed when Speir walked away. I did not recognize him as one of my guests, and of course I was curious what secret business the prince had. Speir walked round to the water's edge, and I saw him gather the mist into the shape of a boat. He stepped onto it and it was solid as wood. I caught his attention before he left, and we struck a deal."

"What was the wording of it?" I ask. I need her to tell me without suspecting what I'll do with the information. "What does he get out of this?"

Mother waves off my concern. "Nothing I wasn't happy to give."

"But what were the terms?" I press. I try another angle. "You've done everything so precisely, I know you must have negotiated an impressive agreement. I want to know how."

Her eyes narrow the smallest bit, just at the corner. She is becoming wary. "You will just need to trust me, my dear."

That's the most I'll get out of her. Any more, and she will know I intend to run.

"Now, to be safe," Mother goes on, "I think tonight you should complain of a headache and go to bed early. I will, of course, make a show of looking for 'Kit'—"

"Tell him that 'Kit' has gone to bed as well," I suggest. I am not sure how my stepfather would feel about my disappearance, but I can't risk him sending search parties out tonight. "He can discover she's gone after we leave."

"Yes, good." She presses my hands, in happiness or excitement or both. I'm distracted for a moment by the feeling of it—the warm gesture that doesn't hurt. I hadn't realized I'd braced myself for pain until it doesn't come.

I force myself to focus. I want to protest, to make my mother see how horribly wrong she is about all of this. But I need supplies. I need to move about the castle without anyone—the king or my mother—suspecting anything of me.

"Very well. I will retire early."

I move to go up to my room, but as I pass the study a voice calls: "Catharine!"

Byrne. I turn, stiffening. He has risen from his desk and is coming toward me with a smile. There is nothing but familial care in his gaze.

"You were gone a while!" he exclaims and leans forward to kiss my hair.

I step back without thinking, my pulse dizzy-fast. His smile wavers.

"We were—" My words sound unnatural in Catharine's voice, more unnatural somehow now that I am speaking to someone who doesn't know who I am. I scramble for the way she would phrase it. "We were delayed in getting Kit's pelisse. It still needs to be hemmed a few inches, and M—Her Majesty wished to have it done while we were there."

"And where is my stepdaughter?" he says, looking over my shoulder.

Mother is in the hall behind me. She sighs. "Kit has set off on a walk, though I told her not to. She will exhaust herself and likely go straight to bed when she gets home."

"Hmm." This seems acceptable to Byrne. He returns his attention to me and I manage to not flinch away. I try to fix a comfortable smile on my face. It feels like a grimace. A knot of confusion draws his brows together.

"My head is hurting," I say quickly. "I think I'll just go lie down."

"Very well." This time, he places his hands on my shoulders before he leans forward. I've no way to escape without jerking out of his grip. It isn't strong—I could easily break it; it's only meant to convey gentle affection, not to imprison. But Catharine would not shy away. Catharine would not shrink from the pine smell of him. When he touches his lips to my forehead, I want to vanish. To fold into myself until I am invisible.

But I hold myself still. Upright.

He leans back again. It must have only been a moment. I feel winded, as if I've just wrestled a horse.

"Rest," he says. "And I will see you when you are better."

"That may not be until tomorrow morning," I say, my voice hollow. "I will probably have dinner brought up to my room."

He nods. "Send word if you need anything." He hesitates, then adds reluctantly, "We can delay the trip, if necessary."

"I don't think there will be any need for that." Again, I try to smile. I cannot afford to draw too much attention to myself.

"A bit of rest will have her bright as a blossom in no time," Mother says, taking my elbow and steering me back to the hallway.

"Mari," Byrne says, "once she is settled, I would like you to come back here. We have matters to discuss before you leave tomorrow."

"Of course." Mother drops him a shallow curtsy and then walks me away.

My hands shake and I clench them closed. In Catharine's body, I am not in danger. But if Catharine had come back in mine…

Mother opens the door to Catharine's room and gestures grandly to the finer bed, the finer furniture. "All the comforts you deserve at last."

I step inside, hardly seeing any of these familiar objects. I can't bear to look at my mother. Anger and disgust roar in my ears, and I can't seem to find the words to release them.

Mother gives me a swift hug, which I do not return. She takes a look at my face and sighs at whatever she reads there. "You will understand one day," she says, patting my arms. "Now get some rest."

She leaves the room. I grab one of Catharine's fine pillows and wail into it, wail until I have no breath. Then I sit there, gasping, the pillow to my chest and tears in my eyes.

My mother is lost to me. She has gone so far from protecting me—she has made it all worse. I never wanted to be free just so someone else could take my place.

I have to help Catharine.

I lay out two bags and select one for Catharine. In her room, I pack everything that seems useful—socks, a blanket, sturdy boots, and small trinkets to sell. Catharine has a map on her desk—I fold it carefully into my reticule. Last, I add Catharine's book of northern folktales. We may need them if we are able to find the Hidden Folk. That's one bag full.

From my old room I take gloves, a woolen dress, and a compass. Catharine does not keep money—a princess does not need coins—but I have some stashed away in my desk drawer. Not enough for comfort, but maybe enough to get us north. I root around in my trunk, searching for a spare cloak. Instead, tucked into the farthest corner, my hands come across a strip of silk. Prince Idris's cravat.

I tug it free. I run my thumb over the crumpled cloth, tracing delicate white embroidery—nearly invisible against the equally white fabric—and remember the warmth of it as he bound my wrist. The heat of his skin, even though he never quite touched me.

I stuff the cravat into my bag with everything else without letting myself consider *why*. Knowing it's there gives me an extra measure of comfort and any further introspection would be a waste of precious time.

On my way back to Catharine's room, I catch a servant and request a hearty meal. My stomach grumbles at the thought of food. I'd forgotten I hadn't eaten anything today, and now it's nearly sunset. But I'll have to be careful not to eat too much tonight.

Once I've wrapped up everything I can carry, including most of my dinner, I sit at Catharine's desk. The quill is easier to hold with Catharine's hand. I'll leave Byrne a note from Catharine to let him know she has run away south. Hopefully that will buy us extra time.

Dear—

The letters come out strangely. Not quite the elegant script Catharine uses, but not quite my hasty scrawl either.

Dear Father—

It's no use. My mind wants to form my own familiar writing, but this body wants to maneuver the pen like Catharine. An ache pounds behind my eyes. I throw the piece of paper in the fire, grab a new sheet and start again. Perhaps, for what I have in mind, it is best that no one recognizes this writing as being either mine or Catharine's.

> *Princess Catharine—*
> *Thank you for your inquiry and deposit. The route via the River Lems will be the safest. Passage has been booked in Burghen. We eagerly await your arrival.*
> *It is three days' journey by foot to the docks and five days' downriver to Chiphaven. From there—Rourne? Garci? Karistan? All ways are open with the right funds. Do let us know if you require more details.*

South. All ways south. While we fly to the north.

Byrne knows his daughter is fanciful. Hopefully it will not be such a stretch of his imagination to believe she has taken off in pursuit of her own romantic story. I stick the piece of paper in one of Catharine's travel books, then set it on the desk for him to find once we are gone.

I settle to wait for night and the cover it will bring. I know I should probably try to sleep, to store up my strength, but I can't stop thinking of Catharine out there, waiting. I told her to get some food from town and I showed her a sheltered grove in the wood where she could hide. She will be dry and warm enough in my new pelisse. But she isn't used to harsh things, to discomfort, to cold. And she is in my body, which I know will ache and protest.

Finally, finally, night comes. The castle quiets. I put the two bags over my shoulders and slip out.

I move into one of the side passages, following the narrow turning steps downward by feel more than sight. I emerge near the kitchens. At this time, the servants will be having their own dinner. Voices murmur, the cook's louder than the others'. I think a quiet farewell to them as I turn to the door. My time here was not all good, but I was cared for. I was looked after. And it will be an adjustment to go back to a life without these luxuries.

I step into the courtyard and skirt the darkest edges to the gate. If I knew for sure there were no stablehands about, I might have taken our horses—but it is enough of a risk just for me, alone, to sneak out. Stealing two mares would be asking for trouble.

The castle gate remains open. Byrne has a hospitable streak and likes the gates open until the main household has gone to bed, so that any weary traveler might have easy access. The guard who will attend the gate through the night isn't here yet.

It is a simple thing to step through. And yet, I find myself pausing. Looking back.

Even before my father died, my mother and I were all we had. She was the one who stayed home with me, who educated and comforted me. She bandaged my fingertips when I pricked them while embroidering. She washed my hair in a basin and taught me how to tie rags to get a suitable curl.

She bet on me, counting on the fact that when it came down to it, I would choose her.

Is it wrong of me to choose Catharine?

I look again at my hand—Catharine's hand. Flawless and strong.

Mother may have been trying to help me, but she has hurt someone else to do it. And I don't want more people hurt. Maybe, someday, I can forgive her. But now I have to protect Catharine. She did nothing to deserve this. And doesn't it make me a little like Byrne if I leave Catharine trapped in the wasting he started?

"Goodbye," I whisper to the castle, and to my mother, and to all the good and bad tangled with them.

✦

Moor, marsh, mountain. Our journey is three days in the taking and many more ahead. We have passed the boundaries of the land I know and now walk through the brown grass with fog and frost tugging at our skirt hems. I keep my compass out, held in this new hand that does not ache. Constantly I check for north-east.

Gray rocks poke out of the next hill like old bones. No, not rocks—ruins. I lift my arm, mutely pointing. Catharine makes a quiet humming noise, agreeing. The day is waning and the wind is picking up. We can shelter there overnight.

I walk ahead of Catharine so that I can spot pools of water or gaping holes hungry for an ankle. This body is sore but hardy, able to be pushed without collapse. In it, I could take a fall. But I know her body—my body—would punish any mistake for days.

We reach the crumbled remains of some long-ago building. As we pause, perched on what was once a wall, I break open a handful of nuts and offer them to

Catharine. In my body, she doesn't seem to mind them anymore. The sharp crack of shells against stone cuts across the wide, wide silence of the moors. The silence of us. The air is crisp with cold and my lungs pinch with every breath.

I search for words, but what do you say when your mother has stolen your sister's face and given it to you?

I pull my wool skirt over my legs—long and graceful and strange—trying to preserve any warmth I can. The nuts taste chalky and aged on my new tongue. I barely keep from making a face. And still we say nothing.

There is only sky and ground, hill and marsh, forever and forever. I don't know how I'm going to get her safe. I'm not sure there is a *safe* out there.

But it's certainly not behind us.

I rise and my boots crunch on rubble. I wonder who lived here, and who they loved, and whether their bones rest easy.

"I'll get some kindling," I say. I am still not used to hearing Catharine's voice when I speak and I pause to clear my throat. "I think we're sheltered enough that it won't be spotted."

Catharine nods. I hesitate, looking again at my sister in my body. Have I always seemed so little? Or is it only that she sits now, hunched, as if she would collapse if she let herself?

"I can make us some beds," Catharine says. She smiles. It's my body, my face, but the smile somehow looks like her. "And maybe see if there's a corner somewhere that has a bit of roof left."

I nod and leave her to it. There is no wood, as it turns out—it's all grass and heather. When I return, Catharine has indeed found a bit of roof and made beds with some moss and our pelisses laid over the top. It is dry, miraculously, and I whisper a thanks for this unseasonable autumn. I sit beside her, shoulder to shoulder for warmth.

"How about a story?" I ask, closing my eyes.

Catharine thinks for a moment. "Have I told you about Mervyn and his impossible tasks? It's been on my mind. They say Mervyn was an ancestor of Prince Idris and Prince Abram."

"No. Go on then."

Catharine reaches into her bag and pulls out the folktale collection. She takes a moment to find the place, then begins:

> *Once there were two sons born together, Mervyn and Erik. Mervyn was the eldest by seconds and the midwife wrapped a blue string round his hand to mark him. Mervyn was weak and his brother strong, so the king told the midwife to move the string to the younger. Thereafter, the king claimed the younger as eldest and heir, but the queen knew the truth. She told it to Mervyn and he grew in resentment of his brother.*
>
> *Time passed and the queen died. As her dying wish, she told the king to honor his real firstborn and give the kingdom to the most worthy. The king made the promise but spent time afterward seeking a way to be faithful to his wife and his inclination. He devised a scheme.*

He brought his sons together and told them, as they were now of age, he wanted to follow their mother's request. Conveniently, he left out her wish that the throne be given to Mervyn, the legitimate firstborn. He alleged that her only desire was for him to choose the most worthy. They were both to go and live three years among the peasants, unknown, and work for wages like every man. At the end of the three years, they would return and present the king with the finest evidence of their labor.

Erik took himself to the southern lands, where the weather was calmer and life easier. He let slip that he was a prince and lived his days on credit and charm. He was apprenticed to a composer, but he played the man's daughter more than any instrument.

Mervyn took himself to the far reaches of their islands, in the heady cold where the wind was never still. There he was apprenticed to a smithy. Though his childhood and adolescence had not improved his weak stature, the rugged landscape and the harsh labor did what nothing else had. Mervyn grew strong, skilled, and handsome. He spent three years crafting a fine sword for his father.

When the sons returned, Erik presented his father a composition that could barely be played for its many mistakes. Mervyn presented his father with a blade that rivaled any master's. There was a clear winner, but the king could not bear to give up on his favorite son.

So the king set them a second task. An heir would need a wife. The son who found the most bonny woman in the land would be given the throne. She must be beyond anything their court had ever seen. Again, this must be done without anyone knowing that they were princes.

Erik left his composer's daughter and went courting across foreign lands. He let it be known that the woman who caught him would win a crown. He wooed and charmed and returned at last with a woman draped in jewels and soft with luxury.

Mervyn stayed nearer the islands, believing that he could find a worthy wife among his own hearty people. However, it was not one of his own that he found, but a woman of a different kind. She sailed the waters with her pirate father, her hands rough with work and her mouth full of every language. She had no fear of the wilds and was only adorned with her stout heart and quick wit. With her came new trade routes and connections to all corners of the world. No one could argue: She was a princess of the seas and when Mervyn presented her to his father he was presenting the world.

The king again was caught in a bind. Erik's spoiled wife already spoke of leaving their unforgiving land and she had not been there a month. Mervyn's pirate wife could match any courtier, broker any deal, and map any path. There was a clear winner, but the king could not resign himself to declare it.

The king set them a third task, a final task. They must both go into the world and find the greatest treasure.

Erik went with his wife back to temperate lands and warm waters. And whether he was lulled by the comfort of that life, or whether he fell to one of the many diseases of the south, who's to say? For he never was seen or heard from again.

Mervyn took his pirate wife and they sailed across torrid seas, gathering and trading. When they returned, Mervyn laid the most beautiful seal skin at the king's feet. The court murmured with approval, but Mervyn said, 'This is not my treasure.' Mervyn lay a golden crown at the king's feet, decorated with rubies and diamonds. The court crowed with approval, but Mervyn said, 'This is not my treasure.' Mervyn lay an illuminated Bible at the king's feet, illustrated in the rarest inks and bound in the supplest leather. The court exclaimed with approval, but Mervyn said, 'This is not my treasure.'

'My treasure,' said Mervyn, taking his wife's hand, 'is the heart of the most courageous woman in this and any land.'

The king took the seal skin and had it made into a royal cloak, which he draped round his son's shoulders. He took the crown and placed it on the pirate wife's head. He took the Bible and swore on it that this son, Mervyn, would be king.

"*And so it was,*" Catharine murmurs.

"Do you suppose the seal skin was a selkie's?" I ask, still trying to nibble through my nuts. It isn't as if I have a choice about being picky out here.

"The tale doesn't say." Catharine flips back to check. "I think it would. And the pirate princess certainly wasn't a selkie."

I shrug. Not all seal skins are magical.

We eat more nuts, drink some of our water. Then we sleep.

And we wake. And we walk.

Our trek takes longer than it would if we had taken the roads, but we don't dare travel openly. Even with the misdirection that had us going south, it's likely that the king will send some men north just in case. So we fight through the wilderness, trying to skirt the mountains when we can. But the valleys are marshy and the going slow. Many times, the most direct route is obscured by gorse, the thick bushes all thorn. There's no getting through those thickets, so we go round them. Sometimes whole miles round.

Along the way, we shelter in shepherds' huts. Occasionally we are lucky enough to find a farmer who will house us in their barn. Catharine is always the one to ask, while I hang back in the shadows. No one would recognize my old body as anyone important, but Catharine's—the one I wear now—is a danger out here. One description spoken to the wrong person and the hills would be swarming with the king's men.

More often than I'd like, as we cross the land in relative silence, my thoughts drift to the princes. Or one prince in particular.

Idris's sudden departure had not drawn my attention before we encountered Speir, but now I wonder. Mother said she saw them talking on the night of the ball. What did the Hidden Folk want with him? When Catharine invited him to dance with me, he looked so unwell—and that must have been after this conversation in the garden. And the next day, the whole family took off without warning. Hardly a coincidence.

I'm not sure that we'll be able to avoid the princes on the main island of Skyare, even if we only use it as a stepping stone to an outlying place. But I don't think it is wise to seek the princes. For all Idris was kind to me, we don't know if we can trust them.

Nevertheless, when I reach into my bag for supplies night after night, I find myself pausing to touch the cravat. A sort of daydreamy feeling rises when I do, but I pull away and cut off my thoughts. I have more pressing concerns.

So I think of other things, until I think of Idris again, and the frustrating loop continues.

✦

When we finally reach the port of Stramp at the end of the mainland, it is little more than a fishing village. Under the cloud cover, the place is as colorless as the sea and the sky. People move about briskly in the cold wind, everyone focused on some errand or task. We receive curious looks but nothing more.

Catharine and I pause at the edge of the harbor. Small fishing boats are preparing to go out with the tide, the men and boys calling greetings to one another. There are a few larger boats as well—some schooners with cargo being loaded.

I feel suddenly overwhelmed, like all the strength that kept me moving has drained out of me at the sight of people. I look at Catharine and see the same frozen uncertainty in her face.

"Can I help you, lasses?" asks a kind voice.

I start and realize an older man has come up behind us. He's carrying a net over his shoulder and his face is creased from years at sea. When he smiles, his teeth are surprisingly white.

Catharine rallies herself. "We are hoping to get to the islands. To Skyare, specifically."

The man nods thoughtfully and glances around at the various boats. He points toward one of the schooners. "The *Marksman* will be going there this afternoon, but they will take a whole purse for fare." He gives us an assessing look—our clothes ragged and torn, our two small bags. "But Tom Westness will take you for less, if you don't mind helping him reel in some herring on the way."

"We can do that," Catharine says with unearned confidence.

I nod more reluctantly. Neither of us has so much as been out on the open sea before, and I know Catharine's wrist still aches. She will have a hard time with any labor. But it can't be too difficult to pull nets in with this well body. Or, at least, I hope not.

The man waves another fellow over. Mr. Westness is even older, with a bright gleam to his brown eyes and a beard streaked with black and white. He takes us on for only a few coins, almost all we have left. Within the hour,

Catharine and I are on his small fishing vessel heading out to sea. On the horizon, the clouds blacken.

The swell is unsettling—lifting the small boat and dropping it again suddenly. I grab my seat with white knuckles, sure at each drop that we're going to plunge beneath the next wave. I swallow hard and Catharine casts me a concerned look.

Unfazed, Mr. Westness says, "Just lean over the gunwale if you need to be sick."

"Gunwale?" I repeat, my neck heating.

"The side, lass."

After more than a week in this body, I'd grown comfortable being the strong one. But even this body has flaws. Soon I'm hanging over the edge of the boat and losing what little food I ate that morning. I feel Catharine put her hand on my shoulder, holding me steady as another swell rises and drops. I retch again.

Mr. Westness had said that we wouldn't get to Skyare until that night. But as the nausea rolls through me, time loses all meaning. I have no sense of how long we have been on this horrible boat, and no way to judge how much farther remains. Catharine helps haul nets. Fish slide and wriggle around my feet. Rain and wind splash my face in turns, and I heave.

Catharine points to something on the horizon, and still I heave.

There's an island in the fog. A column of rock stands apart from the cliff edge, impossible and grand. My heart gives a single hopeful beat and I whisper, "Is that it? Are we there?"

Catharine speaks to the fisherman. Their words are lost in the whirl of my head. To me she says, "No—but we're close."

I bend and heave again.

It may be hours, it may be years, but some time later Catharine is taking my arm and helping me rise. The fisherman is on my other side. My feet land on something blessedly solid. Land. Though it still seems to rock beneath me.

"There, now, careful lass," Mr. Westness murmurs. "We'll just go lie you down."

We enter a house, I think. I only know that the wind stops abruptly and the air warms. A woman's voice asks questions. Her accent is lilting and musical and the words mean nothing to me. Catharine answers. The fisherman says something about the boat and a moment later a door closes. Catharine and the woman clean me with heated wet cloths and help me into a dry dress made of scratchy wool.

"You must change," I say, searching for Catharine, dazed but remembering my old hands. Hands that will punish her for this journey. "You must get dry."

"I am dry." Catharine comes into focus. I'm so nauseated and dizzy, I have to concentrate to hold her still in front of my eyes. "I'm fine."

I'm taken to a small bed tucked into one of the walls. When I lie down, the mattress feels like it is made of thick, woven ropes.

"Rest," says Catharine, squeezing my hand. She winces and looks at her fingers, confused. She then turns her attention back to me. "We're safe now."

I want to open my mouth. We won't be safe until we have reversed this magic. I need to know where we are and where to go next. We hadn't planned what to do once we got to Skyare—the task of arriving seemed so enormous on its own.

But my eyes close. I sleep.

EIGHT

Idris

Father does not take calmly to the news that the enchantment has begun.

"We'll put a stop to it," he says as I finish explaining what Mrs. Westness saw. "I'll lock the door when you go to bed. Then you cannot leave."

I glance aside at Abram, lifting my eyebrows. I told him this would not end well. But my brother insisted that Father deserved to know. Abram misses my look, staring into the distance with a calculating expression.

"Father's right," he says, coming back to the conversation. "You agreed to bear the punishment, but Father did not agree to let you. Maybe just keeping you in place will be enough to stop it."

Father nods. "I will stay with you tonight to keep watch as well."

I sigh. Somehow, I doubt it will go the way either of them wishes.

As it turns out, I am right.

The following morning, I wake to a freezing room. My breath mists in front of me. True whimpers, pressing his cold nose to my palm. I give him an absent pet as I try to sit up. My arms ache. A sharp pain radiates from my leg.

I tug my nightshirt out of the way. A long gash slices down my right shin. Dried blood flakes around the cut. Other smaller scrapes crisscross my hands and arms. I have no memory of how they happened—not even of the pain I must have felt.

A gust of chill air comes through the open window and I lift my head. No, it's not open—it's broken. Shattered from the inside. One jagged piece juts up like a small mountain, stained brown-red across the top. My bed has been dragged halfway across the room, closer to the window, and a rope is tied to one of the legs. I lean up to look over the sill. The rope hangs down almost to the ground two stories below, swaying in the wind. My stomach drops at the sight.

True tries to crawl up on the bed, whining. I move back to make room, but instead of settling beside me he lies down on top of me. My hands shake and I can't seem to stop them. I rub True, checking him for wounds, but he seems fine.

"You didn't come with me?" I ask, scratching his belly. My unease rises at the thought, but I remind myself of the glass and the drop to the ground. "That's probably good."

In an armchair by the long-dead fire, Father mumbles and rubs his face. Seemingly he has been fast asleep the whole time—so still I forgot he was here. He blinks and then stares at the wreckage of my room.

From under True's furry mass, I state the obvious: "It didn't work."

✦

"If you didn't have a rope..." Father muses later, frowning over breakfast. "Where did you even find that rope?"

"Mrs. Muir gave me some after I helped repair the barn roof," I explain. "I was keeping it in a trunk. And I think if I hadn't had it, I would have just thrown myself out." I shift my leg under the table, trying to find a position where the fresh bandage on my shin won't rub against my boots. "Obviously I am going to leave, whether or not you make it difficult."

Abram glances from me to Father. He hasn't said much since he sent for a workman to repair the window. I'm curious what excuse will be given to the man. I'm too annoyed to ask, though I don't know what exactly I'm annoyed about. I drink a gulp of tea to settle myself.

"We could bar the window," Father says. "Make it impossible to escape. Set a guard to keep watch."

"Having you keep watch didn't make much difference," I mutter.

"I apologize for that." Father scowls. "The truth is, I could *not* stay awake. I think the curse affected me."

"Then what makes you think anyone else will be different?" I try not to roll my eyes. "Whatever you do, I'm going to find my way out. Or harm myself attempting it."

"We're lucky Idris didn't break a leg," Abram says quietly.

None of us point it out, but I think we're all wondering whether the Hidden Folk would make me dance on broken bones. I push my food around with my fork, then tear off a bit of ham and slip it to True. He's crouched beneath the table, leaning all his weight against me, even though he normally gets banished to the hearth during a meal.

"Besides," I go on, "I promised. I said I'd do the dances. So…I should just do them."

Father glares at me.

"We can't very well throw him in a dungeon," Abram says, trying to joke.

Father sits up straighter, eyes brightening. "That—"

"No," I cut him off. "I won't agree to that. You can try to make it safer for me to get there and back, but I won't be locked up!"

"Getting a witness might not be such a bad idea." Abram folds and unfolds his napkin. "We could have someone watch over you. I could—"

"No," Father and I both say at once.

Abram frowns at us.

"I can find someone else to watch Idris." Father turns back to me. "Maybe if they aren't part of the family, they won't be affected as I was. And if they can't stop you, at least they can get a sense of where you are going. Servants would talk, but perhaps someone more discreet…"

"Jay might be able to do it," Abram offers. "His ship doesn't leave for another month or so."

Father considers this. "Let me speak with him. In the meantime—" Father points his fork at me—"you need to rest. We must keep your strength up until we can find a solution to this mess."

"And how's that going?" I cross my arms and lean forward on the table. "Found a loophole yet?"

I know Father has been consulting with the storytellers and the wise women.

"No, not yet. Dancing enchantments usually involve the victim becoming trapped—sometimes permanently—within their realm. You seem to be an exception, as you can move between the Hidden Lands and home every night."

"You've told them the whole story?" I ask, surprised. He hesitates but doesn't reply. I smile grimly. "Ah. Not that desperate yet?"

"I am prepared to do whatever is necessary, when it is necessary."

"Why don't you take my room today, Idris?" Abram volunteers, sensing another fight. "At least until the glass is fixed in yours. That is...as long as you won't be bothered by me working in the study."

The bitterness eases out of my smile. Abram's studying is probably quieter than the mouse I've heard a few times in our rafters. "I'm not opposed to rest. That would be nice."

After breakfast, I retreat upstairs with Abram. I thought True might be impatient for an outing—he hasn't had a good walk in a few days now—but he presses close to my side the whole way, apparently determined not to let me out of his sight.

Abram's room smells comfortingly of paper and ink. Through the doors that join this room to our shared study, I can see the floor-to-ceiling bookshelves, his large magnifying glass, and the cases on a table in the room's center. My unruly desk, drowning in papers and books, sits abandoned near the fireplace. His tidy desk is tucked into the corner near the circular window.

"Here," Abram says, turning back the blankets on his bed. He gives an uncertain look at True. "I suppose you want him to..."

Both True and I give Abram our best pleading looks. I say with exaggerated reluctance, "I *could* tell him to lie on the *floor*..."

Abram sighs and shakes his head, moving back. "No, it's fine. Go ahead."

"Thanks." I kick off my shoes and lie down. True burrows on top of me and settles his head on my chest, as if to hold me there.

"Let me know if you need anything," Abram says, starting to close the door between me and the study.

"You can leave it open," I blurt.

Abram tilts his head but leaves the door ajar. I watch as he goes from shelves to microscope to desk, arranging his work. As predicted, his shuffling steps and scratching pencil are quieter than my rodent friend.

The regular, methodical movements, the creaks of our house, and the murmur of voices downstairs combine into a scene as familiar as it is comforting. I try to sink into this feeling and fall asleep.

But the more I attempt to relax, the more I am awake.

Instead of drifting into hazy thoughts and dreams, my mind sharpens with lists. Things I should be doing, should be fixing. The import records I said I would look over last week. Abram's still-missing shipwreck. Meetings I need to arrange. Tasks that were put aside while I was in the south.

Catharine, and what my life might be like now if I had proposed. I consider the best location for a wedding, the arrangements we would have had to make. She would have been lovely. Demure. Quiet. Willing.

But happy? I don't know.

Her sister would have come too. Perhaps her wrist would have healed by then. I wonder whether it has got any better in the time since I left. I wonder if there is something more to that family. Did King Byrne look satisfied after he twisted her through the turn, or do I only imagine it now that I'm looking back? His interest in her felt strange. Yet despite the shadow there, when we were alone she laughed with unrestrained openness. I wish I had been able to dance with her. Someone who laughs like that must burst with life in a jig.

How many jigs have I danced in the nights since my return? Who am I dancing with?

I turn over and stare at the ceiling. Fatigue drags through me, pulling my energy out like the tide. But my fingers fidget on True's back. My toes twitch. The longer I try to lie still, the less I can keep from moving.

At last, I can't stand it anymore. I nudge True off me and roll up to my feet.

Abram looks over from his work, frowning when I start pulling on my shoes. "Id?"

"That's enough napping for now!" I declare, trying to sound more cheerful than I feel.

Abram glances toward the clock in the study. "You've only been down for half an hour."

I could have sworn it was closer to two hours. I try not to let my surprise show. "Well, then I'll try again this afternoon. I have to get some errands done."

But that afternoon—in my own bed, window fully repaired—the same restlessness haunts my attempted nap. I cannot sleep, no matter how tired I feel.

Jay arrives in the evening, late enough that most of the servants have already retired for the night. He rubs his hands together against the cold as Abram lets him into the manor.

"Well, this is mysterious," he says, glancing from Abram to me. "I had word from your father to come by quietly at a late hour, but nothing more than that. Are we painting the tower clock again?"

A few years ago, the three of us had snuck into the Guildhall at midnight and decorated the clock face with a comical expression. It was Abram's idea, of course, though my father would never believe Abram was even involved. It was entirely worth the two weeks confined to the house just to hear the townsfolk—at least, the ones with good humor—have a laugh over it.

"Not something quite so merry," I admit. Abram and I had negotiated with my father to leave the explaining to us. His only requirement was that we must not disclose any family secrets. "It seems I've been enchanted by the Hidden Folk. We were hoping you'd be up to the task of seeing where I go every night."

Jay stares at me a moment, then plants his hands on his hips. "Well, well. And didn't I tell you they were real?"

"You did," I admit. After Jay's first night keeping a full watch on his father's vessel, he had claimed he saw selkies dancing on the shore. Hardly anyone but the elderly—used to the times when the Hidden Folk were more active around humans—had taken his colorful story as fact. The elderly and Abram, that is.

"And what kind of trouble have you got yourself into with them?" Jay goes on. "Been chasing alluring music coming from the dunes?"

"Not exactly."

"The details aren't particularly important," Abram cuts in. "You know how it is, Jay—they took offense and Idris has been caught up in it."

I bristle at the easy way he brushes aside the truth. But I know he's only trying to honor our promise to Father.

"Would you mind keeping a watch over Idris?" Abram asks. "You do not need to, if you'd rather not."

"Are you mad? Of course." Jay smiles. "I've been keen to see the Hidden Folk ever since that night. Maybe I can find something to prove I wasn't lying about the selkies."

"Excellent," I say, some of the anxiousness uncoiling from my gut.

"Don't do anything risky," Abram cautions. "We don't want to complicate the matter. We just want to understand what's happening."

"Aye, aye." Jay claps Abram on the shoulder. "Now, where should I keep watch?"

✦

In the morning, I wake to a dim day. The windows are still intact. True sleeps calmly on my feet. I try flexing my arms and legs. The usual soreness—and the bandaged cut on my shin—is still there, but I don't seem to be freshly injured this time.

Relieved, I crawl out of bed and get dressed. My excitement builds Jay will have answers; I know it. And maybe with those answers, I can find out what is happening to me.

"How'd it—" I open my bedroom door and falter—"go…?"

The chair we set in the hallway is empty. Jay's book and a burned-out candle are on the floor beside it, and a mug of tea long gone cold. True takes a disinterested sniff at the drink and then starts toward the breakfast room.

Right. It would make sense if Jay was up before me, already reporting whatever happened to Father and Abram. Or at least having his fill of food after a long night. I hurry down the stairs to join the others.

But when I enter, only Father and Abram sit at the table. They are speaking in low tones but stop abruptly when I come in. My eagerness turns to frustration. Jay's already told them and left.

"You can talk in front of me," I say, not bothering to hide my annoyance. I collapse into my chair and reach for the toast. "So Jay's already been by? Were you discussing all the horrid details of whatever's going on?"

Abram pales. "He isn't with you?"

"What?" I frown. "I mean, he was meant to be. Last night."

Abram drops his gaze to his empty plate, jaw tight.

"When I got up, he wasn't outside your door," Father explains. "I thought maybe he'd taken a nap on your floor when you returned last night. We were waiting for you to get up before we talked to him."

I draw my hand back from the food, unease creeping through my stomach. "I haven't seen him since we stationed him in the hallway."

Father looks up as a maid enters with fresh coffee. His voice is tight when he says, "Ruth, could you have word sent to the Berd residence? Ask whether they've seen Jay this morning."

Ruth makes a polite curtsy and slips back outside, leaving the pot. None of us fills our cups.

"You think he went home?" Abram asks, doubtful.

"It's possible," Father says. But he sounds as unconvinced as I feel. He rises. "I'll check the guest suite and make sure he isn't around here somewhere."

Abram and I exchange a worried glance. We don't speak while Father is gone, and when he returns, shaking his head mutely, the three of us settle into a tense silence while we wait for Ruth. Heaviness grows between my shoulder blades. I can't eat. I hardly seem able to breathe.

The mantel clock shows half an hour drag past, though it feels longer. Ruth enters the room again with another rushed curtsy.

"Well?" Father prompts, sitting forward.

"The Berds send word they expected Mr. Jay Berd to remain here for the night," she says. "He has not returned home."

Abram closes his eyes. I can't bear the pained expression on his face.

I push back from the table. "We'll look for him."

"Not you," Father snaps. "Ruth, go and get Johnie and Flynn. We'll assemble a search party."

"It should be me," I protest. "This is my fault."

"Yes, it is!" Father rises from his chair.

Mortification and anger flash through me, but I lift my chin and try to ignore Ruth's stare.

"It *is* your fault this is happening," Father continues. "But there are others better equipped to fix your mistake. So, for *once*, listen to me and stay here."

I can't form words around my frustration. I want to point out that *he* was the one who insisted someone keep watch over me. But didn't I allow it? Didn't I let Jay get roped in, even though I've already given myself to the Hidden Folk? I agreed to Speir's offer because I wanted this curse to end with me, not to pull others into its whirlpool of disaster.

I leave the room. True follows in my shadow, and Abram is after me a minute later.

"We'll go to the holms," he says, taking my arm and steering me toward the back door. "We know you sailed past there because Mrs. Westness saw you. If we head out now, we'll have an hour on the others while they get organized."

I glance at my brother, silently grateful for his secret streak of rebellion.

✦

We return to the rocky shore near the holms, where we haul my yole up onto dry ground. On the horizon, a black storm is gathering in the south. Hopefully it will stay down there. I turn my attention to the shoreline. It juts in and out, like torn paper, so I can't see far in either direction.

"We should split up," I suggest. "You go west. I'll go east."

Abram nods, his face set in grim determination. "I'll check the outer holms. You stay on the mainland."

I set off to the left. True runs ahead, sniffing for crabs. Rocks roll and knock together under my feet, and I concentrate on keeping my balance until we're round the first bend.

The tight knot in my chest hasn't loosened.

I dread what I might see at every turn of the shore, in that moment when the next stretch of view opens up before me. The waters are rough out on the sound where Jay and I must have sailed last night, assuming I always go to the same place. Stories abound of selkies pulling sailors overboard, but even without magic it's deadly enough. A single mistake could kill a man. Especially in the dark.

The low tide has exposed rocks farther out in the cove and lumpy seals lie stretched out on the flat stones. They lift their heads with bored curiosity when True and I pass, then flop down once we're safely away. Sometimes, when there's enough distance between me and them, their keening song wails into the air. Sailors say it sounds like a drowning child. A cry that calls men to change course, to lean over the sides of their boats and be pulled under.

I come to another bend. Before me, the rocks blend into pale sand. Seaweed and kelp left by the tide glisten in the dim light. I can see all the way to where the coast curves back out to a point.

About midway between me and that point, a lump covered in seaweed lies sprawled on the beach.

My breath stops. It's nearly man-sized. Man-shaped.

Unsteady, I cross onto the sand and make my way toward the shape. I want to run, to know immediately what the kelp covers, but my legs have gone weak. I force myself to inhale. The air smells of rot and sea.

True goes ahead, curious. He sniffs at the shape with interest, then lies beside it to better investigate. I can't read whether he recognizes whatever is beneath. *Who*ever is beneath.

My stomach turns.

In a time both everlasting and far too fast, I'm standing by the thing. The still-wet fronds drape over it like the wrapping of the dead. I swallow. Then I flex my fingers and make myself bend forward. Make myself peel back one of the stalks of weed.

Before I can look at what's beneath, a cloud of gnats flies out of an exposed wound. I jerk away, trip over a rock, and fall onto my back. True leaves the corpse to jump around me, trying to lick my face.

I push him aside. Make myself look.

It isn't a man. Isn't Jay.

By the rubbery texture of the gray skin, I think it must be a porpoise. Washed up at least a day ago. Something has helped itself to a chunk of meat out of its side, now crawling with gnats again.

Relief and disgust war in me. I turn to my side, almost gagging. My limbs are cold and weak. My vision spins.

A faint shadow crosses my hands on the ground. Someone crouches beside me, and a female voice I recognize asks, "Are you all right?"

The overused question cuts through my nausea and pricks awake my frustration—at this curse, this situation, my helplessness, all of it! I push myself up to snap that I'm fine.

But then I see her.

Kneeling beside me is a girl with white skin, dark hair, and silver eyes.

NINE

Kit

"Catharine?" he says, eyes wide.

True lets out a bark of joy and starts sniffing me all over.

I swallow, hoping I've made the right choice in revealing myself. He seemed distressed. Unwell. And like that first morning, when he leaned into the wind from the castle window, I couldn't leave him on his own. Though this time, I've actually let him know I am here.

"It… How are you…?" The prince tries to push himself up, but his legs give way.

I catch his arm to keep him from falling again. He is cold, I can tell even through the greatcoat. It's almost as if it radiates from within him. His tanned skin is paler than I remember and there's a sleepless gauntness to his face. He's still staring at me.

"It—It's a complicated story," I explain ineloquently. A hook pricks in my throat. Mother said that Speir ensured Catharine and I could not explain the spell, curse, whatever this is, to anyone uninvolved. This is the first time I have tried to go against it and I wonder if this sharp feeling is Speir's magic. Shaking away the thought, I add, "I can explain, but—you aren't well. Are you by yourself out here?"

"Abram." He waves vaguely in the direction behind him.

I straighten, trying to spot his brother, but he's nowhere to be seen. Idris puts a hand on the ground to steady himself. I cannot very well leave him.

"I can send Cath—" The hook in my throat digs at the word, so piercing and sudden I almost gasp. I wet my lips and try again. "I can send my sister to find him. Let me help you. Mrs. Westness's croft is not far from here and she has a fire going."

"How do you know...?"

I stand carefully and take his arm to guide him up. "I'll tell you as we go. Come now."

He stands with my help and then releases my hand to walk on his own. He's still wobbling, like he's been too deep in drink. I push propriety aside and firmly take his arm again. He glances at me, surprised, and I feel my face heat.

"I find the terrain here rather unsteady," I say, lifting my chin. "I would appreciate your assistance."

He laughs, sudden and short. "That's kind of you, but you can just say I'm being a proud fool."

I smile and say nothing. Pride may be foolish when all you need is support, but I know what it is to rely on someone else for something so little, so ordinary, it feels like defeat to even ask.

We make our way onto a path, True bounding ahead. This is where I was when I saw Idris below, bending over that thing covered in kelp. He would have been difficult to recognize, swallowed in his coat, but True gave him away. I meant to hurry back to the croft before he saw me. After all, he could reveal us to Byrne with one simple message. But then he stumbled, almost collapsed, and I made my choice. Now I'll just have to live with it.

After a moment's pause, Idris asks, "So how did you get here?"

"By boat," I joke, stalling for time.

"Better than swimming." He casts me a curious look again. I'm not sure what it means.

"Circumstances were such that we…needed to leave," I say slowly. I'm still not sure how much of the truth is possible—or wise—to confess.

"Is there anything I can do to help?"

I glance at him, leaning on my arm and still struggling over the relatively flat terrain. "I'm…not sure."

"Solving mysterious fleeing-home situations is my cup of tea." He nods toward the ground. "Walking—now, *that's* the difficult stuff."

A sudden, bright laugh bursts out of me. It's the first time I've laughed in Catharine's body, and the pitch of it isn't mine—but there's something familiar in the rhythm. I cover my mouth with my free hand, holding that spark of joy against my lips. I feel lighter for it.

Idris is studying me. "You seem…different."

The hook waits in my throat. Now that I've felt it once, I can sense its presence even without treading near the curse. I wonder, if I gave a sign, if I nudged him in the right direction, whether it would slice my throat. I lower my hand but say nothing.

"How long have you been here?" he asks.

Finally, a question I can answer with no trouble. "Only a couple of days."

We come into sight of Mrs. Westness's croft. Smoke rises from the chimney in a comforting, steady flow. Beyond, the land is rolling and empty, save for a flock of sheep and a few jagged stones cutting into the sky on a far hill. Today was the first time I felt well enough to explore, though Catharine has been out a few times. I slow a little to take in the view.

"What are those?" I ask, pointing toward the horizon.

"Standing stones," Idris says. "There are a lot around here."

"What are they for?"

Idris shrugs. "The sheep use them as back-scratchers, but I'm pretty sure that wasn't their original purpose."

With a smile, I lower my gaze to the small front door of the croft and reach for the latch. True cuts in front of us to enter first. Idris goes in second and I close the door behind us.

"Oh!" Catharine rises from beside the peat fire. She stares at Idris and me, then drops a precise curtsy. "Prince Idris."

"Hello, Princess Katherine—or, should I call you Princess Kit?" Idris looks between us. "That must get confusing."

Catharine opens her mouth—to correct him, I think—but winces suddenly and touches her throat. There is an awkward moment of silence.

"Is Mrs. Westness gone?" I ask, brushing past his question. I help Idris into a straw-woven chair by the fire. Mr. Westness left last night to return to the mainland, saying something about getting in before the next storm.

"Yes, she went out to gather peat." Catharine goes to pour a drink, but I catch her. She hasn't tried to maneuver a heavy stoneware jug in her aching fingers yet and I know it's far from pleasant.

"I can do that," I offer, "if you wouldn't mind going to find Prince Abram. He's out on the shore, down west." I glance at Idris for confirmation and he nods. "He'll likely be worried if he discovers Idris is gone."

Catharine's eyes brighten at the mention of Abram. But she lowers her voice. "I'm not sure that would be entirely… I wouldn't want to leave you unchaperoned."

Heat rises in my cheeks. "It will only be for a few minutes."

"Well, I suppose," Catharine agrees reluctantly. "I'll be quick while you see to Prince Idris." She emphasizes the *prince* bit gently, more a reminder than a correction.

"Right, of course." I help her into her pelisse and latch the door behind her.

My body tenses unexpectedly. With my back to Idris, I am suddenly keenly aware that I am alone. Enclosed. That he is a few feet away from me. That he is watching me. But the poison of terror isn't coming from Idris. It is the shadow cast by my memories of another man. I force myself to breathe. My fingers find my collarbone, and I start tapping. *I am safe. And I can leave if I want.*

I don't want to leave. I want to help him.

A drink might be a start. Mrs. Westness cannot afford tea and the water here isn't good on its own, but she has an extremely weak ale that she calls "small beer."

Still tapping, I collect the jug of small beer and take a mug from the shelf. The movement uncoils my fear and the room comes back into focus. Prince Idris's keen gaze follows me. I wonder whether the attention is just something this body inspires, whether it is this way with all men and Catharine. But I hope he is seeing something more than that, something of the truth.

As I pass him a full mug, I am struck by how the weight of the cup does not strain my fingers.

"Can I ask why you left home?" he ventures.

"It was no longer safe for us." Even that simple statement tugs the barb in my throat that prevents me from speaking. From what my mother said, he spoke to Speir—so he must know something of the Hidden Folk, and maybe something about how to break a curse. But how can I ask when I can't speak enough words to hint at what truly happened? I sit in Catharine's chair, cradling my own mug between my hands. True lies down on the floor between us, his rump near Idris's foot and his nose on mine.

Idris frowns at the fireplace. The flames put a glow in his face that only darkens the skin beneath his eyes. He has pleasant eyes, remarkably serious when he doesn't smile. I wonder what has caused this change in him, but I don't know if it is my place to ask.

Before I can decide what to say next, he glances at me. I dart my gaze away before we can make eye contact. My heart pounds.

After a moment, he asks, "Did something happen at the ball? Something—with the king?"

I sit up, surprised. Perhaps he is more observant than I gave him credit for.

"Your father," he begins and I wince at the words. He pauses and then goes on, uncertainly, "I thought... I wondered whether he was...entirely kind to Kit."

"Please don't say that in front of my sister." I glance toward the door. I haven't told Catharine, still. How could I tell her, after my mother has done this to us? It would seem as if I was trying to make our parents equal in their wrongness. I would be taking away Catharine's last comfort. And, worse than all of that, I would be asking her to believe me—choose me—over her only living family. I have made that choice for myself. I have chosen her, but I dread what she might decide.

True sniffs at my boots and I reach down to pet his forehead. Instinctively, I move my shawl to cover more of my chest before I bend, though in Catharine's body I don't have to worry so much about the neckline flouncing open. Her dress—even this simple, plain travel dress—is fitted, and her chest is smaller. I realize I don't have to be so cautious and let the shawl hang where it will instead of holding it in place. I glance at Idris, to see if he's noticed, or if he sees more than he should. To see how I feel about him seeing.

But he is sipping his drink, eyes closed. The tightness in my shoulders eases. He isn't watching me like prey, waiting for a bit of skin to be exposed in an unguarded moment. It has been some years since I felt I could just sit in the presence of a man and not check my every movement. But I feel strong in Catharine's body. Maybe almost safe.

It makes me sad for the girl I was in my old body. For the girl I'll be again when we switch back.

"Well, how can I help?" Prince Idris asks, putting down his now-empty cup. "There must be something my family can do to ease your stay here. Do you know how long…or what you are hoping…?"

He stops and a blush turns his ears red. I feel the same heat spread over my face. I am in Catharine's body and he is wondering if we have come with the purpose King Byrne suggested—come to beg for a proposal.

"I don't know how long we'll stay," I answer hurriedly. "But it must be kept secret. We cannot afford for the king or queen to find us."

"I can promise for myself and Abram, at least." He spreads his hands across his lap, palms up, exposing a network of small crisscross cuts.

"Thank…" My gaze catches on one of the scabs that has broken recently, leaving a bright streak of blood.

Idris notices me looking and tucks his hands under his elbows self-consciously. But I'm struck by an idea. I jump up and go to my bag. Hardly daring to breathe for fear the barb in my throat will sense my intentions, I dig to the bottom, close my hand round my find, and return to Idris. I hold out the cravat.

"Give me your hand," I instruct.

He stares at the strip of cloth and then at me. Slowly, he holds out the hand with the broken scab.

I begin wrapping the cravat round his wrist, then loop it up over his palm to his thumb and back again. In my mind, I play through the steps he made only two weeks ago.

Wind and tuck. Tight enough to hold, but not to restrict. I am clumsier than he was and my fingertips graze his skin sometimes. He is fire-warmed now and a faint heat rises from him. My cheeks burn.

Finally—and yet, too soon—I finish. I tie off the bandage. Before I can step back, he closes his fingers round my hand. Not to hold me in place—just to ask. My breath catches and I can't move. I dart a glance at his face, but I can't make myself meet his eyes.

His brows are drawn. Connecting, questioning. "A prince's cravat?"

I repeat the line he told me: "Think of all the stories you could spin."

Idris blinks. Slowly, he asks, "Kit…?"

A swell of gratitude warms my insides. I am seen. But the barb is back, scratching against my throat, close enough to pierce. I don't dare shift, don't dare lift my eyes to his. I stare down at our joined hands without answering.

"You cannot speak of it?" he guesses.

The barb presses tighter. I'm not sure if I imagine it, but I think I can feel a drop of blood slide down my throat.

The door opens, thrown out of Catharine's hands by the force of the wind outside. It slams against the wall. Both Idris and I jump. I back away, nearly knocking over the second chair in my haste to make space between us.

"I apologize," Catharine says, stepping in. True springs to his feet and dances around her. She backs away from the dog nervously but still manages to make a formal curtsy to Idris. She lifts her hand to indicate his brother. "I found Prince Abram."

True pivots to his new favorite, leaving Catharine to relax. Abram has to stoop to get through the door. He gives a swift glance around the room but focuses on Idris. "Are you all right?"

Idris holds himself straighter. The serious glint in his eye has gone, replaced by a friendly annoyance. The line of his mouth has turned up in a good-natured expression that looks almost unnatural. It takes me a moment to realize there's no dimple in this smile.

"I'm *fine*," he says in almost a singsong voice. "And hello."

Abram frowns at him. "Princess Kit said you were feeling poorly."

"I only needed a drink." Idris pushes himself up and stands with apparent ease. If it weren't for a moment where he leans, off-balance, before he corrects himself, I might have thought he was completely normal. "I am now fully restored!" The grim expression returns to his face for a moment. "No sign of Jay?"

Abram shakes his head. "No. And the weather's turning."

I glance at Idris, wondering whether they are speaking of Mr. Jay Berd. But as neither have explained, I'm not sure it would be polite to ask.

Idris turns to me. "I should get back to the search." He rests a hand on True's back. "Is there anything I can do to help with your—situation?"

I choose my words carefully. "We are seeking remedies in stories and in the stories' origins."

Idris nods. "I'll see what I can do."

Abram shifts, perplexed.

Idris leans forward and I stiffen involuntarily. He smells of the cold gale off the North Sea. Fresh and windswept.

Quietly, he says, "Abram reads more than me and might have a better idea of spells and such. Is it all right if I tell him what I, er, guessed?"

The barb does not cut into me when I nod.

"Good." He smiles and the dimples return. "Otherwise it would have been dashed confusing to keep your names straight when I talk to him."

I can't help a little laugh. Catharine's gaze catches my attention—and I remember that I ought to be more formal. I try to school my expression into something polite and not *too* friendly. "We would value your discretion further afield," I add.

"Understood." Idris doesn't look away from me. "Don't worry, princess. I'll see what I can find out."

I nod, grateful. But for some reason, deep down in my bones, I do not feel completely pleased. A small, secret, twisted part of me feels—disappointed? I push my thoughts away before I can be allowed to fully recognize them. I want Catharine to be in her body, to be free of mine. That is the right thing to want. Anything else would make me like my mother.

"Get some rest, prince," I say to Idris.

Abram nods to me. "It was, um, good to see you, Princess Catharine."

The sweet shyness in his voice charms me. I try to give him Catharine's more encouraging smile. "And you, Prince Abram."

He ducks out and Idris follows. True dashes after them.

Catharine closes the door and I move to pour a drink for her.

"Kit?"

I turn at the whisper. Catharine is staring down at her hand. She is very still, almost as if she does not breathe.

"Is this…normal?" she asks.

She lifts her hand to me. The left index finger is bent. As I watch, she presses her lips together.

I reach out to touch her hand. "What's wrong?"

Her voice is almost soundless. "It won't straighten."

The middle joint on the finger is swollen worse than I've ever seen it. I touch the inflamed spot, and Catharine sucks in a quick breath between her teeth. I don't dare force the finger open.

"What happened?"

Catharine's hand trembles in mine. "I don't know. I didn't even notice until I went to close the door. It just won't—I can't move it."

I cradle her hand—my old, swollen, breaking hand. This has never happened before. I don't know what to do or say, but I'm filled with the need to comfort away the panic in her voice. The panic I feel mirrored in my chest.

"We'll wrap it up until Mrs. Westness returns," I decide. "Maybe she'll know what to do."

I take a cloth ribbon from a basket by the chairs. It wraps round the finger many times over, enough to add plenty of cushion. Once I have it tied on securely, I usher Catharine to one of the chairs and give her a small mug that she'll be able to hold with one hand. Then I collapse into my own chair.

"I never knew it was this bad, Kit." Catharine lifts her gaze to mine. Her gaze that comes through my old face. "Why didn't you tell me?"

"It wasn't always." I pull my shawl closer and nestle into the shelter of my woven chair. My thoughts rush. The wasting seems to be getting worse, even though I'm safe now. Catharine's safe now. Byrne doesn't have any power here. Wasn't that how it worked in my mother's story? My grandmother escaped from her terrible sister and she got better?

Until she got worse, all at once.

I flex my fingers—Catharine's fingers—and concentrate on the ease of the movement. On how nothing clicks or strains or pinches.

I need to find a way to put us back in our right bodies. Catharine doesn't deserve what's happening.

Neither do you, whispers a part of me that sounds like my mother—the mother who cuddled me when she read with me, the one who danced through the halls while we waited for my father to come home. I long, suddenly, for her to be here. For her to brush my hair with the gentle, steady rhythm that never tugged or hurt.

I push the thoughts away. It's my mother's fault we're in this situation. And I shouldn't want her—not after what she's done.

"I'll get you out of this, Catharine," I say. "I'll find a way."

TEN

Idris

The weather forces Abram and me to return in the early evening, pelted by hail and with no sign of Jay. Father pretends not to notice I was out—an impressive feat when I am soaked to the skin and dripping puddles. His own search found nothing. Jay has just vanished.

No one suggests assigning another person to watch over me that night. I barely seem to lie down before I fall asleep. I dream like a fever and wake before I've begun to catch my breath.

It's still drizzling outside, but the worst of it seems to have again shifted to the southern horizon. I take toast from the kitchen so I don't have to see Father in the breakfast room. "No news of Jay?" I ask Ruth while I slather it in butter.

She shakes her head. "No, sir."

I tear off a bit of crust and toss it down to True. "I'll be out on a walk if anyone asks."

My feet ache. All of me aches, actually. A dry heaviness weighs in my head, like the aftereffects of a nightmare.

I want to curl up in bed again, but I have a feeling I would end up just being twitchy and irritated, and then I'd start thinking about Jay, becoming more and more anxious… It is better to walk.

My thoughts turn to Kit as I head through town. It seems my family isn't the only one dealing with enchantments. The cravat—the one I gave Kit and she gave me—is still tied round my palm. When she approached me yesterday and she was only Catharine, I had been confused. My vague suspicion seemed delusional. Then she spoke my words back to me and the air around us changed. Her stillness as she bent over me, her breath held, answered without sound or movement. *Kit.* I had been indifferent about Catharine's closeness—but when it was Kit, everything sharpened. I felt with surprising fierceness exactly how near she was, exactly where her fingers rested on the cravat over my skin.

I shake away the feeling. It was a strange moment, nothing more.

While I don't think I can handle another full search for Jay today, the least I can do is poke around for something that might help the princesses. The best source of folklore isn't in our archives or the library—it's Merlin Muir.

As usual, he's outside the Stromwell Hotel, smoking a pipe and chatting with people on their way in from their nightly work or out to their day's tasks. He's finishing up a story about the finfolk as I walk up—some cautionary tale for a pretty local girl who appears to be on her way to gather kelp, judging by the woven basket at her side. It's a story I don't recognize and I wonder whether Abram knows it.

Perhaps I should have told Abram where I was going. He might have wanted to come along.

A foggy image rises in my mind. I am in a boat and someone sinks into the space ahead of me. A dark shadow.

My pulse is pounding suddenly. I try to shake it off—this fragment of a nightmare.

Yesterday, I told Abram what I was able to piece together from Kit. He had a great interest in it all, but he'd been distracted by the search for Jay. He will probably want to go looking again today. Maybe I should be doing that, too, rather than seeking stories.

"So don't you be turning your back to the ocean," Mr. Muir concludes, "especially not when you're between the tide lines."

The young woman nods seriously. "I wouldn't do such a thing, you can be sure." He gives her an approving salute with his pipe. She leaves a coin on the table—"For your next round of pleenk—and nothing stronger, hear? It's barely sunup!"—and goes on her way.

"Good morning, princeling," Mr. Muir calls to me. With a wave to the dark clouds, he smiles. "What lovely weather we've had, aye?"

"Indeed." I take a seat on the bench beside him. My legs feel instantly relieved. "Has everyone made it off the water safely?"

"No one harmed last night, not that I've heard. And no one's coming from the mainland if they have any sense. Wisest to wait it out." He takes a draw on his pipe and leans back. "Have you brought some stories to trade?"

"One, maybe." I rub my knees while True settles protectively in front of me. "It's a bit of a story, a bit of a question."

"Let's hear it, then." Mr. Muir faces the busy harbor and sea beyond, ready to listen.

I think for a moment. Kit was only able to convey the barest part of whatever is happening to her and her sister. Someone has put a spell on them that's switched their bodies, but why and how is something only they know. Maybe the background of it isn't so important—maybe it's just the way out that matters. To weave it into a story for Mr. Muir, I have to fill in the gaps I don't know. And I need to make sure it's unrecognizable, just in case Mr. Muir takes this tale and spreads it around. I don't know how it'd get back to King Byrne, but it's not a risk I'm willing to take.

"There was once a rich miller up near Bursey," I begin. "He had a natural daughter and a stepdaughter, one perfectly proper and one with wild simmering just under the surface."

I go from there, feeling my way through this retelling of a barely told tale. The daughter can spin the finest wool, but the stepdaughter can sing to the water, and the water listens. She is the secret to the family's prosperity, and the miller cannot bear it. Jealousy and resentment consume him, because his proper daughter should be the one with the power to make the water flow. So he conspires with the henwife, who weaves a spell to switch the girls' bodies. Then the natural daughter will be able to sing to the water, and the stepdaughter will be trapped in a normal body. The miller expects the girls will accept the change submissively, but instead they run away to seek their own fortune.

I trail off at this point.

Mr. Muir takes the pipe out of his mouth. "How'd they break the curse, then?"

"Curse?" I ask, surprised.

"Curse, spell." Mr. Muir shrugs. "Seems it was meant to do harm to the stepdaughter more than it was meant to elevate the natural one. Either way, the harm's done to someone. Sounds like a curse to me."

"Yes, well." My thoughts turn. My curse and Kit's came so close together. Could there be a link between them? "That's as far as I've got. How would you expect it to go from there?"

Mr. Muir tilts his head, considering. People pass by, calling friendly greetings. Some stop to water their horses at the trough in front of us. The cathedral may be at the center of the city, but this spot is the pulse. Anyone from the main harbor or the eastern land has to pass through here.

"Tricky one, this," Mr. Muir muses. "You hear of a body being warped or changed, but not so often of two souls swapped."

"That's what I wondered." I bend to give True's head a scratch. "I hadn't heard of anything like this before and I thought maybe you would have."

"Hmm." Mr. Muir lifts a hand to a passerby. To me, he says, "Not sure I have one that fits exactly."

Uncertainty coils in my gut. If even Mr. Muir doesn't know, how can I hope to find a solution? I can't unravel my own curse. How will I help Kit? I wish again that I had brought Abram along. He would know the right questions to ask, the right places to prod for answers.

"If I were one of the miller's daughters," Mr. Muir says thoughtfully, "I'd take myself to wherever the magic comes from. Follow the water to its source, so to speak. Maybe literally. Have a chat with the Hidden Folk, or trows, or whoever roams that part of the land. Bursey, you say? Perhaps the trolls, if you could make a good enough trade for their favor."

I pause. "I'm not sure who rules magic there."

"Not Bursey, then?" Mr. Muir lifts one bushy eyebrow.

My face heats. "Not exactly."

Mr. Muir turns his gaze back to the sea. "Hmm."

I scratch my neck, trying to ignore my blunder. I don't know the stories of the south so well. It's so far from the water, it's hard to believe the Hidden Folk are active there—especially when they are withdrawing even from our islands. But if Kit's curse and mine happened less than a week apart, it is too strange to be a coincidence.

Maybe if I learned how to stay awake while I dance, I could ply the Hidden Folk with questions. I could even ask Speir. Frustration crawls under my skin. I have access to perhaps one of the last pockets of magic and I can't even use it.

"You let me know when you find out the end," Mr. Muir says, reaching down to rub True's ears. "I'll be curious to see how they get out of this one."

"Right, I will." I rise, still thinking. "Thank you for your help, Mr. Muir."

He lifts his eyebrows. "Not sure how my musing helps, but happy to do it any time you need." His expression changes, a little serious, a little concerned. "Take care of yourself, princeling."

I nod, absent.

"Hello, lass," Mr. Muir calls. "Pleased to see a new bonny face around these parts."

I glance in the direction he's facing and start in surprise.

It's Catharine. Or—Kit, in Catharine's body.

She's wearing a plain dress, with a simple straw bonnet, but even so she's turned a few heads on the street. Strangers aren't particularly rare in a city so full of trade, but normally they are men.

"This one's our prince," Mr. Muir says, pointing. "Very eligible."

"Mr. Muir!" I snap, mortified. My whole face burns.

Kit bobs a curtsy. "Good morning, Idris, erm, Prince Idris."

"Good morning," I reply.

True trots across to her and nuzzles her hand.

"Hmm, so you know each other?" Mr. Muir motions me to go. "Show the new lass around the city then, why don't you? Give her a bit of our island hospitality."

I shoot him an annoyed look but follow True to Kit's side. "Sorry about him," I mutter.

She shrugs, not exactly looking at me. Embarrassed, too, I think.

I clear my throat. "Is there, ah, something you need in town? Maybe I can help."

"I was hoping to sell a few things," she says. "And I need to find a physician."

"Are you hurt?" I glance over her, but she seems fine.

"No." She adjusts the coarse shawl round her shoulders. It's knitted and well used—one of Mrs. Westness's, probably. "My sister had a minor injury."

"Oh, I'm sorry." I glance down the road. We have a small market by the cathedral and the Guildhall. My father and Abram are probably around there, overseeing the search for Jay—at least, if Abram isn't out searching himself. I warn Kit, "My father will probably be about."

She blinks. "I didn't think... That is, King Byrne conducts all his business in the castle."

I shake my head. "It's a bit less formal here."

"Well." She looks past me and steps back. "Well, maybe I won't..."

"You might try Kirkness?" I stick my hands in my greatcoat pockets for warmth. "Though it's across the island. Almost a half-day's walk."

Kit frowns, wavering. "Do you know where these things could be sold here?"

She opens her bag and shows me an assortment of items. A pair of deerskin gloves, a bundle I think is a dress, though it doesn't look particularly fine, and a simple necklace. I do a sum in my head.

"How bad is the injury?" I ask.

"A broken finger, I think." Kit closes the bag again. "But—it might be more than that."

"I'm not sure this will be enough to pay for more than one visit," I admit. "However, I'd be happy to—"

She's already shaking her head. "No, that's not necessary. I can…I can find a way…"

"I have an idea," I blurt. "My friend—Jay—has gone missing."

"You mentioned something about that the other day." Her hands twist the bag's string absently. "What happened to Mr. Berd?"

I'm surprised she knows his surname and then remember he was with us at the ball. "You were introduced to him?"

"He danced with me when you, um, couldn't." She looks away again.

That was right after my talk with Speir, I think. I suppose it must have also been our first interaction. Mortification burns my ears. I fumble for an apology. "That must have seemed horribly rude."

"Not *horribly*," she says, her diplomacy making her sound like the real Catharine. "You weren't well."

I wish I could reach back and cuff my former self over the ears. Kit had deserved better. "I'm still sorry."

"It is in the past." She waves away my concerns. "You said he is missing?"

"Yes." I hesitate. We are still in public, and even though a curse doesn't bind my words I'm reluctant to say them. "We're conducting a search. If you'd like to help, I'm sure we're compensating the people looking. I could check, if you want."

"How long has he been gone?"

"About two days now." A tiny part of me wonders if she's interested for a reason beyond just common decency. But if she is, it's not my business. "He vanished the night before you found me."

She thinks a moment, then nods. "I'd like to help, but I don't want to be paid out of pity."

"I promise it would be the same treatment we give everyone. In fact, if you want to be sure, I'll ask my father in front of you."

"Can he be trusted...?" She gestures to her face. "Wouldn't he send word to King Byrne?"

I want to assure her that Father is very good at secrets, but I have to admit that I don't know what he'd do if the secret wasn't our family's. I pause, thinking. "He's in the Guildhall right now, I believe," I tell her. "There's an archive right beside one of the audience rooms. It's terrible for reading—you can hear everything going on in the next room. I could put you in there and you could eavesdrop without being seen."

Kit wavers, weighing the risks.

"We pay quite well," I say, fairly sure it's true.

Her mouth tilts up in a small smile. "I guess I'll find out."

"This way." I head off the main thoroughfare and take to the alleys. True bumps his nose against my palm to let me know he's here. The three of us duck between houses and slip past sheltered courtyards.

"I'm working on your problem, by the way," I say over my shoulder. "But I haven't made much progress."

"Oh, thank you."

It seems mad that I would have no memory, at all, of a full evening. If I could stay conscious through the night,

I might be able to get answers. And I could find out what happened to Jay.

I try to think back to last night, to probe through the blank for anything. It's like trying to recall a forgotten dream. Snatches of feeling—dread, fear—and the vaguest of sensations. A shadow behind me in some cold, dark place. Blurred words drowned by music.

My head feels heavy and a wave of exhaustion crashes over me. I stop in the middle of a narrow backstreet, barely broad enough for my shoulders not to brush each wall, and lean against one for a moment.

"Idris?" asks Kit, an anxious note in the way she says my name.

"I'm fine," I tell her, but my voice comes out breathless. I'm not sure I've ever been this tired in my life.

True, who had been ahead of us, shuffles backward until he can sit against me. It's too narrow for him to turn round. The sight of his unnatural movement makes me laugh and some of the exhaustion lifts.

I nudge True with my foot so he'll move forward again, then follow him out. Kit comes round beside me. It's odd, because it's Catharine's face I'm looking at, but what I thought was cool and formal on Catharine turns open and expressive with Kit. Her scrutinizing gaze makes no secret of the way she studies me and finds whatever she sees to be worrying.

"I've been ill," I admit, not exactly sure why, except that I don't want to dismiss such unguarded concern.

"I thought so." She tilts her head. "And you aren't on the mend yet, I don't think."

I shake my head. I don't say there's no mending me.

True taps his nose against my boot and I give his back a rub with one hand while I point with the other. "That's the Guildhall."

Kit turns to look at it. The building is grand, though dwarfed by the red-stone cathedral just down the street. The Guildhall was built only recently and looks surprisingly modern among the characterful houses that surround it. The stone is smooth, the windows huge. It's designed more for show than practicality, as the wind finds many gaps to whistle through that aren't such a problem in the old buildings.

I hope Abram is inside. I'd like to talk to him about Mr. Muir. If he has gone off to look for Jay, I won't have a chance to see him until the evening.

"Come on," I say, walking forward. "My father will probably be in one of the studies, not the main hall."

Just to be sure, I pop my head in before we enter the building. Some guild members from the islands are standing around in discussion with foreign traders and representatives. To the left, I recognize one of the newly elected officials from the western independent nations. His voice is over-loud and he stands with his hands on his hips, clearly hoping to make an impression. On the right, an elderly chieftain from the south shows a string of glass beads to a middle-aged woman in the garb of an eastern earl. All corners of the world are here, with their different cultures and governments, but their foreignness will be an advantage for Kit. They won't recognize her.

I wave Kit in and escort her up the servants' stairs to the archive. "Do you mind waiting a few minutes?"

"Not at all." She glances at the shelves of books with mild interest.

"Perfect. Just a moment."

I close the door behind me and call a servant to the audience room where I know Kit will hear everything. The servant informs me that Father is here and I ask him to see if Father will join me for some tea. Then I settle with True by one of the large windows. I can see all the way out to the harbor from here. Abram's yole is moored in its usual place, so I suppose he hasn't gone searching far if he's out.

I call the servant back. "Is Abram here too?"

The servant shakes his head. I let him go, a little disappointed.

Father comes after a few more minutes, looking weary. I lift my hand in greeting and confusion lowers his brow. "Idris, why do you have a cravat on your hand?"

I drop my hand again, flustered, and start untying the cloth. "No reason."

Father massages his forehead. "What are you doing here? I thought you'd snuck out with Abram again."

"No, I came to town instead." I stuff the cravat into my coat pocket. "How is the search for Jay going?"

Father sighs and sits opposite me. "No news. No one has found a sign of him."

But then, sometimes the sea takes a man without leaving a sign.

My stomach tightens and I turn my gaze back to the harbor. Where am I going at night? Where did I lead Jay?

"How is Abram handling it?" Father asks, his voice gentler.

"He's distressed. He can hardly help that." I tap my foot on the floor. "I haven't had a chance to talk to him today."

Father frowns. "He isn't with you?"

I gesture at the otherwise empty room.

Father shakes his head, impatient again. "I mean, he didn't leave the manor with you?"

"No, I haven't seen him."

Father casts an anxious look out at the harbor. "His yole is still here. It's not like him to leave no word when he goes out."

Abram probably sneaks out more than Father suspects, but he isn't wrong—at a time like this, Abram wouldn't have wanted to cause anyone to worry.

"He wasn't at the manor?" I ask, an uneasy sinking in my chest.

"No, I looked for both of you before I set off." Father gives me a severe look. Reproaching me for leaving without a word. For leaving at all.

The fidget in my foot gets faster. I remember Kit in the next room and what I promised to ask. Hoping to change the subject, I say, "Are we still looking for people to search for Jay? I think we were paying, right?"

But Father has turned again to the harbor. His brows draw close together. "Has anyone seen Abram today?"

"I—don't know." True nudges my hand. I give him a scratch. He nudges more persistently and I realize he's not wanting my hand—he wants my waistcoat pocket.

I feel inside, thinking I might have some dried meat left over from a recent walk. My waistcoat is one of my finer ones—and now that I pay attention, I think from the smell under my armpits I might have been wearing this last night. I just grabbed it without looking this morning. I wonder, reddening, whether Kit noticed.

But then my fingers meet a strange object in my pocket and all other concerns flee.

Slowly, I pull out a pair of glasses. Gold-rimmed. Round.

Abram's.

I stare, my pulse tight and rapid in my throat. A sickly, feverish heat rushes through me from my hands to my head. I shut my eyes and see a shadow pressing something into my pocket. A shadow that speaks words I can't understand in a voice as familiar as my own. I am walking away, and True runs from me to the shadow and back, whimpering. I am getting into a boat and True is scrambling in, barking frantically. I am leaving.

The shadow stays.

I open my eyes, breathing hard. My ears start to ring. My voice sounds very far away when I whisper, "He followed me?"

"What?" Father looks at me, and his gaze fixes on Abram's glasses. "Why do you—"

My head swims. I want to keel over and gag, but I can't move. I feel a shaking horror so deep in my bones it fills my whole awareness. Father is asking questions but it's all a smudge on my consciousness. My eyes are blurring and stinging and my head pounds a rhythm of *he followed me* and *they trapped him.*

Father pushes himself to his feet and paces, both hands digging into his hair. I still cannot move. He hurries suddenly to the door and barks orders at a servant. "Check with everyone! Who saw Abram last?"

But I know, deep in the center of my quaking soul, that Abram is gone.

"I'll get him back," I say, my voice toneless. Another useless promise.

"I can't—" Father clenches his jaw, still standing by the doorway. "Idris, if you only—"

He stops himself again, mouth pressed shut as if holding in his tirade through sheer force of will. I wish he would shout. I wish he would say it out loud.

This is your fault.

"Who can go with you tonight?" Father says instead. "You still can't remember anything, can you? We need someone reliable. They don't have to go into the realm with you but they need to keep watch. We need to know where you are going and if Abram is there."

"I don't..." I swipe at my eyes, rubbing wetness away. I don't deserve to cry over this. It's my fault. "I don't know who would..."

"I will."

We both start. Kit has opened the archive door and stands framed by the darkness behind her.

She lifts her chin and repeats, "I will keep watch."

"What—?" Father takes a step toward Kit and then looks at me. "What is she—?"

I push myself up. My legs burn and I feel another wave of weakness. I want to sink back down.

"She and her sister are seeking refuge here," I say, trying to save Kit from having to explain. "There has been trouble in the south."

Father blinks. He is trying to pull himself back into his formal, official expression. Exhaustion suddenly overshadows every other emotion as he says, "I don't... Princess, we will help you in any way we can. But I don't want you to endanger yourself."

"I want to do this." She steps into the room. She's untied her bonnet and holds it tightly in her hands. "But I do have two conditions: You must not tell my family where I am and you must pay me with a bag of silver coins."

"There are better ways to make that money," I say, though I'm not sure where else she could make so much so fast. "This isn't worth it."

Kit turns blazing eyes on me, and then on my father. "I can do this. You will not have to worry about me spreading rumors—you'll keep my secret, and I'll keep yours."

I shake my head. "I don't want to risk anyone else."

At that, my father's eyes harden. "You already have, Idris." To Kit, he says, "I accept your terms."

ELEVEN

Kit

I pull on my pelisse and pause to check the contents of my reticule. A ball of yarn, in case I need to track my way in or out of a place. A flask of water and a few hazelnuts, the only food I was able to forage today. An iron ring, in case any of the Folk get a little too close. A cutting from a rowan tree. A small Bible, loaned from Mrs. Westness and weathered with use. Religious texts aren't a deterrent in most tales, but Mrs. Westness insisted, just in case it turned out some devilish creature lives in the Hidden Lands. In case I need a more practical weapon, I slide a short dagger into my boot.

Catharine leans over my shoulder. Her hand is bound with the local physician's best bandage. The remainder of my pile of silver sits near the hearth, plenty for another visit and even some left for repairs to Mrs. Westness's roof—our gift for her hospitality.

"Is there anything else I need?" I ask Catharine. She's the one who gathered this assortment of items, all meant to keep me safe. King Hugh told me I'm only to keep watch *outside* of the realm, but if I want answers, I'll have to get closer. Catharine is the storyteller, the collector of these tidbits. I never thought her reading would become a matter of life and death. As I glance at her furrowed brow I feel another swell of gratitude. She is doing whatever she can to keep me safe, even if she doesn't agree with my decision.

"That's all I can think of." Catharine bites her lip and leans back. "Are you sure you want to do this? At worst, it will be dangerous. At best, you'll be risking your reputation."

"Well, most people will think I'm risking *yours*," I try to joke, gesturing to my face.

Catharine wrinkles her nose. "I don't mind that."

"I know." I take her hands, though I don't squeeze. "And I am sure Speir was one of the Hidden Folk. I might be able to find him there and make him undo our curse. And even if I can't…" My head fills with Idris's drawn face, Abram's shy kindness, and Jay's ready smile. "Well, there are a lot of young men who seem in need of rescue."

Catharine nods, serious. "Don't try to do too much on the first trip. The most important thing is to be sure you know how the rules work, so you can stay safe. Once we know how to play the game, we can free the boys."

I nod and give her a quick hug. "I'll see you in the morning."

Catharine wraps her arms round me. "I'll have breakfast ready."

It's already dark when I arrive at the manor house, although the evening has only just begun. I follow Idris's instructions round to the back of the building, the servants' entrance. He seemed embarrassed when he suggested it, but I'm grateful for any way to avoid being seen. Catharine's face might not be widely recognized here, but King Byrne would know her description if it got back to him somehow.

A maidservant—Ruth—shows me to a private parlor and leaves me with some soup and bread. The bread here is strangely flat, with a grainy texture that fills me faster than the loaves I'm used to. I eat and move closer to the fire. The night is black and cold, and it will be hours until we're even halfway through.

For all I acted assured in front of Catharine, my stomach is now in a tight knot. There are a thousand ways the evening could go wrong, but it isn't the journey to the Hidden Lands that fills me with anxiety. It's the time I'll need to spend alone with Prince Idris. We decided that I will stay in his room, to keep word about me being there as limited as possible, rather than for me to sit in the hallway all night, where any servants might see me.

Still, we will be alone. For hours.

He'll be a gentleman. I'm sure he will. He's never made me doubt that. But I am not used to it.

A part of me feels something more bubbly and excited than nerves. If I could only lean into the feeling, let my heart acknowledge it fully, it might be... anticipation? Perhaps tonight could be whole hours as perfect as our clearing at the ball.

But a shadow lurks in the corner of my mind and my lungs tighten.

Trying to shake off my unease, I take out one of my nuts and crack it. The pieces still taste chalky and unappealing in my new mouth, but the action of cracking and eating makes me feel more settled. The shadow fades back to a place where I don't have to feel its cold touch.

The door opens and I turn, tensing. I expect to find Idris there, to tell me he's going to bed and to invite me to my watching place.

But instead of the prince, it is Ruth. She has returned carrying a candle. She looks uncertain. "Miss? I believe the prince wanted to greet you himself, but he seems to have fallen asleep. I can show you where you're meant to stay, though."

I nod, rising. Ruth takes me down the hall and opens an ordinary-looking door. My throat is tight and my breath is shallow. I've never had a reason to feel unsafe with Prince Idris and some part of me knows I need not be afraid of him. But even this healthy, unharmed body can't seem to understand that. I am a rabbit, poised to run at the first hint of danger.

"Thank you," I murmur. I make myself step into the room.

True lifts his ears and hops off the bed, wagging his tail. I avoid looking at Prince Idris asleep under the blankets. But all my attention focuses on him. My hands shake. My heart and my head tell me there is no reason to be afraid, but an ancient and feral part of me screams *run.*

I grab the door and turn the handle, wrenching it back open—all instinct, all need to escape. But a noise behind me cuts through the panic.

A noise like an exasperated horse.

I turn slowly. The noise again—a heavy sigh with a flapping raspberry ending. Idris is snoring. A comical, horsey snore.

I snicker and, just like that, I'm in control again. I look at the door, still open, and my hand on the latch. This isn't like before. I am choosing to be here, choosing to stay in this room. Choosing to stay with Idris, the same way I have since I first saw him.

Quietly, I pull the door shut. I tug one of the chairs closer to the fireplace and stir the peat. When I sit, True leans against my legs. It feels good to bury my hands in his fur and listen to the *thump thump* of his tail on the floor. My heartrate slows to a normal pattern and I take deep, deliberate breaths. The room smells of sea and books.

The wind gusts outside, whistling past the window, and now and again rain or ice hits the panes. I stay near the fire, absorbing its warmth. Idris sleeps and as I listen to his occasional horsey snore, the hours take on a golden glow. A peaceful clearing in an icy forest. I find myself hoping, foolishly, that maybe Idris won't get up tonight. Maybe he'll just sleep, and I'll sit here, and morning will come with nothing more than that.

Time creeps by slowly and then all at once. I've been staring at the fire for hours when, somewhere in the house, a clock chimes. I count the bells. *Ten…eleven…twelve.*

There's a creak behind me, and I jump, standing. Idris pushes himself out of the bed. Even now, as he grabs clothes from his wardrobe, he's strangely quiet. He never looks at me.

He's only dressed in his nightshirt and, without noticing me, he grabs the collar and starts to pull it over his head. Quickly I turn my back, staring at the fire with burning cheeks. I listen as he fumbles around. It's a matter of minutes before I hear him open his door and snap to True. The dog trots after his master. Idris has grabbed a different outfit than he wore yesterday and he's left Abram's glasses on his bedside table. I grab them before I follow him out.

Idris moves fast, and even with my new height and long strides I have to half run to keep up. The house is eerily still, as if we're moving through a painting. Idris pushes open the front door and steps into the wind, indifferent. I catch the door before it can close and dive after him. The cold stings my skin, my nose, my lungs. Even my pelisse doesn't keep it out. I notice for the first time that Idris hasn't put on a greatcoat. Bizarrely, he's only dressed for a dance.

He doesn't seem to notice the gale. He doesn't even pause before he's off to the road, taking the route toward the city with an urgent stride. I keep after him.

"Idris?" I call, once I'm close again. But he doesn't respond, and when I try to get a look at his face I can't make out his expression in the dark. His eyes gleam, though. Open.

True nudges my hand as if to remind me I am not alone out here.

Idris cuts straight through the town and to the dock. He starts untying a small yole. My stomach churns and I feel like a fool. Of course this would involve water.

If I get sick like before, I'll be useless on the other side of wherever we're going. And the sea looks much rougher tonight than it was when we sailed to Skyare. The harbor water is disturbed by small waves, but the churning sea beyond the breakwater roars in my ears.

True jumps in the boat and Idris himself is preparing to get in. It's too late to back out now.

Gulping a breath, I push in front of him and clamber to the bow of the boat. I sink down at the same time Idris jumps aboard and takes in the mooring lines. He pushes off from the dock with an oar and starts raising the sail. I grip the gunwales on either side of the boat, waiting for the rocking to start and my nausea to follow.

But even when we come out of the sheltered harbor, the boat remains remarkably steady. Almost like we are on a separate, still water. My nausea doesn't rise. Cautiously, I relax my grip and look around. There is no moon tonight, not with this cloud cover, and sea spray and rain lash me in turn. Yet the boat hardly rocks.

A shiver runs down my back. *Enchantment.*

Despite the lack of light, I can make out Idris's face a little better now that we're sitting across from each other with only a thin mast between us. He is pale as a corpse. His hair is dark and matted to his forehead with sweat, despite the cold. His eyes are fixed on some distant sight, glassy like a man mad with fever. He stares right past me. I wave my hand in front of his face. He blinks, though his eyes don't follow my movement.

"Idris?" I try again. "Are you there?"

He blinks again. A flicker of recognition crosses his face. But then the wind fills the sail and his hands are busy correcting our route. Whatever started to wake in him has gone again, his body rigid in attention to some invisible order.

I poke his knee, just to see if he'll do anything. He doesn't react.

I swallow. I'm out at sea with someone who doesn't seem to be in his body at all.

The boat shifts suddenly, caught in a new current, and I grab the sides once more. I can see whitecaps on the waves around us, but we continue as smoothly as the gentlest of canters. Smoother even than a carriage. Waves slap the hull and the boat creaks, but otherwise it is unnervingly silent.

A splash. I look to my left but resist the impulse to lean over the side. Catharine has told me enough stories about creatures waiting to drag a person overboard. I stare at what I can see without getting nearer the water, and it takes another few minutes before I make out a slick movement rising and falling through the waves. The next time it surfaces, two huge eyes as dark as ebony observe me. A seal.

Soon we are surrounded by them—I count at least six, but their rising and diving in the darkness makes it difficult to be sure.

I cannot tell how long we have been at sea when a shadow darker than the sky looms ahead of us. Cliffs rise from the water, steep and impossibly high. The sea thunders against the rocks and the white foam of the breaking waves is startlingly bright in the murk of black on black. Idris turns the tiller and aligns the boat straight at the cliffs.

"Um," I blurt. "Idris?"

He shows no sign of hearing me. We pass a rock jutting through the water, its sides slick and tip sharp. One of the seals jumps up on it and flops forward inelegantly. A moaning, wailing sound fills the air—the seal singing.

The cliffs grow closer, stretching far above us. I tighten my grip on the boat. "Idris!"

He gazes past me with no show of concern. No awareness whatsoever. Every swell throws us closer to the rocks.

I am about to lurch for the tiller when he speaks.

"Open!" Idris calls, voice hoarse and loud after his long silence. "Open, black cliff, and let the young prince in and out with his boat and his hound."

Swiftly, I add to Idris's command, "And his lady before him!"

A *crack* loud enough to split the air sounds behind me. I spin, gaping as the cliff rends itself apart. A gap glimmering with distant light opens, small but growing larger. Larger but still impossibly small against the face of the cliff. In the faint light, I see rocks like jagged daggers slicing the water to shreds. More seals hop up on these sharp perches and take up the wailing song. The noise is almost unbearable—the breaking rocks like a landside, the waves like thunder, and the wailing like the loudest funeral mourning. True hunkers lower in the hull of the boat, ears pinned back.

The gap in the cliff is still opening, but our boat hasn't slowed in the slightest. If anything, we seem to be moving faster. I hold my breath, waiting for a shift in the water to crash us into any of the thousand dangers around us. But the boat sails calmly forward, serenely steady in the midst of whirlpools and a screaming sea.

Then we are at an entrance. Rocks splinter and fall above us. I shut my eyes, tight, waiting for falling stone to smash and sink us. I can swim, but I learned in the calm lochs of my home; this wild water would overpower me in moments.

I feel the air change as we pass into the opening—suddenly humid, close, and warm. I crack an eye open and gasp.

It isn't so much a cave as an archway. As we come free of the low ceiling, the walls suddenly open without anything to obscure the sky. And the sky itself is no longer covered over by clouds. Stars glimmer, more than I've ever seen in my life, and while I gawk upward a shimmer of bright green wisps lazily across them.

"The dancers," I breathe. Lights that color the northern nights. I've heard of them, but had never seen them myself.

Reluctantly, I pull my gaze back down. Steep cliffs rise either side of our small boat, but the water is calm here. It gurgles softly, like a cooing child. Ahead of us, white sands glow on a peaceful shore. Beyond the shore is another cave, where silver light shines.

Idris grounds the boat on the sand and splashes out into the water, pushing it farther up onto dry ground. As soon as he stops, I climb out with True. The temperature has warmed, and I have a ridiculous desire to pull off my boots and sink my feet into the fine sand. Heat radiates from it, as if it's been baked in the hot summer sun.

Idris strides toward the second cave. His walk is familiar and I realize he moves like himself, even though he is in a dream. There's something disconcerting about it. I wish he moved like a sleepwalker, that there was something odd in his gait. Instead, it's as if he were still there, conscious, even though I know he isn't.

I spare one last glance at the sky. Pink and blue wisps tangle together and fade. I only promised the king I would keep watch, that I would find out where the entrance was. And I have done that—though I'm not sure I could trace it on a map. I could stay here, in the balmy sand, and watch the lights and wait.

A strand of spectral music drifts out of the second cave. When I turn, Idris has already disappeared inside, but True waits on the threshold. The dog wags his tail slowly as if to encourage me to follow.

I take a deep breath. I haven't come just to keep watch. I need to find answers.

Slowly, I step out of the starlight and into the strange silver glow. True wags his tail more fiercely and joins me, keeping pace at my ankle. His presence reassures me, but my heart still beats erratically.

The ground slopes down gently as I move step by step. I stay close to the wall on the right, trailing my hand along it, while True remains at my left. The light grows brighter, the music louder, and as the space beyond comes into view I nearly forget to breathe. I stop at the edge, pressed to the stone, and stare.

The underground chamber is larger than our dancing hall at the castle—maybe larger than the castle itself. I lift my gaze. There is no ceiling, just a vast sky filled with an enormous moon. I've never seen it in so much detail, not even at harvest time when it rose large and orange over the horizon. Staring at it now, I can make out craters and mountains, patches of bright white and mild silver.

A heady, dizzy feeling sends me off balance and I press my hand harder on to the wall. It is a dark, smooth stone, polished as if by a thousand tides over a thousand years. Limpet shells cling to the surface, glowing white, yellow, and orange. When I look across the hall to the far walls, I see the limpets are stars. There are stories in the constellations they form, but I cannot read them.

Then, as I watch, a bright-green light glimmers across one wall. It melds into vivid cranberry, then purple, spreading all the way across the perimeter just like the northern lights did across the sky outside. When it reaches me, the color is a cool mist that passes over my skin and fades, only for the colors to begin again at another point.

I pull my gaze from the surroundings to the people. The Hidden Folk seem to be made up of three different sorts, though they all mingle together in their dance. I search my mind for the sea folk Catharine has read about and make my best guess as to which is which: mermaids, finfolk, and selkies.

Mermaids are the tallest, with long legs instead of tails. Their hair color ranges from emerald green to wildfire red. They decorate their heads with scarves of seaweed or hairbands of seashells. Their skin color is similar to a human palette. I could easily imagine them lounging on sun-burned rocks, waiting for a sailor to lure. They wear dresses with petticoats clasped just under their chests and a skirt that clings to their hips before it flares out around their knees. I don't see any mermen among them, but then I can't remember stories of male merfolk.

Then there are the ones I think might be finfolk. They are about the height of an average human, though their limbs are thin and just a bit too long. There is an eeriness about them that's subtle but unsettling. Their skin is also similar to a human's but touched by strange shades. Vivid blue around their cheekbones or autumn gold at their fingertips. Their clothing is made of a shimmering, scaly material that almost looks like fish skin. Though the overall effect is silver, the material reflects a rainbow of colors whenever they move through a patch of light. The tips of their ears end in a subtle point, sometimes decorated with gold hoops. Though I search for him, I do not see Speir among the crowd.

The selkies are the shortest, some of them not even five-feet tall. They have luscious hair—normally black, but sometimes brown or golden—and wide dark eyes. Their clothing is like sea-foam silk, draped across their bodies in sensual folds. The men are clean shaven and the women don't have so much as a freckle to mar their pearly skin.

Children dart in and round the dancers, sometimes stopping to spin with an adult or perform a cartwheel. They are not plump and toddling like human children—their lean bodies move with uncanny grace. Two children are occupied chasing a sparrow, waving a stick in the air at the bird.

I don't spy anyone who looks like a small troll creature—a trow or hogboon—and I suppose they must be tied to their landlocked homes.

This dance is themed, I realize, with all the costumes in silvers and whites. I'm suddenly conscious of my dark-plum pelisse. Quickly, I undo the buttons at my chest and bundle it up in my arms. At least my dress is a delicate cream, instead of Catharine's finer, darker gowns.

Idris isn't hard to spot in his blue coat and breeches. He is sitting on one of several luxurious chaise longue near a long table piled high with food. The sight of pink salmon and bread wrapped in crunchy seaweed and colorful pastries as fluffy as a cloud makes my mouth water. A woman—a mermaid, I think—kneels in front of him in the tightly packed white sand of the floor. She bends over his feet, grinding pearls in a stone bowl. I slide into the room and follow the wall, trying to get a better look. The woman dips her hand in the shimmery white powder, then sprinkles it over Idris's bare soles. He stares past her at the dancers. The dull vacancy in his gaze sends a shudder down my back.

The woman rises and gives Idris her hand. She is impossibly beautiful, with hair more golden than the sun, left loose in long curls down past her hips. Her hand is delicate and skin a sun-kissed tan. Idris lets her lead him into the dance. His movements turn fluid, naturally paired with every lift and fall of the dance.

The notes tug at me as I watch him and I take an involuntary step from the wall. My bag's contents clink against my leg, reminding me of the danger, and I hug my pelisse tighter to my chest as I retreat.

I need to find out how to break Idris's curse, and my own. But I've never been more conscious of my appearance. In a room of these extraordinary beings, even Catharine's beautiful body must seem ordinary. Plain. Human. I'll be spotted if I draw their notice, and I'm not eager to test the mercy of folk like Speir.

There is a small crevice in the wall, deep in darkness. I climb into it, shoes slipping and sliding over the time-polished rock. It's wide enough that I can crouch and watch, with the rock ledge offering some protection. True waits long enough to check I'm settled, then trots off to sit by Idris's abandoned shoes.

No, don't go! I want to shout after him. But I bite my tongue.

Maybe it's better, anyway. Someone might notice if True stood guard by me.

Still, uncomfortably perched behind the slightly damp rock, I can't help feeling alone.

I check the supplies in my bag, reassuring myself I should be able to leave, and turn my attention back to the chamber. The dances are strange and lovely, a never-ceasing movement that flows from one partner to the next. I blush a little to see how close the couples stand—the men's hands on the women's lower backs, sometimes on bare skin. It is far more intimate than the balls I've attended.

Unbidden, an image of King Byrne surfaces in my mind. The tightness of his hand as I stepped into that last turn. The smell of him and the pain cutting through my wrist.

I close my hand over my wrist now, feeling the narrowness of it, the ease with which it turns and bends. A body that's never been punished for simply existing.

A body that isn't mine. That I'm trying to give back.

Again, bitter sadness rises in my throat. I swallow it down. Catharine does not deserve to be in my true body, my breaking body.

But do I?

I push the thought away. The wasting is mine. *Bear what must be borne.*

Someone dressed in color catches my eye as he appears from a side room. I hadn't noticed, but there are low openings in the wall that must lead somewhere else. This man has to hunch to get through and he straightens again, squinting as he surveys the dance.

Without his glasses, it takes me a moment to recognize him. Abram.

He looks unharmed, wearing a simple, unrumpled brown suit. He's barefoot, like Idris. He's too far away for me to see clearly, but I think from the intentional way he seems to be scanning the assembly that he is in his right mind. Looking.

True hops up and lopes over to Abram, wagging his tail. I slide one foot out of the crevice and carefully begin to ease myself free. Abram is kneeling to pet his brother's dog. I eye the crowd between me and him, unsure of the best way to attract his gaze without drawing anyone else's. But before I can decide, a selkie maiden catches his arm and tugs him into the dance. He doesn't resist, though he scans the faces of the people he passes.

I press against the wall and wait for another chance.

A few turns take Abram close to Idris.

Abram straightens, his face brightening. "Idris!" I see his mouth move, though I can't hear the name above the sound of the music.

Idris doesn't so much as blink. I watch disappointment and concern chase each other across Abram's face. Then two more turns separate the brothers again.

But the dance is bringing Abram closer to me.

I lift my hand, waiting, waiting for my chance. When he turns in my direction, I risk a wave. He frowns and I'm not sure he knows who I am. I lower my arm, not wanting the Folk to notice.

The dances don't exactly end or change—they seem to meld one into the next. Partners are exchanged seemingly at random. It's some time later when Abram reappears, moving along the wall to me. I exhale a relieved breath.

When he gets closer, his expression changes to surprise. "Catharine?"

"Ah." The barb appears in my throat again, sensing my instinct to correct him.

He shakes his head. "Sorry. I mean, Kit?"

The barb sharpens. I don't dare nod, but I hold out his folded glasses to him.

"Thank you," Abram says eagerly, grabbing them and slipping them on. He blinks a few times, then turns his worried expression back to me. "Why in the world are you here?"

I briefly explain how Idris and his father figured out Abram had disappeared. How I had offered to come and keep watch tonight.

"It's too dangerous," Abram says. "You shouldn't have. Catharine needs you."

I'm surprised and a little touched by his concern.

"You'll be trapped now, like me," he goes on, his face etched with anxiety. "I can't step out of the cavern. Not even onto the beach. Every time I try, I feel—I feel a bit like I'm unraveling."

"I've taken precautions," I assure him. "I should be able to leave." *I think.* "Is Jay here?"

Abram's brows lower again. "No. I haven't been able to find him."

I chew my lip. "Maybe he never made it this far."

Abram doesn't answer, but I can see in his uneasy expression that he has thought the same thing. I remember the rocks outside. The violence of the sea.

I shake away the thought. "How are you holding up?"

"All right, more or less." His voice sounds dry. Now assisted by his glasses, he scans the crowd again. "I've managed to keep the mermaids from tricking me to drink or eat."

"Mermaids?" I echo, curious to see if my guesses were correct.

"They untie their tails for the dance." Abram gestures to the tall women in their long skirts.

"The fabric is their skin?" I ask, looking again at the strange material.

Abram shakes his head. "I'm not sure how it works. I've heard when they want to walk on the shore outside of the Hidden Land, they have to remove the tail entirely—like a selkie, I think. We have stories of men stealing their tails to claim a mermaid in marriage."

"That's horrible." I remember the selkie-wife tales. I know what it is like to feel a man claim your skin for his own. Now, standing in front of these real women, ethereal and otherworldly, in a skin that isn't mine at all, I feel pity and anger. No one should have their body stolen, no matter why.

With some effort, I pull my thoughts back to the present. Idris is stumbling on the white sand, growing clumsier with every turn. I hug my folded pelisse to my chest.

"You said they were trying to trick you?" I ask Abram. "What would happen if you ate or drank?"

"I'm not entirely sure," Abram admits. "But I know in some stories, taking food in the Hidden Lands seals your fate as a captive. That hasn't happened to Idris, obviously, since he is able to come and go, but I don't know if I'm afforded the same protection he is. And mermaids are known to enchant men if they can."

I glance at him questioningly.

"If they marry a human man, they never age," Abram explains. He rubs his arm, embarrassed. "Idris is clearly not on offer, but they've been...pleased by my situation."

My stomach churns and I'm not sure how to answer. Skin stolen for a marriage or an enchantment woven to create love—I'm not sure that one is any better than the other.

"Here." I dig into my reticule. "I'm sorry I didn't think to bring more, but these should be safe." I pass him the flask of water and what remains of my hazelnuts. "I'll try to bring more tomorrow."

He smiles and takes a deep drink of the water. "Thank you."

Out in the dance, Idris suddenly stumbles and collapses to the ground. I take a step forward, but Abram catches my arm.

"Stay here," he says, leaving the flask and hurrying on without me.

Reluctantly, I move back against the wall. I can still see everything as it unfolds. The Hidden Folk drag Idris to the chaise longue. His face is colorless and his head lolls. They hold his head back and tip red amber liquid from a glass into his mouth. My heart nearly stops, but I remember Abram's words: Idris can still leave. He's protected by rules that may or may not extend to Abram and me.

Abram reaches the chaise longue just as they begin to haul Idris back to his feet. I hear Abram's words faintly over the wild music.

"Let him rest," he's saying. He reaches for Idris's arm. "Let him be, for God's sake!"

But the Hidden Folk pay him no attention, and Idris is shoved back into the crowd. Abram stops at the edge of the ring, helpless, and then a mermaid with hair blacker than coal pulls him into the dance as well. I think I see him hold back, but it's only a moment before he's in the thick of it too.

I crawl back into my hiding place, thinking. The dances go on and on. The music—played by performers I cannot see—shifts and changes between one piece and the next. First, it is a meandering tune, as rhythmic as the waves, and then it turns into a stormy frenzy, loud and fast. The next jig rises joyful as a seagull cresting a cloud, before plunging like an osprey into serene depths. The instruments have a sound similar to ours, but with an unnerving edge to each note. It vibrates in my ear, somewhere between a comfort and an itch. A fiddle tuned a notch too high. A cello whose sound carves into me. A flute that's rusted with seawater. A whistle that hits two notes at once.

I can't tell how much time has passed before Abram extracts himself again. He weaves his way toward me, glancing at the Folk often to see whether they are paying any attention. But before he can get far, the music abruptly cuts off.

The Hidden Folk turn as one to the larger of the open tunnels. The instruments were so loud that in their sudden silence the final notes ring through my ears. Faintly, I can hear the cooing babble of the water in the cove. But otherwise, there is no sound, not even the breathing of the crowd. Abram stops, turning as well. Idris has his arm draped over the shoulder of a selkie on one side and on the other a finman—

No, not *a* finman. It's Speir.

My hands clench into fists. When did he arrive? How had I missed him?

Speir takes a handful of Idris's hair and uses it to turn him. When he lets go again, he gives Idris's head a pat, the way one might a dog. My blood boils.

The near-colorless moonlight makes it seem everyone has turned to stone. I cannot move without breaking the moment and there is no way I can reach Speir without making a scene.

Then there are shuffling steps and from the tunnel march four finmen with a sedan chair on their shoulders. A woman—a queen, I think—sits in the chair, upright and proud. On her head is an elegant crown of white coral and amethyst gems. She wears a long gown, glowing white silk tinged with the pale pink of a pearl. The skirt hangs over the edge of her chair and a breeze from the cove behind me ripples the hem like a wave.

Underneath the skirt, I glimpse lumpy metal shoes. They seem too tight, biting into her skin and sending blue streaks up her legs. I wonder why she wears them.

Then the dress settles again, covering her feet. The men set her sedan on a raised dais, where she can preside over everyone. Her gaze drifts past Abram to Idris, where she pauses with a measuring look. She lifts her hand, graceful and pale.

Then she stares right at me.

I freeze where I am, hands tightening on the edge of my nook.

She is across the large hall and I should not be able to see her as I do—all clarity and closeness. Her eyes are wide and vivid, her irises nearly black. Selkie eyes. Her hair is palest blonde, left loose and long enough to brush her ankles. Her cheekbones cut shadows into her face that in the daylight of an autumn afternoon would have made her beautiful. But in the light of the moon, she is left hollow. Skeletal.

She holds herself upright with a rigidity I recognize. It is the sheer will of determination in the face of invisible pain. It is in the stiffness of her fingers, still lifted in some sort of signal. It is in the angle of her head, exactly straight rather than relaxed one way or the other. It is in her eyes that are like black mirrors. They hold mine in a question.

I am back at the ball, Byrne reaching for me. I am staring at those around me. I am asking them, *Can you see me? Am I real?*

Then the queen slides her gaze away. Back to Idris. She smiles, less mirth than grim satisfaction. She lowers her hand. The music resumes.

I sink back into my hiding place, relieved and confused.

When I look again, Speir is gone.

TWELVE

Idris

My thoughts

are

frag

ments.

Space

forms between

each

moment.

I am

s t r e t c h e d

and

dis tant.

Gone.

The blur and burn of color fog in my mind.

There is a familiar face. Light on glasses. A dog's nose pressed to my hand. Words called. *Cannot leave.* And then a woman speaking: *Tomorrow, tomorrow.*

Cold cracks in lungs. Heat sizzles on skin. Mouth tastes of wine and salt.

An unsteady surface, rolling beneath. Firm again. Uphill. Steep. Air that cannot find room. A chest too small.

Then sudden softness. A bed. A warm shaggy body lying on burning feet.

Peat smoke, comforting and familiar. A shadow by the fire.

Quiet.

Clink clink scratch, clink clink thud.

I keep my eyes closed, reaching for the last threads of sleep. Trying to tangle my mind in them, to fall back into rest. But my body—though pulsing with pain—becomes wide awake. Something scrapes on the wall. *Clink clink scratch, clink clink thud.* It won't stop.

I open my eyes reluctantly. Morning cracks through thick clouds. I'm in my room, in my bed. True lies on my feet, his brown eyes watching me, though his head isn't lifted. His tail thumps on the covers, but that's not the sound I heard. I press my palms against my aching head. I want to strangle whatever is making that noise. I want to bury my face in my pillow. But as soon as I turn over to try to sleep, I hear it again.

Clink clink scratch, clink clink thud.

Groaning, I flop onto my back. Movement catches my attention. Kit, leaning over the fire and stirring it.

"Are you making that noise?" I ask, my mind clouded by irritation and exhaustion.

She stops. "Oh, I didn't mean to disturb you."

"No, not that. The clinking." I cover my face. Momentarily, the darkness of my arm makes the ache in my head subside.

But then here it is again: *Clink, clink. Clink clink clink clinkclinkclink...*

"Make that infernal noise stop," I mutter. It seems to echo in my brain, plucking at my eyes.

A pause. "There...isn't any noise, Idris."

I shift my arm and shoot her a glare. She lifts her hands, apologetic. Her hair is still tied up, with wisps falling around her face. Spots of darkness shadow her eyes. I realize she's been up all night—and, just like that, my mind clears.

She's still here.

I sit up quickly, ashamed of my temper and desperate for her news.

"What happened last night?" I ask, my face heating with embarrassment or eagerness or both. "What did you find out? Is Abram—?"

"Abram's all right," she says quickly. "Or...as well as he can be. He's still trapped, but he's not been harmed."

"And Jay?"

"He—I don't know."

I push myself out of bed. True grunts in annoyance. In only my nightshirt, the morning air is cold despite the fire. Right. Nightshirt. My face flames and I grab the blanket from True to wrap round me.

"Would you like to...get dressed first?" Kit asks, eyes averted. "I thought I might slip out and perhaps speak to you and your father in town?"

I check my impatience. There is nothing proper about our circumstances and I've already risked Kit's—or, Catharine's—reputation enough by asking for her help. The least I can do is make sure we talk somewhere safer for her.

"Right, of course." My legs tremble, and I sit again. "Do you need help getting out?"

"I think I know the way." She picks her pelisse from her chair and pulls it on. "Where should I find you?"

"The Guildhall," I offer. "Same as last time."

She nods and slips through the door. I rise as soon as she's gone. But this time, when I stand, I notice that there's something different about the floor. I look down. My feet are bound in cloth. Cuts or blisters sting against the bandage when I shift my weight. I feel a swell of gratitude, and something else that seems to blend embarrassment and warmth. Kit must have done that.

I take my clothes and dress quickly. True huffs a sigh when I open my door but comes reluctantly after me.

"You can stay if you want," I tell him. He looks up at the sound of my voice and wags his tail halfheartedly. I run my thumb up the space between his eyes, so that he closes them in a doggy smile. Softly, I say, "Thanks."

Father is pacing the breakfast room. When I enter alone, what little color remains in his face drains away.

"She came back," I say quickly. "She's fine. Abram is still trapped but she said he's well."

Father exhales. "Where is she?"

"I told her we'd talk at the Guildhall. We thought it might be more—proper."

Father is walking past me to the front door before I finish my sentence. "Take some food and come."

I snatch a napkin and load it with ham, toast, and sausage. I "accidentally" drop one of the slices of ham onto the floor and True gobbles it up. Holding the rest, I hurry after Father. My feet pinch and sting. It takes me a few minutes to catch up, and by the time I do, my feet have dulled to about the same ache as the rest of me. I can walk without a limp, at least.

Father maintains his icy silence on our walk to town. I use the opportunity to eat. I'm famished, but even when I'm done I don't feel stronger. My hands have a slight shake to them, I think. I wipe them clean and stick them in my pockets before I can be sure.

We are let into the Guildhall and informed someone is waiting for us in the audience room. I ask for tea and hot rolls to be sent up. If Kit beat us here, she probably did not stop to eat.

But when we enter, Kit isn't the person waiting.

A young man stands and turns to us.

"Jay?" I gasp.

Jay comes to me and takes my arm. "Good lord, Id—"

Father catches my other shoulder just as my knees go weak. The morning tips toward black and I move my legs in an attempt to walk wherever they're taking me. My pulse pounds against my skull and a woolly, thick humming clouds my ears. I breathe deeply, forcing my lungs to expand, and slowly my vision returns. A rush of heat and cold sweeps through me, and I can't tell if I'm shivering or sweating.

Clink clink clink clink.

Jay closes my hands round a cup. I drink. It's tea. The wool in my ears loosens, and I catch the words spoken between my friend and my father.

"…so much worse?" Jay is saying.

Father gives a short nod. "It seems to progress faster every night."

"I'm fine," I rasp. I clear my throat. "I just—Jay! What are you doing here? How—?"

Jay pulls another chair close and sits, his brown eyes still concerned. There's a bandage round his head and he looks tired. "If I knew it'd be such a shock, I would have told the servants to prepare you. I got home last night—I wanted to be here when you came today." He glances at my father, and I'm not sure if he's addressing this to me or him. "I didn't want to disturb the house."

Father pours out two more cups of tea. "Where have you been these past two days?"

"Mainland." Jay takes his cup and holds it between his hands.

I blink. "What?"

"I followed you, Idris." Jay exhales. "You got out of bed on the strike of midnight, dressed, and took off for the harbor. You've been taking your yole. I boarded with you, and we set off due west. After about half an hour, you turned north. I saw an island I've never seen before, either in person or on a map. The cliffs were sheer—even taller than Verron's—and you went straight for them. I tried to take the tiller and…"

A memory struggles to surface. Hands grappling with mine. Someone shouting. All my strength gathered in a shove.

"I pushed you over?" I whisper, horrified.

Jay nods. "Seems that way."

Father rubs his face.

"Weren't we near the whirlpools?" I ask, trying to trace his directions in my mind. "How…how in the world are you not drowned?"

"I don't know that part of it." Jay points to the bandage on his head. "You didn't just push me over. You pushed me into a rock."

"Joseph have mercy," I breathe. "I'm sorry."

Jay smiles. "No harm has come of it in the end. I blacked out. My recollection isn't the sharpest from there. When I woke, I was on the shore. Thought I saw a whole colony of seals in the water—more than I've seen that close before—but I'm not sure. They could have been rocks… I was near Port Stramp and managed to get into town. I've been there."

"And the weather kept you unable to send word?" Father guesses.

Jay nods. "Until yesterday afternoon not even Tom Westness would venture into the open water." Jay frowns. "Stramp was buzzing with some strange news, Idris. Mr. Westness had got rather wrapped up in it…"

Someone knocks on the door. A servant glances in and makes a bow. "Excuse me, Your Royal Highnesses, but there is a woman who says she was directed to speak with you?"

Father glances at me quickly. I nod for the servant to let Kit in. "Jay can be trusted to keep a secret," I say to my father.

"More secrets?" Jay gives me a smile. "How many are you collecting?"

But then Kit steps in—Kit in Catharine's body—and Jay starts to his feet. "Princess!"

Kit blinks in surprise. "Mr. Berd!"

Jay makes a hasty bow. "Are you well? I heard a disturbing report—"

"I'm fine." Kit turns to me uncertainly.

"Jay can be trusted," I say again. "Have a seat, princess."

Father helps Kit to the last empty chair. She sits, smoothing her wrinkled dress over her legs. I offer her a hot roll and a cup of tea. Suppressing a yawn, she accepts them. But she doesn't make a move to eat or drink.

"I'm glad to see you well," Jay says to Kit. "The mainland is in an uproar about what happened. Your father has been desperate to ascertain you were not harmed."

"Harmed?" she repeats. Her fingers absently crush one side of her roll. "Harmed by whom?"

Jay's eyebrows lower in confusion. "Your stepsister, of course."

"What?" Kit and I say together.

Jay blinks at me. "You haven't had the news? I suppose the foul weather set in right as the notice arrived in Stramp."

Father perches on the edge of his chair. "What did you hear?"

"The king sent out word that his daughter—" Jay nods to Kit—"had been kidnapped by her jealous sister and stolen away. There were concerns that some harm was intended. I spoke with Mr. Westness. He had recognized Princess Catharine's description in the king's edict. He told me he'd brought both girls across. He saw how ill you were, princess." Jay turns to her again. "How, on the ride over, you never spoke a word and you deferred to your sister."

Kit stares at him. "My sister didn't do anything to me. We left together."

A pause. "You did?"

"Why would you think—?" The color that had faded out of Kit's cheeks returns in force now. Her hands grip the plate. "What would give you any reason to think that my sister would ever hurt me?"

"At-at the ball," Jay says uncertainly. "Your stepsister seemed jealous of the attention you received. She wouldn't speak a word to me. And your father told me that while he expected you would soon leave the castle, he had no reason to believe your stepsister had any prospects."

I stare at my friend. I had no idea he harbored this idea of Kit. On the journey home, Jay talked about the ball with Abram and me. But I was so distracted by my own problems, I didn't pay any attention. Did he mention these suspicions then? Could I have corrected him?

"I'm afraid you have wholly the wrong way of it!" Kit says sharply. "No one was kidnapped. Harm befell my sister and me at the hands—" Her voice slices into silence as she winces.

I lean forward, wanting to help, but she throws a hand up to hold me off. Father studies her closely.

In a moment, she continues cautiously. "We…could not stay…for our own safety. But we left willingly *together*."

"I'm sorry," Jay says. His ears have gone red. "I wish—I shouldn't have made any assumptions."

"No, you shouldn't have," she agrees icily

"At least no harm came from it," I put in, trying to ease the tension.

Jay doesn't speak, but the dread in his expression makes my chest tighten.

“That’s not the end of the story,” my father observes, his voice low and quiet. “Is it?”

Jay shifts in his seat. “Mr. Westness wasn’t confident enough about his passengers to get involved with a king, so he hadn’t said anything to anyone but me. And I…I wasn’t sure… But when I got home and saw how my family had worried for me, I felt… I thought I ought to relieve any parent of such suffering, even if it was only a slim chance Mr. Westness had actually escorted the princesses.”

Kit is frozen, staring at my friend in horror.

“I wrote to the king last night.” Jay clears his throat. “I’m afraid the letter will have reached the mainland this morning.”

I touch Kit’s arm—an instinctive gesture of comfort—and she all but explodes under my hand. She jumps to her feet and springs away. A visible tremble shakes her as she drops the plate onto a side table.

“I—” She swallows. “I’m so sorry—please excuse me.”

And she is out the door.

Jay looks stricken. Father half stands, but I dart after Kit. She’s stopped in the hall, turned toward the stairs one moment and then facing another way the next like a trapped animal. This time, I check my impulse to put a hand on her shoulder.

“That room there should be empty,” I say, pointing to one of the judgment rooms.

She flinches away from me, as if she hadn’t realized I was there. “I don’t—that is—”

Something about her flitting unease makes me think of the way fish will twist and panic as a net tightens. It seems suddenly foolish to suggest she go into another, smaller room. A smaller trap. I move past her and grab a door at the far end of the hall. My feet sting with renewed force after the time spent sitting, but I try not to limp.

"Here." I open the door and step aside, so she can see a stone staircase to the small garden. "Maybe some fresh air?"

Kit nods and rushes past me. "Just a moment, please."

I think about staying with her. She's so distressed, it seems wrong to leave her alone. But I remember what it has been like to have Father and Abram breathing down my neck the past week, their worry and concern adding another burden on top of everything else. If I cannot relieve Kit of her pain, then I won't add to the weight of it by making her attend to my feelings as well. I close the door softly, letting her have her privacy.

I stay by the door, though. Just in case she wants someone. Or in case someone else tries to go outside.

After a few minutes of quiet, I shift to lean on the wall, trying to get some of the weight off my feet. In my head, I do my own counting. If Jay sent the letter yesterday evening, it will have gone with the morning sail to the mainland. It will be in the hands of King Byrne in another two days. And I imagine King Byrne will set out the moment he gets it, meaning he will arrive here in four days or less.

I'm still not sure exactly of the nature of his relationship with Kit. But I think I have the measure of Kit's character. She followed me into the Hidden Lands last night. If she talked to Abram, she must have entered. And if someone could go in and out of the Hidden Lands and be sat calmly by the fire in the morning but react with so much fear at word of her stepfather—then I trust that she has good reason.

My eyes ache. I close them, trying to sink into the moment of respite. The relief of the darkness behind my eyelids makes my shoulders relax and…

Clink clink thud.

My head nods and I jerk upright. The floor seems to slide under me—then I'm steady again. I rub my hair, looking around for whatever is causing that confounded noise. But there's no one in sight.

✦

After a quarter hour or so, Kit opens the door. She looks composed, but still more anxious than she has been the entire time I've known her. Though she is in Catharine's body, and it's Catharine's face that betrays her fear, there's something in the knit of her eyebrows and the way her gaze slides away from mine that reminds me of the night of the ball, when I bound her wrist.

"I'm so sorry," she says, "but I feel I must go and tell my sister about this. I know I haven't fully let you know everything about last night, though, and…"

"I'll sail you back to Mrs. Westness's," I offer. "You can tell me on the way."

"What about your father?"

"I can handle him later." I shrug. "Let's go."

"Are you sure you're well enough?" she says, keeping pace when I begin to walk. "Shouldn't you be resting?"

I shrug again. "I'll give that a try this afternoon. I'm fine to sail."

True trots alongside us as we head outside. I take Kit down to my yole and give it a push down the grass noust and into the shallow water. I offer my hand to help her in. She hesitates, then puts her hand in mine as she steps onto the boat. I remember the calluses on her hand—her real hand—at the ball. Catharine's hand is soft and smooth. I wonder if Kit misses the calluses—the work built up around her skin to protect her.

Kit settles in the bow and True hops between us. I take in the lines, settle at the tiller and use an oar to push us into deeper water.

"We took this route, I'm guessing?" I ask her.

She nods, tugging her pelisse closer round her. I raise the sail and guide us onto the open water. The boat gives a rock when we pass out of the harbor. Kit tightens her hands in her lap, her face drawn in concentration.

"Do you want to talk about last night?" I can't tell whether her unease has to do with whatever happened.

"I—Yes." Her voice comes out clipped and strained.

I wait, worried I've offended her somehow. She holds herself completely still, rigidly fixing her gaze on the horizon. Her jaw is locked tight.

"Are you…?" I begin.

But before I can finish, she dives for the edge of the boat and heaves over the side. I'm so surprised, it takes me a moment to move into action. I shift my weight to keep the boat from listing too far and turn us quickly toward shore. She keeps her head over the side, even when she isn't heaving.

We get to the shore barely a mile out of the town. I beach the boat and haul it safely ashore. Kit has started to straighten up, and I offer her a hand to help her over the side. Her face is pale and she avoids looking at me.

"All right?" I ask, worried. I guide her to a rock. "Just sit here for a moment."

She sinks down and takes shallow breaths. I let True snuggle against her while I go back to the boat to secure the sails. When I return, she seems less pale but more ashamed.

"I'm...sorry," she mutters, pressing the backs of her fingers to her cheeks. "I didn't get sick last night, and I thought maybe...I'm afraid I get horribly seasick now that I'm—"

"Don't worry about it," I assure her. I sit on the sand beside her. "I've done far, far worse than that."

She glances at me doubtfully.

I grin. "You don't live on an island and not experience your fair share of...*displays*."

A smile tugs at the corner of her mouth, and she looks away. It strikes me that I'm sitting here with a princess talking about sick, and the oddness of the situation makes me almost laugh. More than that—with Kit, it doesn't feel taboo. She's still a bit embarrassed, but I don't feel any awkwardness now. I'm not sure it'd be the same if I was sitting here with Catharine.

Kit swallows. "I don't think we should try to sail me all the way home."

"I could walk you—"

"Absolutely not." She draws herself up. "I saw the state of your feet. You need to go home and rest."

It's my turn to blush. "Well..." I'm surprised to find myself a little disappointed to let her go so soon. "Just take a moment to recover, at least. You don't need to go marching off at once."

Kit nods. She takes a few more breaths, then begins, "About last night..."

She tells me about everything she saw. Our journey, the cliffs, my words, the dancing. Abram and the woman in iron boots carried in halfway through the evening.

I stiffen. "She was there?"

Kit nods, confused. "Do you know her?"

I hesitate. "I think she's the queen who cursed my great-great-grandfather."

Kit lifts her eyebrows. "She's the one doing this to you?"

"Yes. Well..." I hesitate. "I don't know if it's her fault really. I mean, the curse she placed is why all this is happening, but she had a reason for it. My great-great-grandfather sort of...bound her feet in iron."

Kit's eyes widen. "I thought the Folk couldn't touch iron."

"They aren't meant to." I shift my weight, brushing some sand off my boots. "Did you manage to speak to anyone? Figure out anything about your own...situation?"

"I only spoke to Abram." The wind rises off the sea and the wisps of her hair dance around her face. "Speir was there—"

"Speir?" I turn to her. "How do you know Speir?"

Her expression tightens and she doesn't answer.

"Oh." He was the one who cursed her and Catharine. But how had he become involved with them? And why would he care to switch their bodies? I can't ask her any of this, of course—already she is stiff, her neck tight with whatever keeps her silent. I add out loud, "He is the one who delivered the queen's curse to me."

She nods, not surprised. But apparently, however she knows that, she cannot tell me.

"He was there for little more than a moment," she continues, picking up from where I had interrupted. Her voice starts hoarse but grows more comfortable as she speaks. "I wasn't confident about making myself known, though I think the queen did see me. But she didn't do anything about it. Maybe tonight I'll have more luck."

My stomach twists. "I've already asked so much of you, Kit. I don't know about..."

Kit lifts her chin. "I promised I would help you and your brother, and besides...I still need to find a solution for my sister." In a joking sort of voice, she adds, "Though I'll require a bag of gold this time."

I look down at True and rub his ears. "Jay said I pushed him overboard. I couldn't live with myself if something happened to you."

"I'll be careful," she says confidently.

After a few minutes, I venture, "What will you do about King Byrne?"

Kit's hands tighten on her knees. "We will have to leave Mrs. Westness's house. And, perhaps, go to one of the more remote islands." Her gaze settles on True. "But I can't leave now. You're my best chance of finding a way out of this. I don't know what I can do to—"

She closes her mouth abruptly. Her skin tightens over her collarbone while her throat constricts. I wonder what it is that cuts her words—what it feels like when she is silenced.

After a few moments, she adds, "I don't know any other way."

"I understand," I tell her.

We sit in silence for a little while, both in our thoughts.

"I should let you get home," Kit says, rising. "When would you like me to come tonight?"

"Eight?" I offer, getting up too. My feet immediately sting in protest. "Sorry I was asleep when you arrived last night. I'll try to be awake this time."

She shakes her head. "Sleep whenever you can. You need it."

I think about what it might be like if I wasn't asleep when she came to my room. The awkwardness of trying to fall asleep with a woman there. My face heats and I simply nod.

Kit hesitates, as if unsure how to part. "Thank you for bringing me…at least part of the way."

I nod again. "Give your sister my regards."

She glances up, an uncertainty in her look that confuses me. It's an uncertainty that is almost, maybe, something like hurt. But in a moment it's gone. She drops a curtsy and turns to leave.

I watch as she gets farther and farther away. Beyond her, the hills rise up against the cloudy sky. My legs are weak, and I lower myself to the sand, suddenly winded. True presses against me. I lie down, closing my eyes, wishing I could sleep.

But as soon as I start to slip into a dream, the noise begins again.

Clink clink thud.

THIRTEEN

Kit

Catharine isn't sitting by the fire when I reach the croft. I close the door and look around. She's still curled on the makeshift mattress Mrs. Westness pulled out for us into the corner of the main room, the blanket up to her chin. She opens her eyes when I step over.

I kneel beside the bed. "Are you all right?" I've never known Catharine to sleep so late, even when she was younger and unused to rising with me for chores.

She blinks, eyes watery with sleep. "What time is it?" She pushes herself up. "I was meant to have breakfast ready for you!"

"It's fine." I put a hand on her arm.

Catharine looks toward the window. "It's late, isn't it? I'm so sorry. I thought—I don't know how I slept so long."

But I know. I remember the way a cloud of fatigue would steal over me and I couldn't seem to get enough sleep. Habit and need would drive me up anyway, even when my body felt like it would cave for the want of rest. I always pushed through. But Catharine isn't used to it.

I take the pillow from my side of the bed and try to prop up the two together so she can sit comfortably. It's nothing like the pillows at the castle. When Catharine leans back, these flatten to barely more than a blanket.

"I should get up, anyway," she says with a little smile. "I want to hear how it went."

"I can tell you just as easily here. I'll just warm the room and get you a cup of small beer—no, you stay." I smile to make the command gentler. "Just rest."

Catharine sighs but doesn't try to get up. "You're the one who should be resting."

I ignore her as I check the fire. Mrs. Westness must have relit it before she went out for the morning. I stir the peat, my eyes stinging in the smoke. King Byrne is coming. May already be on his way. My heart hammers. The Hidden Lands seem like a dream—a story I slipped through—in the face of the fear that nips at my chest now. *This* is real. *This* is danger. I know it isn't rational, but the risks I took last night feel like nothing in comparison. *Worse* is coming. *Hurt* is coming. Just the thought of seeing him again makes my lungs close.

"Kit?" Catharine's voice is soft behind me. "Is it… Did you always feel this way?"

"What do you mean?" I ask, facing her.

Catharine has her bandaged hand resting on her chest. Slowly, she says, "I feel as if I can count every breath. As if I have to concentrate to draw them in. As if…my skin is too tight and small. My eyelids too heavy." She lifts her gaze to mine and it strikes me as strange all over again—my face looking at me, my eyes worried and sorrowful and…afraid.

"Did you always feel like this?" Her voice whispers, cracks. "How could you bear always feeling like this?"

I leave the fire and sit on the bed, wrapping my arms round my sister. But not just her—round myself, too. My frightened, broken body.

"It's not always so bad," I say, my throat tight. "It comes and goes. I got used to it—but you won't have to. I'll have you back to yourself before you have to."

Catharine tightens her hold of me, crushing her face into my shoulder. "I didn't know, Kit. I didn't know."

I can't speak around the hole in my chest. Even with my love and my sadness engulfing me, I'm struck by the ease of my breathing. The lightness of my bones. The joints that don't hook and pierce when I squeeze, when I clutch the back of Catharine's dress in my hands. *No one has known,* I realize. *I didn't even know.*

I am a whirlwind of feeling. Afraid of this breaking thing I'll soon be trapped in again. Proud of myself—my small, younger self—who did her duty no matter how much her body wanted to curl over and sleep. And sad. Sad, sad, sad. Sadder than I've ever let myself know.

I pull back from Catharine, wiping the wet from my cheeks as I return to the fire. I pour the drinks into mugs. The movement settles me and the gulf of sadness fades back to a place less vivid. A place I can tuck away. I grab some flatbread while I'm up and then join Catharine again on the floor.

"Here," I say, handing her mug over. "It's my turn to tell you a story. It's stranger than the ones you've read and true as the sky is gray."

"You've missed an opportunity to rhyme," she says, rubbing her knuckles under her eyes. "The sky is blue."

"I've yet to see a blue sky here." I lift my eyebrows. "Now listen. There was once an enchanted prince..."

I tell her the story of last night, trying to weave it into the style of her folktales. Somehow, framing it in the way of the stories we read in her books makes it feel at once clearer and safer. When I finish, we both sip our small beer and fall into a thoughtful silence.

"Pain doesn't wake him up," Catharine says at last.

"What?" I ask, drawing myself back to the room. I had begun to think of King Byrne again, though I hadn't yet found a way to bring him up.

"Prince Idris. His feet were bleeding by the end, you said, and he'd collapsed a few times." Catharine tilts her head and scrunches her nose. I didn't know my nose could wrinkle like that. "He must have been in pain, but it didn't wake him."

"Maybe he can't be conscious while he's in the Hidden Lands."

"You said there was a spark, a moment," Catharine points out, "when you were in the boat together. Maybe his daze isn't a part of the curse. It would certainly be useful to have him awake next time."

"Hmm." She could be right, but I don't know what else would cause someone to be so disconnected from their surroundings. My thoughts wander again to tonight. I'll need to free Abram. And find a way to help Idris if I can. And find a cure for Catharine's and my curse. We'll need to leave as soon as we can after tomorrow, to put some distance between us and Byrne.

It's as good a time as any to let Catharine know the news. I clear my throat and explain that Jay has returned. Catharine brightens, pleased that he's safe.

I hesitate. Dread pools in my stomach at even the shape of Byrne's name on my lips, but I make myself say it. "King Byrne has been looking for us. He sent out word that I… kidnapped you. Jay believed him and has written to him with our location."

I expect horror to spread over Catharine's face. For her to shrink back like I did at the news.

"That's an odd thing to think." She looks thoughtful and then smiles. "But this is good! If Father gets the news before your mother finds us, then he can help."

My fingers tighten on my mug. "What?"

"We needed to run to put distance between us and your mother," Catharine explains as if I've forgotten a basic piece of the past. "In case she tried to do something worse. But if my father gets here first, then she can't harm us anymore—she wouldn't dare. Not that I want her to be punished for what she did," Catharine adds quickly, misreading the dismay on my face. "Of course, I don't want my father to know your mother was behind it all. I'm sure she must have been confused about what the spell was—she couldn't have meant to hurt us."

I feel winded by the innocence, kindness, and naivety of Catharine's understanding of our situation. For the first time, I realize we haven't really *talked* about what we were doing. We just ran. I assumed she knew that we were running from both our parents, but she assumed we were running from my mother and to protect my mother from the consequences of her actions. She only has half the picture.

"I..." My skin flushes with heat. I feel every part of me, every word that tries to form and dies in my mouth. I wish I had just told Catharine the truth months ago, years ago. Wouldn't it have been easier to blurt it out the first time it happened? Couldn't I have done it better then?

But I was only fourteen. And I didn't understand. And in the two years since, my reasons have only become more complex. They tangle, threading through the things I wish I could say, silencing every sentence before it can begin.

I cannot speak the truth. So I try to find my way to it from an angle, to circle toward the heart of it without letting my mind know that's what I intend in the end.

"I think your father might still punish my mother if he realizes we have been cursed," I say slowly. "Even if we did not reveal she was involved."

Catharine takes my hand, all earnestness. "I won't let him hurt your mother. I promise, Kit. He'll be angry, probably, but I can help him forgive her."

I resent Catharine now more than I've ever let myself resent her. Because she believes it—she believes that there are angers and hurts that can just be loved into peace, that with enough goodness all the bad will be washed away. My envy is sharp and bitter and I try to shake myself free as soon as the feeling strikes me. I don't want to think of my sister this way, to be angry like my mother, but I *do* want to grab Catharine and say, *Look at the body you're in! Look at what he's done!*

But I try a different tactic, toeing my way a little closer to the truth. A little closer to the raw, open wound of the thing. "He's told the whole country that I kidnapped you. What if he punishes me? Or—you, in my body."

Catharine shakes her head. "He's mistaken. We need only tell him that we left together." She presses my hand. "He would never hurt you."

I'm on my feet before I know I've pushed back. My skin burns. My mouth tastes sour. Catharine stares at me in surprise and part of me knows I should stay. I should speak now. I should just come out with it.

But my stomach turns over and shock runs through my limbs like icy lightning, and the croft is too small and too dark and I can't trust her. I can't tell her. *I am alone and the door is closed—*

"I—need—to step outside," I say quickly. "Just a moment."

I dive outside and into the cold. I've forgotten my pelisse but I don't care. The frigid wind seers my own freezing insides and I am half in my body again. I walk, quickly, taking to the hills behind the house. There is a door in my mind, and it is locked, and there are hands reaching for me, and I am so, so small.

I try to shove the memories back. That is past. That is behind. I am not there anymore.

I am here. I am *here.*

But the door in my mind won't open. The bolt catches it, holds it shut. I pull and pull and it won't budge.

I concentrate on the crunch of frosted grass under my feet. The smell of sea and sheep. The tendrils of hair tickling my neck. The tight burn of each breath in my lungs. I count them: One and two and three and four…

A hand closes on my shoulder. Is it in my mind, or is it happening now? A voice chiding me. *Don't be afraid, little girl.*

I uncross my arms and put my right forefinger against my collarbone. I tap quickly—*one, two, three, four, five*—and I make my breaths stretch out, so that each one takes five seconds to inhale and then again to exhale. The slope grows steep under my feet, but I keep tapping and counting.

His hand is not on me. He is not here.

I crest the rise, my heart pounding with the exercise instead of panic. My blood boils with heat. The standing stones loom scattered before me, dark-gray with streaks of black from the rain. A few sheep lie in their shadow or tucked against them for protection from the wind. They eye me with cautious interest.

I begin tapping again, making myself pay attention to everything around me. I turn in a circle. The landscape unfurls below me like a map—part mist and part patchwork of fields and stone walls. The silver sea blends to silver sky. A boat is out there, vanishing into the cloud.

The past sinks into the past. The girl and the man and the door lose their sharpness, become just a memory again. I am in my body. I am whole, and here. I stretch my neck and feel settled, again. Myself, again.

The memory has receded to where it belongs. I am awake.

It would certainly be useful to have him awake next time.

I look down at my still-tapping finger.

I think I know how to help Idris

FOURTEEN

Idris

Cold drops land on my face and I claw my way out of a dreamless sleep like a drowning man seeking air. I'm in my room, breathing hard, and my eyes struggle to adjust to the darkness. The fire has died down and Kit is a shadow, stepping back from my bed. My body heats as I realize she must have been leaning over me.

"Sorry," she says. "You weren't waking up."

"Right." I blink, trying to clear my thoughts. "That's fine."

We made this plan—for her to wake me just before midnight, in the hope that if I started the night conscious I might be able to stay that way. I give True's head a pat and sit up. My body aches and my head feels heavier than a millstone. I'm still gathering my strength to stand when the cathedral bells toll.

A tight binding streaks through my muscles, pulling me to attention, and my head swims into a fog. I am up. I am changing. I am going to the door.

Someone grabs my hand and words buzz, muffled and distant. It takes effort to concentrate on them.

"...describe it? What are you feeling?"

Kit. Kit's voice. I run a hand over my face and I'm surprised how cold I am. Outside. We're outside and walking toward the harbor.

"I feel cold," I say, the words slurring.

Her grip on me tightens. "Yes? What about—the ground under you? What does that feel like?"

The ground seems very far away, entirely disconnected from me. My feet ought to be hurting, but I can't feel them. I can sense the slope of the hill under me, though, so I answer, "Steep. Firm."

"All right." Kit holds up something—bulky fabric. My greatcoat. "Can you put this on?"

I take it without stopping and swing it over my shoulders. My legs itch to keep moving. I barely feel awake and it is enough to concentrate on staying here without trying to stop the invisible force that pushes me forward. I ought to be colder than I am, or I ought to feel warmer with the coat. But everything outside of me is a haze. I focus instead on the weight of the coat, the brush of the fabric against my arms. True nudges my leg with his nose and a little more of the world becomes clear.

My grasp on time and place is disconcerting. One moment, I am walking down the hill toward the town. Then I seem to sink into black and emerge at the edge of the water, my yole at my feet. Then I sink again and wake at the crest of a swell. But before we drop, the water smooths into a glassy path. We glide forward with only the slightest rocking.

I run my hands along the tiller, concentrating on the firmness of the wood against my palms. I am here, awake.

I try to settle into my body, to feel every part of me. But my spirit struggles to stay. I feel the command of the enchantment—a rod directing my movements. My thoughts slip toward blankness. It would be easier to fall into the empty place. Holding myself together takes all my energy.

"Still here?" Kit asks, leaning round the mast to look at me.

I nod. "So far."

She smiles. The clouds are thin tonight and moonlight gently illuminates her face. I'm not entirely sure how to think of her, how to interpret the way a little warmth sneaks over me under her bright look. It is Kit, but in Catharine's body. Should I want to reach across the space between us and touch the dimple in her cheek?

The thought jars me. I pull my gaze away, giving myself a firm command to stop it. Whatever *it* is. Dimple curiosity? I want to groan at my own foolishness. With everything that's happening, I shouldn't have it in me to be so stupid. I'm not a lad pining after some young lass. I'm in the thick of a curse and being danced to death by the Hidden Folk.

"We should talk," Kit bursts out suddenly. "It might help. But I'm not sure what to talk about."

"I'm not good for making conversation right now." My hand on the tiller brings the bow left. I don't know where I'm taking us, but my muscles apparently sense the way. "Ask me something."

She looks down at my dog curled between us. "Why did you call him True?"

I reach out and let True lick my fingers. My mind feels sluggish. "You know the story of the babe, the wolf, and the hound?"

Kit tilts her head. "Is it one of your folktales, or is it true?"

"Is there a difference?" My tone comes out more seriously than I intended and my question takes us both by surprise.

"The way I heard it," Kit says slowly, "there was once a king who loved his firstborn. And he had a hound, who loved the baby just as much. But one day, the hound would not come away when called for the hunt. The king returned that night and found his son's nursery torn apart, splattered with blood. The hound came out from under an overturned crib, his mouth covered in red. In a rage of grief, the king struck the hound down."

I nod. "But then a baby began to wail."

"The baby was fine," Kit continues. "The king found his son well and whole, lying beneath the crib. And beside the baby—the corpse of the wolf who had tried to consume him. The hound had protected the child, but it was too late. The hound was dead."

"My father told me that story when I was a boy," I tell her. "He'd say, 'The hound was true to the end—it was the man who judged too quickly and made a mistake that couldn't be undone.' Father thought it a good lesson for me. I was too impulsive." I pause. "Well, I am still."

Kit leans forward to pat True's back. "So you named your dog after the one in the story?"

"I loved that story." I look down at True, with his wide, dark eyes, and he thumps his tail. "I always thought the dog deserved better."

"It's a sad story." Kit pauses in thought. "I wonder if it was the king or the baby prince who told it eventually."

"What do you mean?"

"It's the ones who live who tell the stories." Kit pushes back a lock of hair. "Well, unless it's just a work of fiction. But Cath—my sister always says there's something real in a folktale."

I shrug. I hadn't considered it before.

After a beat of silence, Kit goes on, "There was a woman in the Hidden Lands with her feet bound in iron. You said she has something to do with your curse?"

We talked about this earlier. Father would probably be annoyed, but I see no harm in telling her what Speir showed me. Kit is deep enough in my family's secrets to know. Her gaze remains trained on my hands, her brows drawn together in thought as I tell her.

"That's different from the story I heard about Mervyn," she says when I finish. "I wonder if he found the selkie before the pirate princess."

I hadn't thought about "Mervyn's Impossible Tasks" in some time. It's a story every child in Skyare knows. Thinking out loud, I repeat, "It's the ones who live who tell the stories."

My hand on the tiller alters our course, the compass in my chest realigning with some unseen beacon. My thoughts blur again—True, sitting in front of me with his ears perked up and alert—True as a puppy, small enough to curl up on my chest after his first bath—haze and shadow, memory and dark.

This time, it is my own voice that startles me back to the present. I hear myself shouting, "Open, black cliff, and let the young prince in and out with his boat and his hound."

"And his lady before, and his brother within!" Kit adds quickly.

A terrifying, marvelous sight comes into focus before my eyes. Cliffs cut into the sky, their face shadowed from the moon, and we are already near enough I would not be able to save the boat if I tried. But then a jagged split thunders down the space just in front of us and stones slide away to reveal a hollow between two looming sides. My hand guides us straight for it, and I am breathless with wonder as we narrowly slip past rocks and whirlpools. In the rationality of daylight, I would never attempt this gap. But the enchantment sings in my veins and I find myself grinning as we steer into the cave, slicing between dozens of hazards that would dash us to flotsam and chum.

The next thing I know, I am on firm ground. Sand—then rock—and my thoughts are wisps that trail away.

Music and turn and spin and touch and breathless and fall and Abram—

I blink, struggling my way back. Abram leans toward me, and I'm on the ground—no, on some sort of couch. A mermaid grabs my chin, forces my head up, and pours something thick and sweet into my mouth. I cough on it, almost choking. Abram's hand catches my arm and he's speaking quickly. The glass moves away and I struggle to catch my breath.

"Hey," Abram says, his over-large eyes searching my face from behind his glasses. The purple-pink light makes his skin look bruised. "Are you—?"

I try to nod. "I'm all right."

It's such a lie, I laugh at myself—but it turns into a hacking cough. My muscles feel unwound and my bare feet are raw.

The drink, whatever it was, sizzles through me, lighting me up with restless heat. Even though I don't feel like I can stand, I find myself pushing to my feet. Someone is taking my hand and pulling me forward. I want to collapse into the blankness again to escape the pain of my battered body.

Abram tightens his grip on my other arm. I'd forgotten he was here.

"Let him have a moment," Abram says to the mermaid, his tone harsher than I've heard before. "For goodness' sake, let him rest."

The mermaid, who now holds my hand, lifts her eyebrows. Her appearance swirls in my addled mind—her skin is a striking black, like rocks left by old lava flows, and she has raven hair tinted blue hanging in narrow braids down to her knees. My mouth goes dry and a part of me wants to lean forward into her inviting smile. But Abram pinches me and I flinch back toward my brother.

"Idris, why don't you sit again?" Abram says, gentle now.

My legs itch and it's all I can do to hold still. I shake my head. My voice rasps when I speak. "You all right?"

"I'm surviving. Kit brought me some food, which was much appreciated."

"Where is she?" I try to focus. The floor is a dark stone shot through with gold. I tilt my head back. There is no ceiling—just a glorious twilight, with lavender and golden clouds drifting across a velvety sky. All of the colors are a little too vivid, a little too bright.

My head spins. "Is this what it always looks like?"

Abram follows my gaze. "No, it changes every night."

White sparks flash across my vision. I close my eyes tightly. Abram's hand steadies me.

"You asked about Kit—she's hiding." Abram pauses. "I think they know she's here and they don't seem to care, but she's still being cautious."

I nod. The music shifts from a slow melody into a jig. The itch in my legs is unbearable. "Sorry, I have to—"

Before I can finish my sentence, the mermaid has pulled me away from Abram. Every step is like treading on glass, but I try to press into the vividness of the hurt. Try to stay in this room and shrug off the blankness. I don't know how long I've been trying when suddenly everyone around me stops. I careen into a finman and arms come up to catch me. They face me toward the end of the room, holding me up, and even with the help I sway like a listing ship.

A woman is carried into the hall. The midnight-blue fabric of her dress seems to float around her, like a mist over stars. A circlet of silver and pearls adorns her long white hair, which hangs in waves down to her ankles. She meets my eyes, hers solemn and cool and black. Untouchable.

I become acutely aware of every drop of sweat on my forehead, the smell of my armpits, the damp stickiness of my hair.

In those large black eyes I recognize something. Even though I never saw her face in the memory, I know her.

The Hidden Queen. The selkie my great-great-grandfather bound in iron.

When her retinue sets down her chair, she lifts her white hand and beckons me forward. I stumble when the Hidden Folk around me move, supporting me step by painful step.

They release me in front of her and I let myself sink into a kneeling position. It's all I can do not to collapse on the polished floor.

The silence of the chamber thrums in my head louder than the music did before. Patches of light and shadow chase their way over my skin. I lick my lips, searching through the cloud of fatigue for something to say to her. Some way to apologize. Or beg mercy.

"What a bonny face," she says quietly. Her voice is unexpectedly deep and melodious. "You certainly have his blood."

I find myself staring at the silver-embroidered hem of her long gown, which ends at my eye level. In the stitching, seals—selkies?—chase each other through waves.

"Did you never retrieve your skin?" I blurt, looking up.

Her mouth tightens. There are no lines on her skin, but there is an ancient smell to her. Like sailing near the deepest parts of the sea.

I swallow. "I—I am deeply sorry for what was done. I hope—I mean, is there anything—?"

Her eyes narrow, ever so slightly, and I am starkly aware of how little sense I'm making. I feel like I'm trying to converse in a language even I don't understand. My head swirls and my surroundings feel very far away. *What is happening?*

"Control." Her lullaby voice remains soft. In her black eyes I see myself reflected—small and pitiful. "Even now, that is all your mind craves."

My thoughts blur and I struggle to remain, to feel my knees on the hard ground.

"What are you doing to me?" I croak.

"Me?" She smiles. There is no mirth in it. "I summoned you here. But your mind seeks to take back your body. After all, isn't removing yourself a type of control? I am not responsible for this dissociation—you are. However," she continues with a bored wave, "I did not bring you here to talk."

A strand of her long blonde-white hair falls over her shoulder as she leans forward. An animal urge in me, an impulse that only seeks to survive, screams that I should flee. I am a minnow in front of a force of nature. But I'm frozen to the spot.

She presses three fingers to my forehead. Her skin is a cold that cuts through the burning in my head.

Almost in a purr, she says, "I brought you to *dance*."

My sight goes sharp and my pain vanishes. I spring to my feet, and the music is playing again, and I grab for the first person I see. A mermaid with algae-green hair. I pull her into the dance, and she's laughing, and I feel nothing but the need to move, the pulse of the music in my veins, the maddening urgency for *more* and *faster*.

Partners change and I lose track of the shifts in music, the tunes that bleed into the next. I spot Abram to one side, expression worried. The woman beside him shakes her head. He speaks to her and points at me. I am turned away and my vision smears. The over-sharp sting of too-vivid color sears my eyes and black tinges the edge of my vision.

Then I am brought back round the circle of dancers and new hands take mine. Hands that are warm instead of cold, and strong instead of delicate. It takes a moment for her face to register in my mind. Flushed skin, dark hair—Catharine. I am back at my birthday ball, back when dancing was a pleasure and my future stretched out in front of me.

"Idris?" she asks. Her fingers tap a steady beat on the side of my hand as we move through our steps. The rhythmic touch disrupts my thoughts. I close my eyes tight, putting all my concentration on the touch. *I am here. I am enchanted. I am with Kit. Not Catharine, Kit.*

"Thanks," I breathe, opening my eyes again. The mad flurry of movement seeps out of me and I slow. Mercifully, the tune has slowed with me. My chest is tight and my breathing ragged. "Should you be out here?"

Kit glances at the other couples. They seem to be paying us no attention. "Abram said they already knew about me and that he's been able to stop dancing, so I probably wouldn't get trapped, and…" She shakes her head and turns her gaze back to me. "We were afraid you…"

"I'm fine," I say through force of habit.

Kit smiles gently. "You don't have to lie, you know." Her fingers drumming on my hand pause. "There is nothing *fine* about this whole situation."

My body still moves in the dance, instinctively knowing it, even though it's nothing like our formal ones on land. This brings me and Kit close, my left hand on her waist and my right holding hers, always, not just the touch-and-go of our balls. I had not noticed the closeness when I danced with the Hidden Folk—though I hadn't noticed much here, at all—but with Kit I'm aware of everything. The exhale of her breath on my neck, the brush of her skirt against my trousers. I am fully here again, but in a strange, unsteady way.

"Why did you agree to this?" Kit asks.

I try to bring my thoughts into order. "To what?"

"Why did you agree to take the curse?"

"The question everyone seems to be asking me." I force a tired smile and tell her what I told my father and Abram. Someone had to do it. If I didn't, it would fall to someone else. Better me than them. The words are so familiar now, I hardly have to reach for them. My attention drifts—to the twist and turn of the couple next to us, to the swelling of music, to an absent thirst.

"Why better for it to be you?" Kit asks. She starts tapping on my hand again. "Why should *you* have to pay for what someone else did?"

"The harm he did should be paid."

"Yes, but it should have been paid by him." She frowns at me, more interested than critical. "Why do you think *you* need to be punished?"

"I—I..." I fumble to find the right words. "When I accepted the curse, I wasn't thinking about myself. I did it because it was the best thing, the right thing, to do. There should be justice for the crime."

"That doesn't explain why you want to carry the brunt of that punishment." When Kit spins, a strand of hair comes loose from her careful bun. I like her better for that imperfection. "I don't know that there is justice for this."

I blink, taken aback. "What do you mean?"

"Your ancestor stole something that cannot be replaced." Kit faces me again, the steps bringing us within a hand's breadth of each other. Her eyes dart up toward mine, and then she turns her head away to create more distance between us. "What he did will never be undone, no matter how much you dance. No matter if—if you die. She remains bound in iron, and the years of that pain are not erased. Can there be justice for something that has gone on for so long?"

"It is the price she has asked," I counter. "Shouldn't the one who was harmed be the one to name the cost?"

"I don't know." After a moment, Kit whispers, "Perhaps it is in the realm of men to take and women to suffer." Before I can reply, she adds quickly, "No, I'm sorry. That wasn't fair to you."

"I don't think you're wholly wrong." I adjust my hand on her back. She stiffens, ever so slightly, and I loosen my hold. "But I think, maybe, you do not give yourself credit for resilience. You suffer, and you rise above it. You fight for what you love. You don't sink."

"Women are not saints. We rise and fall like anyone."

"But *you* rise." I bend a little, trying to catch her gaze. She won't meet my eyes. I want to put a link between us, to have her feel my earnestness, as if feeling it would make her believe me. "Look at where you are, Kit. Who else would be trying to fix so much?"

When she speaks her tone is suddenly hollow. Lonely. "There's no one else to do it."

"There's me, and Abram, and Catharine." I keep her close as we turn. There's a twist to her mouth that speaks of her skepticism. I feel the protests to my words, which are nearly empty. The words of someone who knows nothing. We four are connected, but aren't we four still caught in this mess? I reach for something more, something truer. "And maybe…some things can't be fixed. And maybe… that is all right."

"How is it all right?" Her jaw hardens with a challenge. "Everything is *wrong*."

I waver. We are in the Hidden Lands. I am dancing myself to death and my brother is trapped here. Kit is wrapped in a body that isn't hers. Everything should be wrong, but in this moment, with her near me and her fierce grip on my hand, I feel none of the wrongness. I feel strangely alight. Whole.

"Maybe," I agree softly. "But you are not alone."

She deflates a little at that. When she speaks, her voice is low and quiet, as if she were dragging the words from a very great depth. "I am tired."

The exhaustion that radiates from her twists in my chest. I want to pluck it from the air. I want to tuck comfort round her like a shawl.

"I wish…" But what do I have to offer? Limited days and collapsing youth. I am so overcome by my own troubles, I have dragged her into them. I am drowning and the best that I can offer is to not drown her with me. "Have you had a chance to find a cure for your curse?"

Kit shakes her head. "Abram's asked various Hidden Folk, but no one has offered any useful information. And I haven't been able to glean much from eavesdropping. Speir hasn't been here tonight."

I glance around the chamber, realizing she's right.

"We need to find an answer so you don't have to keep coming," I say, half to Kit and half to myself. It is easier to track my thoughts if I speak them. "I could ask—"

My legs choose that moment to go weak and I nearly topple over. Kit steadies me, bearing my weight until I can pull myself back into order. My feet still move with the dance, almost on their own, forcing us to keep going.

"What if you just stop?" she says, tapping the side of my hand again. "Just stop dancing. Can you?"

"I'm not sure…" I try to still my feet, but the music grows louder in my head and the beat pounds against the back of my eyes. I stumble my way back into the dance, nearly stepping on Kit's skirt in the process. She moves swiftly out of the way and manages to follow me. My vision goes murky and my head feels heavy. "I—I don't think so."

Kit lifts her hand and hesitates, fingers curling with uncertainty. But then she touches her fingertips to the fabric of my shirt over my collarbone. She taps, firmly. "When I am lost," she says, "this helps the most."

The tapping centers me in this moment, pulling my attention to the present. I'm aware of my heart's erratic beating, beginning to steady now to match Kit's rhythm. Her skin is warm and, as my eyes focus again, I realize we've come closer. She smells of heather and earth. Her eyes are wide and silver and she's tilted her head back to study me. A small, concerned crease between her brows smooths away.

Her eyes flick up and, for the first time, meet mine. A breathless charge surges between us. My heart jumps, then beats harder still. I've met Catharine's eyes before—with her, it was only as a matter of course, a social norm. With Kit, all the world vanishes. Meeting her eyes is a gift I'm not sure I've earned. It wakes a burning I did not know slept in me.

Her lips are full and the sound of her voice—so soft I might not have heard it if I were not so near—reminds me of the low sigh of waves in a cove.

It takes a moment for her words to register: "You've stopped."

I keep my gaze on her and this time she does not look away. It would be an easy thing, to lean forward. It would take the space of a breath.

I am here, I want to say to her, *with you.*

Will you stay here with me?

FIFTEEN

Kit

We are stillness in a crowd of churning color. A clearing in a forest.

I ought to move my hand back to his arm, the way the others hold their partners. Even that is much closer than our balls, where the most contact I must brace for is a simple touch and release.

I steel myself. I promised I would bring him back. And I know what it is to be wandering so far and alone in yourself that you cannot see through open eyes.

I keep my hand deliberately on his shoulder, near his neck, and push the coat and waistcoat aside, sliding my fingertips under his cravat so there is only one layer of fabric between my skin and his. My thumb comes to rest at the edge of his clavicle. I feel it tense, pronounced, whenever he shifts.

I have never willingly been this close to a man.

Idris is merely a hand's breadth away. He smells of sweat and his hair is limp with it. But there is a bright fondness in his face.

I lift my gaze to meet his. His eyes are a deep brown, the color of loam. They are kind and warm and full of summer promise. Safe. So safe that my heart twists in painful hope. Heat raises the hairs on my arms.

I don't turn away. I admit the thought: *He likes me. He likes looking at me.*

Joy sparks in my chest. For a moment, I feel shining and pure.

But only for a moment.

A crack seems to open in my mind. On one side, there is me and Idris wrapped in our dance and our newfound closeness. On the other, there is a shadow. Another man's greedy look. A hand in the dark. A dark, inky taint.

An instinct so deep in me it feels ancient shouts, *Careful, careful!*

I squeeze my eyes shut. I am safe with Idris—it is a truth as sure as a compass. Idris doesn't want to hurt me.

But my feral heart shrieks, *Danger, danger!*

I can't make sense of these two sides. I want to be in this moment—I want to be a normal girl dancing with a kind and good boy. Forcing my eyes open, I try to prove to my mind that I'm *here*. I'm with *Idris*. I'm all right.

He frowns, the smallest line of worry between his brows. The closeness that thrums between us tightens, and I try to let myself feel it. Attraction? Shouldn't this be pleasurable? But the warmth has become more nausea than joy. A soupy, wobbly unsteadiness churns in my stomach.

The crack in me widens. Each splinter is a memory—an iron grip on my wrist, insults in my ear, a leering smile.

Proof upon proof upon proof that I am not normal. I will never be normal.

Stop! I beg myself. *Let me be here!*

It is a battle against panic to feel anything at all. I have Idris's arm round my waist, but it isn't him that I feel. I feel the door in my mind, locked, and I am beating against it. Excruciating pain tears through my chest. I want to lean into Idris's touch but that ancient feral part screams for me to claw him off and run.

A shudder quakes through me. Idris must feel it, because the worry grows in his brown eyes and he pulls back. I want to take his face in my hands. If I were me, in another world, with another past, I would pull him to me and kiss him. If I were a different girl, I would loop my arms round his neck and lean into his embrace.

But I'm not a girl at all in this moment. I am terror, so coiled and tight that my lungs won't expand. I release him, and before I can change my mind someone else has seized his hand. A selkie pulls him away. He stumbles into her arms, and his feet resume the dance, and I know I've lost him again.

Breath rushes into my chest with a rattle. A tear drops down my cheek and I slap it away. Hollowness carves through me. Shouldn't that have been like all those romantic moments in stories? Shouldn't I be happy? I *was* happy, for a moment. Wasn't I?

All I feel now is tired, and empty, and sad.

Someone jostles me from behind, and I stumble out of the way. I retreat to my place against the wall, trying to force my breathing to steady. I want to go home—to curl under a blanket and forget everything.

But, beneath it all, a small part of me still glows. He looked at me in a way no one else has and it was warm and kind and *good.*

Don't trust it, the ancient in me warns.

The fragile glow is all but swallowed by the shadows lurking in my head. I want to reach into myself and yank them free, like weeds in a garden. I want to only feel the glow and none of the fear. I want to cup my hands round the light and hold that moment separate from everything else: when he *saw* me.

He didn't see you, whisper my thoughts. *He saw Catharine.*

The glow fizzles and dies. I look down at my own hands—Catharine's hands. Beautiful, unmarred. I am in Catharine's body, one that has never known hardness. That has never been violated.

But *I* still carry the taint in me.

"It seems your mother's gift goes unappreciated," says a voice in my ear.

I start, jerked out of my thoughts. Speir stands beside me casually, as if he's been there this entire evening. His bright-orange eyes sweep me from head to toe.

"You!" I exclaim, heart pounding.

"Hmm, yes. Me." He tilts his head. "You don't seem to be enjoying the new body your mother procured for you. How odd."

I rub my eyes, head spinning from the whiplash of emotions—mine all in a roar and him calm as an otter stretched out in the sun. "This isn't my body to keep."

"You wear it." He shrugs. "Simply enjoy it."

I shake my head. This is the chance I've been waiting for. "We want you to undo the curse. Catharine and I want to switch back!"

His eyes glint. "Careful. Do not lie in the queen's court."

I stare at him. "I—I'm not lying."

"Oh? You would have me believe you wish to reclaim that diseased body?" He frowns a moment, then his face brightens with the keenness of a boy who has discovered a secret. "Do *you* believe that is your wish?"

A flush spreads over my cheeks. "I want what is best for Catharine."

"Ah, but that is not the same thing as wanting the curse broken." He leans back, hands spread. "And I am not one to go back on a deal."

All of Catharine's stories, all the lessons about never negotiating with the Hidden Folk, crowd the back of my mind. But I ask, "Can't you make a new deal with me?"

"Not if it contradicts an earlier one. Besides..." He moves behind me and round to my left. I stiffen involuntarily. "I'll let you in on a secret about magic. A spell works best when the participants step willingly into it."

My heart thuds in my ears. "What do you mean?"

His orange eyes have no warmth to them. Only the calculating curiosity of a botanist pinning a specimen to a board. "*I* did not cause the switch, dear. I merely opened the door."

Dread sinks into my bones. I remember looking into that strange mirror—remember seeing all of my flaws in a sharpness that was impossible to ignore. Even at the memory, the sickening heat of loathing rises in my stomach. I had hated myself—hated my body.

Did I do this to us?

He hasn't looked away from me this entire time. I'm not sure he's even blinked. "If I opened the door again, now, would you go through?" he asks.

I am the one to turn away. I cannot answer, and my confusion only fills me with more distress. This should be the moment I fix everything. I should insist. I should fight. I should make him reverse it.

A sparrow suddenly flutters past my ear, making me jump, and then two small beings dart past us in chase. The boy waves a stick aloft in the air, his fair-boned fingers round the wood nothing like a plump child's. I close my hands round each other, concentrating on the way they do not hurt.

"So you won't help us?" I ask, watching the children. The boy finally manages to poke the bird with his stick. The golden clouds above cover everything in a shifting pattern of dappled light and the bird changes from gray sparrow to white seagull. I blink, trying to make sense of it.

"I would rather see what you will do." Speir lifts one finger. "A warning, though: No curse can be broken with an unwilling participant."

He pats my back with mock sympathy and I jerk away. I want to protest that I *am* willing! But I'm no longer certain that it is true. I was prepared to switch back for Catharine's sake, but for my own? My toes curl in my shoes.

The girl lifts her hand and the bird alights on her palm. Grinning, she speaks into its ear. The bird's feathers grow, shift, and turn silver. Where there was a seagull, there is now a small falcon. My insides twist at how easily she enchants the poor thing.

"The stories say humans are unpredictable," Speir says, his gaze following mine to the children. "Yet only one human has ever surprised me."

The falcon takes off and the children twirl past Idris, the boy waving his stick. Speir's shoulders tighten. It's the first time I've seen him express any discomfort.

"Go on and see if you can break the curse." He steps away, but then turns again to face me with a cynical smile. "Just try not to be boring about it."

Then he strides off and catches the children. I spot him gesturing at the bird and the crowded ballroom, but I can't make out his words.

Deflated, the children nod. They wander away from the dancers, toward one of the passages that leave the cavern. The girl holds out her arm and the falcon alights on it. With a sigh, just as they are stepping out of the room, the boy pokes the bird with his stick. And, suddenly, it's a seagull again.

My breath catches. I dart a look at Speir—but he is making his way toward the queen of the Hidden Folk on her throne, not paying attention to me.

Speir clearly was warning the child.

He did not like that the stick was near Idris.

They just enchanted the seagull. And then they broke the enchantment.

I edge my way along the walls. Tonight they are covered in thousands of tiny, spiraled seashells. They range from bright orange to dark purple to startling white. I think there must be creatures in the shells, because if I look away and back the mosaic of color rearranges itself subtly.

I continue, trying not to attract anyone's attention. Abram was right that the Folk don't seem to care about my presence in general, but whenever the Hidden Queen is in the room I can't help feeling as if she were watching me. I am always aware of where she is, and I wonder if it is the same for her.

The young ones have left the ballroom. I peer through the gaping opening where they went. It is a dark tunnel, like the one Idris and I came through when we left the cove. Unease raises the hairs on my arms. There are plenty of stories about foolish mortals who went exploring in the Hidden Lands and never came back. But then, from the other end of the tunnel, I hear a seagull's inelegant *squawk—squawk—squawk—*

Then: *Trill.*

The cheerful tune of a warbler.

Clenching my jaw, I move into the dark. There are no torches, but a faint glimmer of light shows from round a bend. I follow the turn—and stop in surprise.

The sky is the underside of water struck through with moonlight. Blue-white light filters down in a pulsing pattern. It has a shine to it that reminds me of diving into the loch with my eyes open—that otherworldly gleam that turns your own skin unfamiliar. I realize I've stopped breathing and inhale cautiously. My lungs still work here thankfully.

Enormous white mountains hang from the sky, their centers a glowing blue and their edges jagged with upside-down cliffs. A shadow crosses above me. A magnificent humpback whale serenely swims over my head. Its underbelly is creased like an enormous fingerprint. Barnacles cluster below its chin. The way it moves apparently effortlessly in the water tugs a longing in me I don't understand.

My stomach *swooshes* as if I've just missed a step on a staircase. Swallowing on a dry throat, I lower my gaze.

The ground at my feet is the same warm, white sand in the cove. But some way ahead, the land drops down into a valley. A forest of kelp stretches nearly as far as I can see, clustered around one main path. The stalks grow taller than a croft house and the green-gold fronds sway weightlessly in the air. Far in the distance, on another hill, I can just make out white structures. Some kind of buildings?

A rustling from the kelp fronds whispers secrets I can barely hear. *Kingdoms* and *cures* and *come to us*. My foot lifts to take me forward a step.

"*No*," I hiss, pinching my fingernails into my palms. "Focus."

I pull my attention closer, to the beach. The children are sitting on the sand a short way from me, paying me no mind. I take a deep breath. I'm not here to explore the Hidden Lands—I'm here to break my curse.

The boy again pokes the bird and it again becomes a seagull.

I feel in my reticule for something interesting to catch their attention and my hand closes round one of the nuts. I crouch on the sand and toss it toward the children.

They stop their conversation to watch it. Then the girl gives a shrill laugh and pounces on the nut, rather like a cat, batting it around. The seagull squawks indignantly and flies to a nearby bolder. I grab a second nut and toss it, slightly less hard, so that it stops closer to me.

The boy comes for that one and picks it up to examine it. He taps at the shell with a fingernail.

"I can show you how to crack it," I say.

The boy looks at me. For a moment, his face is entirely serious, like an old man's. Then he breaks into a grin, coming forward. "Yes, if you would."

The girl follows, holding hers now. I take a third from my bag and crack it in one quick, sharp motion on the rock beside me. I turn the nut so they can see the crack down its side, then work my fingernail into the small opening.

"What are your names?" I ask.

"I'm Pri—"

The girl hits the boy's arm and hisses, "Not your real name."

"Oh, yes, you may call me Talfryn," he says. He gestures to his companion. "And this is…Aderyn."

I pull the shell off and help myself to the insides while I think. I remember that before he worked his curse, Speir told my mother that sharing a name was not so different from sharing a soul. I suppose there must be some magic in a real name. Just as well I go by my nickname, then. "I'm Kit."

They both nod. "We've heard of you."

I'm not sure if that is good or bad, but I extend my hand to them. "Have a go at cracking your nuts."

The children make several attempts before they hit the shell hard enough. As they gobble up the nuts, their faces brighten with delight. Like Speir, they have strange eyes—Talfryn's are vibrant as a lime and Aderyn's are salmon pink. I think they must be finfolk children.

I take out another two nuts so they can try again. I only have three left now.

As they give it a go, I ask as casually as I can, "Talfryn, what was Speir saying to you earlier?"

Talfryn has his gaze fixed on his nut, concentrating hard as he brings it down on the rock with one hand while he holds his stick in the other. "He said, 'Take care—it is too crowded here for throwing around and breaking enchantments.'"

My heart quickens. "The stick can break enchantments?"

Talfryn wrinkles his nose. "It's a *wand*."

I swallow tightly. "What would you say to a trade?"

Talfryn tilts his head, nibbling on his nut. "What would you give me?"

I reach into my reticule, but Aderyn interrupts.

"More nuts!" she says. She pulls at Talfryn's sleeve. "Ask for more nuts! We won't be allowed to go to the land for another century—we might never get any again!"

Talfryn considers. "More nuts," he agrees. "*And* you tell us where you found them. None of the humans who've come before had nuts."

"There have been other humans?" I ask, scooping my remaining supply out of my bag.

"They wander in sometimes." Talfryn snatches the last of the nuts from my hand and passes one to Aderyn. "And the place you found them?"

"There's only one spot on Skyare that I've discovered so far." I describe a small grove of trees near Mrs. Westness's home. The hazelnuts are still in season now, but not for much longer. "You have to go during the autumn months," I tell them. "When the trees change color."

"Trees?" Aderyn repeats the word as if she's never heard it before.

"She means when almost all the gannets have flown south," Talfryn informs her. He holds out his wand. "A trade made in good faith. We will look for these nuts when we come of age."

I hardly breathe as I take the wand. I thought it was a stick, but when my hand closes round it, I realize it is coral—one long white piece of coral. It sits in my palm with an unexpected heaviness.

I slip it into my reticule. It is just short enough to fit, with the drawstring closing over one end.

"You should go back to the hall," Aderyn advises cheerfully. "We are in the Betweens here, but mortals who go deeper don't leave."

"Maybe she *wants* to stay," Talfryn says. There's a glitter to his otherworldly eyes that reminds me of Speir.

"Thank you, but perhaps next time." I rise and wipe the sand from my skirt. My gaze longs to return to the view, but I keep my attention fixed on the strange children. For a moment I teeter, unsure how to properly say goodbye. I settle on a curtsy.

They burst into giggles, but at least they aren't offended. I hurry into the tunnel, their laughter echoing behind me.

As I emerge into the ballroom, the musicians begin to slow, the music turning grave. As one, the Hidden Folk stop their dancing. Four finfolk take the four corners of the

Hidden Queen's throne, lift, and begin the promenade from the room. I recognize the signs—last time I was here, they did this just before Idris returned to his boat.

I search the crowd, a pinch of worry in my chest. But there is Abram. He has a hand on Idris's arm and is supporting him toward the exit. I hurry to follow.

Speir appears again at my side only a few steps later. "I suppose tricking a pair of infants is *mildly* clever," he says, casting a bored look at my bag. "Though it only solves part of your problem."

I tighten my hand over my reticule.

"Oh, no need for that." He waves away my anxiety. "I will not take it from you. You were given it freely and *we* are not thieves." A gleam of curiosity makes the orange of his eyes brighter. "I do wonder, though—which one of the curses will you choose to break?"

I lift my chin. "The children did not seem limited with this wand."

He huffs. "They broke simple enchantments. Hardly the stuff of your curses. You will have to choose one of the three."

"Three?" I echo, my throat drying. Idris's curse and my mother's are the only ones I have thought of.

Speir lifts a shoulder. "Didn't your mother tell you the wasting is a curse?"

My heart pounds as if it would throw itself against my rib cage, as if it would break free.

"Cure your sister of the wasting," Speir says carelessly. "The wand will no longer work, but you can keep her body and she will not suffer in yours. Isn't that what you want?" He leans forward. "To leave your old body, your old life—shed it like a skin that never belonged, and escape?"

I cannot speak. I can barely breathe. But I won't give him the satisfaction of seeing me unsettled. Idris and Abram are moving toward the tunnel to our cove. Idris looks back at me and his eyebrows lower when he sees Speir. I think there is something protective in his face and a rush of pleasure mixes with my confusion. I remember earlier—how we danced close and how his eyes softened when he studied me—me, in Catharine's body.

But it wouldn't be Catharine's body anymore if we truly switched for good. It would be mine.

I don't bother bidding Speir goodbye. I rush after the boys as if I could escape Speir's words. Still, I wonder: Is there a way out of all this where I can be truly free?

I push the thought aside, angry with myself. Angry that any part of me would consider taking Catharine's body. *It isn't my idea*, I reason, walking to join Abram and Idris. *Speir just put it there.*

When I catch up with Idris, he asks, "What did Speir say?"

I hesitate. I need to talk to Catharine before I decide what to do with this wand, with this offer of one broken curse. Even then, guilt coils in my gut. Shouldn't I just pull it out now, tap Idris, and save his life? Shouldn't I at least tell him that I have it?

But my indecision tangles in my head and instead I say, "He wasn't helpful."

Idris nods. His face is ashen with weariness. I follow him as he makes his way to the cove. Abram walks beside me, his steps small and nervous. Braced for resistance.

But my amendment to Idris's command seems to have worked: Abram walks freely onto the sand. He grins at his brother—who returns an exhausted smile—and then helps make the boat ready to sail. I wait on the side, my hands clasped round the strap of my reticule. The wand inside burns a hole in my mind. I owe it to Catharine to talk to her first—and I cannot bear the idea of the hope and disappointment that might come upon Abram and Idris if they knew what I have.

Idris offers me a hand up into the boat. Remembering earlier, a blush rises to my cheeks. But if he's thinking of it, he seems unbothered. In fact, when I dart a glance at his face, his eyes seem glassy. I take his hand lightly. His skin burns with fever.

We settle on the benches and Abram pushes the yole off. As with the first night, the calm water guides us back toward Skyare. I should be tired—and I feel I am, in some deep part of me—but my nerves buzz. Idris rubs his face, looking miserable and flushed. His curse is only getting worse.

I have the cure to all of it in my bag. Just a hand's breadth away.

✦

I part ways with Abram and Idris at the harbor and strike out for Mrs. Westness's croft. The dawn sky is unexpectedly clear for the first time since we arrived. Clouds wisp away in pink and gold. There is so much blue here, I find myself dazed by it.

When I come to the croft, Mrs. Westness is crafting with straw near the fireplace. Catharine sits across from her, watching the intricate movements of the old woman's fingers. They both start when I open the door.

"You're back!" Catharine says, relieved. She rises and hugs me.

"You'll be wanting something to drink?" Mrs. Westness guesses, moving to get the jug.

"Thank you." I look at Catharine. Pride, delight, and nerves all mix inside me. "We need to talk. Do you feel up for a stroll?"

Catharine nods. "I have news for you too."

She grabs a shawl from on top of the bed, pulls it over her shoulders, and loops her arm through mine. Together, we step into the cold morning. The sun makes such a difference. Even now, it transforms the wild landscape into something welcoming, something more gold than gray.

"Look." Catharine holds her hurt hand out for me. The bandage is gone. She flexes the finger that had frozen, and it bends and straightens.

"How—?" I touch it for myself. The joint still has its distinct bowed swell, the same way a boat curves wide and then narrows again. But Catharine gives no sign of pain.

"I took the bandage off to have a look and I tried to bend it." Catharine demonstrates with her finger. "It made a loud clicking noise and then it just…started working."

I'm relieved. Confused. Is it a sign that my health might improve on its own?

Or is it just the wasting curse being cruel? Pretending to let my body mend, only to break it more thoroughly, more permanently, some time in the future?

"Well." I'm not sure what to say. My mind circles to practicality. "I guess we don't need that whole bag of gold coins, then. I wonder if Mrs. Westness would like a new barn as well as her roof repaired."

Catharine beams. "I'm sure she would."

As we continue to wander the coast, I tell her that Abram has been saved and that my idea for Idris worked. The brothers are both home safe. Or, at least, as safe as can be hoped right now.

"That's wonderful!" Catharine exclaims.

We leave the grass for the beach. I let my gaze scan the tide line, where shells and rocks and seaweed have been left. I gather a deep breath.

"There was something else, Catharine," I begin. "I think—I've found a way to break a curse. I spoke to Speir and made a trade with two children for this." I draw the wand from my bag. The heaviness of it surprises me again. The pockmarked surface is brittle, nearly ready to break, but the thing itself weighs more than a pot of tea. "They told me that one tap of this would break a curse."

"Kit!" Catharine beams at me. "Why didn't you say that first? This is perfect! You've done it!"

I hesitate and her grin fades. "Well, you see, it only works on *one* curse."

Catharine's eyes widen. Softly, she says, "Oh."

I let this settle between us. When she doesn't speak, I find myself babbling to fill the silence. "We can use it to undo the curse between us, or we can give it to Idris, or—" I cringe at the selfish hope in my tone—"we could cure the wasting."

"I don't think there's much of a choice," Catharine says, looking a little confused. "We must give it to Idris, of course."

"Of course," I echo. Her goodness makes me ashamed. That she would choose the kindest action with only a moment's consideration. I scold my treacherous heart. I do not deserve a sister like her. I slide the wand into my bag. "Right. That's what I felt…"

"We'll just find another solution for ourselves," Catharine says confidently. "I know you can do it. Perhaps Speir could be convinced to help."

I don't mention that I've already tried—that Speir hinted there might be multiple clever ways to undo our curse, but it requires me to *want* it. I look at Catharine in my old body. I imagine being back in that skin, which has been the vessel for so much shame and hurt. No matter how small and fragile and plain I was, it didn't protect me. Instead, it invited the king's attention.

If I return to my old body, I'll be exactly where I started. And even if I manage to escape Byrne, I can never escape the curse he opened in me—the wasting.

Perhaps I could convince Speir to open the door, to let Catharine and me switch, and then I could use the wand to make my body healthy. But even this is a selfish thought. Catharine and I are in an inconvenient state—my diseases are slow and survivable, for now—Idris's curse will claim his life. And it might claim that life soon, judging by his deterioration.

"I will take it to him, then," I say. Exhaustion creeps over my muscles, paired with resignation. I have my path laid out before me—but I am tired, in both spirit and body.

Catharine must sense some of this in my empty voice, because she turns us toward the croft. “Why don’t we get some food in you first? And maybe you should lie down for a little bit.”

“I’ll go in the early afternoon,” I agree, too weary to argue. “He should be home and safe until then.”

I still need to arrange our flight from Byrne. I still need to find a way to convince Catharine we *need* to flee. But I let her lead me inside. Despite my victory in gaining the wand, I feel defeated.

SIXTEEN

Idris

When Abram enters the breakfast room, Father springs to his feet and grabs my brother in a tight hug. I haven't seen Father embrace anyone with so much warmth since we were children—if then. I stand apart, awkward and strangely jealous. True leans against my leg and his weight is comforting.

Finally, Father stops hugging my brother and holds Abram at arm's length. His eyes are misty. "You're well?"

"No worse for it," Abram answers, smiling. "Kit's idea worked."

"What did we promise her this time?" Father asks, glancing toward me at last. "Gold? I'll double the size of the bag."

I nod and don't point out that I doubt Kit did it for the money. She deserves whatever she asks for, anyway. That and more.

Father ushers us both to the sideboard, which is laden with enough food for a feast. Abram eagerly fills a plate and then takes his seat. True crawls under the table to await scraps. I take my chair and close my eyes.

As soon as my head nods, the infuriating clinking noise starts up again. I open my eyes and look around, but, of course, there is no source. Father and Abram talk as if they hear nothing.

"They were fairly hospitable, actually," Abram is saying. "They never tried over-hard to convince me to eat or drink, and they showed me a place to sleep during the day."

"Kind of them," I mutter.

Father ignores me. "Did you learn anything that might help break the curse?"

"No, unfortunately." Abram casts a curious look at me. "I was never able to speak with the Hidden Queen, but she spoke to Idris last night. Do you remember, Id?"

"Yes. She still doesn't have her skin." I pour myself some tea and cut a glance up at my Father. "Do we have it somewhere? Did Mervyn keep it?"

Father frowns. "Skin?"

"In the memory Speir showed you and me, Mervyn has a selkie skin." I try to recall the details, but I'm only left with a foggy recollection. "He says something about her not honoring the old ways? I think he meant he had stolen her skin, but she would not marry him."

"Are you sure?" Father asks. "I thought he only bound her with the iron shoes."

A flare of annoyance blazes in my chest. "Yes, I'm *fairly* sure. I did see the memory more recently than you."

"Mervyn had a seal skin," Abram chips in. "At the end of 'Mervyn's Impossible Tasks,' he shows a fine seal skin to the king. And then, later, they use it as a cloak."

Father winces. "Regardless, I have never heard anyone in the family mention the selkie skin—even in that story, it's only called a seal skin. And I certainly haven't come across any special seal skins around here."

"Mervyn built this house, didn't he?" I ask, glancing up at the ceiling. "He might have hidden it somewhere."

"Does it matter?" Father asks. "Even if you returned the selkie skin, she would still be bound in her shoes."

"But the gesture might make a difference to her," Abram says thoughtfully.

My voice comes out tight. "And maybe it's just the right thing to do—to return it!"

Father frowns at me. "Maybe it's that sort of thinking that got us into this mess." He raises a hand before I can reply. "There's no reason to explain it to me again. But *if* he did keep the skin, we would know. The tale says it was used as a cloak? Why isn't it with the treasury or in the archives of Mervyn's possessions?" He shakes his head. "I fail to see how searching for something lost long ago is a good use of your energy."

"I can look for it," Abram offers, "while you get some rest."

"How often do I have to say it?" I grind out. "I cannot sleep during the day. When I attempt to lie still, the idleness itself is torture. I might as well do something useful. I should be the one doing it, anyway."

Abram studies me, and I turn away before I have to see the concern in his eyes. Quietly, he says, "You don't need to keep trying to do this alone."

"The last time you tried to help, you got stuck in an enchanted world." I push back from the table and stand. My feet immediately double their constant stabbing pain. "Maybe you both should just let me do what I need to."

I leave the room, True at my heels. This was not the homecoming I'd imagined for Abram—the triumphant reunion of our little family, the settling back into old rhythms. Disappointment stings in my throat and I'm only more frustrated. Frustrated with my temper. Frustrated that everything I touch turns to ruin.

Before I leave the hall, I catch a murmur of my name. I pause, listening.

"…kinder to him," Abram is saying.

"You are young," Father responds, voice clipped. "The young always see heroism in a martyr, but in time you'll understand—there is nothing noble in needlessly taking an unjust punishment."

Whatever Abram replies, I don't hear it. I stomp up the stairs and go to tend my wounds. *Am I not* your *son?* I think as I angrily pull off my shoes and get a cloth for the open sores. *Didn't you teach me the duty that's driven me to this?* If I had had a different father, a different family, perhaps I wouldn't be the me that felt this way. The me who chose sacrifice.

If Mervyn had never stolen a skin he had no right to, there wouldn't be a price that had to be paid at all. There would have never been suffering that required justice.

I send the servants to draw a bath and set out my own change of clothes. True, sensing that a wash is imminent for someone, slinks away to hide behind my bed. In my current mood, I barely find it funny.

Kit's question during our dance rises in my mind: *Why do you think* you *need to be punished?*

I thought I was doing this just through selflessness, through a sense of right—but maybe she and Father are correct. Maybe there is a selfish part of me that wants to be broken.

✦

Once I'm clean, I dress in fresh clothes and turn my attention to the places Mervyn might have hidden a selkie skin.

In the stories I grew up on, the selkie skin was often tucked in the space between rafters and roof or hidden under a loose flagstone in the floor. Sometimes it was buried under a tree or in a field. If Mervyn hid it outside, I have little chance of ever recovering it. Better to focus my search on the manor.

Unfortunately, Father is right about one thing—I've never happened upon anything in my home that looked like a seal skin. And in my younger teens I made a habit of scrambling into every nook I could find. If I didn't stumble across a secret hiding place then, it must be extremely well hidden.

I start by questioning the servants. The oldest in our service would know where something would most likely be hidden. Though they look at me askance as I describe the glossy fur I'm looking for, I'm directed to the attic—an obvious choice—and the kitchen, the only part of the house that hasn't had the floors replaced in the past twenty years.

For hours, I examine the ceilings, looking for gaps and poking my hand into every one I discover. I find only dust and dirt every time. More hours are spent in the kitchen, ignoring the cook's glances while I stomp around, listening for flagstones that might be loose. One tilts under my weight and eagerly I dig it out of the ground, but, underneath, there's only the building's foundations. The whole time I search, the clinking echoes in my head. I keep seeing shadows in the corners of my eyes—a cat, or True, or a child who vanishes when I turn to look. The lack of sleep is driving me mad.

Finally, with nothing to show for my effort, I retreat to the library. I expect Abram to be there, but from the snores in his adjoining room I take it he's still sleeping off the night's adventure. I turn my attention to the shelves. If memory serves, Mervyn kept a series of journals during his time as king. I pull them down—three in all—and sit to flip through them.

The words blur in front of me. Most are to do with landowners, crop reports, progress on construction in Stromwell. Various personal scribbles are in the margins.

In the stories they now call Adelaida the "pirate princess." She has been a good queen. Perhaps not as remarkable as my first choice. But suitable…

By the second volume, my gaze just slides across the pages. But I keep turning, telling myself that if I see something helpful I'll know it.

Male goosander spotted near Glett. Brilliant black feathers. Rare to see one these days…

Adelaida found out about the trophy. Not sure how. Rather put out with me…

Could he be speaking of the selkie skin? Could that be "the trophy"? I am suddenly alert.

The Coastal Jewel is blooming early this year. Bodes well for a warm summer…

Adelaida still upset. Will need to find a new hiding place…

This could be helpful—if only he'd mention *where…*

About midway through, I open to a sketch of a map. It shows the southeast region of Skyare, with careful attention paid to the coast. I stare blankly for nearly a minute before my mind registers what I'm looking at.

Mervyn's notes point out natural harbors. Doodles of ships are scattered across the ocean. And in one cove, near Mager Head, he's sketched a seal. A circle is drawn round the sketch, twice.

I'm on my feet immediately, startling True from his resting spot. I hurry past him and down the stairs, not bothering to wake Abram. I scribble a hasty note to leave on the dining table: *Gone to the Mager.*

✦

The sun tilts toward the west by the time I moor my yole at the cove. I hop over the side and drag it farther onto the shore, holding it steady while True splashes out beside me. He goes off sniffing the seaweed and I take a moment to get my bearings.

The cove is enormous—almost a bay. Small rocks turn into larger boulders near the cliffs, which tower higher than our cathedral's tallest spire. Red soil and gray stone blend together, and caves loom taller than my manor house.

I've almost certainly explored this part of Skyare before, but it was long ago.

I pull out Mervyn's journal to check the map again. I'm definitely in the right area. If this is where he hid the skin, I have no shortage of places to look and no particular place to start. I begin at one side of the stretch of beach, slowly making my way along, like Abram when he searches for wreckage. I don't know exactly what I'm looking for.

There is an area on the far side that stretches out smooth and wide. I pause at the edge, struck by a sense of familiarity. My toes tap a beat and I imagine the echo of a song in the air. As I glance back to the sea, in my mind I see the moon rising full on the winter solstice. It would come directly out from this cove and bathe the whole beach in silver.

That's what feels familiar about this place—the stretch of even ground is the same size as the Folk's dancing area. In fact, I think one night the hall shaped itself to replicate this very spot.

I move on, combing the rest of the beach. When I find nothing, I look around. Perhaps the selkie skin isn't down here, after all. It could be buried on top of the cliffs.

There's one pillar of land that's become separated from the main part of the coast to form its own tall island. I'm drawn to the path that winds from the rocky beach up its side, narrow and steep. True follows me, scrambling over the rougher bits. The wind catches at the edge of my coat, trying to pull me over the edge and into another darker cove below. I pause, wrap an arm securely round a rock, and lean out over the drop. My heart races and for a moment I feel truly awake for the first time in weeks.

I close my eyes, letting the wind tear at me. But soon the cold turns sharp and uncomfortable, and I retreat into the shelter of the hill. I take a deep breath and continue my climb.

At the top I step onto a small field of tall, golden grass. The ground under my feet is soft here, almost squishy. Deep with moss. True squeezes past my legs and trots ahead, nosing at some of the rabbit holes. I follow him unsteadily. The terrain is covered in bumps and dips. I wonder whether these were once houses, some long-ago settlement reclaimed by the land. We have a lot of those on the islands. Abram might know.

I have been searching for some time, and the sun is steadily lowering toward the horizon, when the clinking in my head shifts and morphs into a word. A word repeated in the wind.

"Idris!"

I blink, turning to look round. At the place where the path meets the hill's crest, Kit is waving to me. My heart lifts in surprise—and something warmer. Once she sees I've spotted her, she continues forward, holding her skirt to one side to avoid tripping. The wind claws at her hair, pulling some of the dark strands free. True bounds toward her and I have to call him off before he barrels into her, sending her over the side.

She is smiling by the time she reaches me, one hand resting on True's head. Her gaze goes past me to our surroundings. "This is amazing."

I glance in the same direction, trying to see it as she does. The cliffs curve and jut into the ocean, and the blue of the water is matched by the blue in the sky, so that everything is big and wide and open. Birds circle overhead, and gulls cry out at us, and the breeze never stops blowing. The way the grass bends and shines under each gust makes me feel strangely settled, and the dance of Kit's loose strands of hair across her cheeks is more beautiful than all of it.

Realizing I might be staring, I clear my throat. "How did you find me?"

"I went to the house and one of your servants directed me to Mager Head." She gestures toward the mainland of Skyare. From here you can see for miles back inland. A gray horse is grazing on that side of the gap. "They let me borrow a horse so I could catch up with you."

I shade my eyes to get a better look. The dappled pattern across the horse's hindquarters confirms my suspicion.

"They let you take *my* horse?" I say, amused. "I didn't realize my servants were so bold."

"I think they were more concerned," she says.

I choose not to hear this, turning my attention to the bumps in the grass. I nudge one with my boot. Whatever lies beneath is solid, like a stone.

Kit opens her mouth and I imagine she wants to ask all the logical questions. *Why are you out here? Is it really a good idea to exert yourself? Are you sure this is the right thing to do?*

"I thought maybe I could find the queen's selkie skin," I explain before she can speak. I wave the journal's map in her direction. "My great-great-grandfather had this place marked. But I haven't found anything yet."

Kit takes the book from me and frowns, studying it. Slowly, she says, "I'm not...sure that this is evidence that the selkie skin is here. His sketch could just mean he saw a seal?"

"Maybe," I admit. "But seals are commonplace. Why record it?" I put my weight against the nearest bump in the grass, pushing until a small gap opens in the ground. Just dirt. "If I could find the skin, she might release me from the curse. And even if not, it should be returned—not hidden out in the wilderness somewhere."

"Have you found anything promising?" Kit passes the book back to me.

"No." I sigh. "But I don't really know what I'm looking for. I just thought…"

The foolishness of my search sits between us, though Kit is too kind to point it out. Even with the tentative clue on the map—which could be nothing, after all—there is too much land to search. Too many places to hide something little bigger than a cloak. And it isn't as if Mervyn would have constructed a monument to mark the place where he hid his prize. For all I know, the last person to know the location of the skin died when Mervyn did.

"Idris," Kit says. The wind snatches at my name, pulling the sound away from us. "I found a way to help you."

I lean closer to her, partially to hear and partially because the wind is a physical force pushing against my back. True lies at our feet, watching us keenly. The grass waves and shadows dart and drift across the horizon. Everything smears in and out of focus around me.

Kit brings a narrow stick of coral from her reticule. It's not very long—perhaps about half the length of her forearm.

"Speir told me that this wand would break one curse," she says. She lifts her silver eyes to meet mine. "It just takes a tap."

She extends her arm, ready to touch my chest with the wand, but I step back. "Wait—"

My foot hits one of the buried rocks and I almost fall, but Kit catches my arm and yanks me forward. As we stumble together, my nose touches her hair and I have an impulse to press my face against her neck. Heat burns through me and I straighten, making space between us. The wind cuts my flushed skin.

"Are you all right?" Kit asks, her hand still on my arm. She releases her hold and reaches up, brushing the back of her fingers against my forehead. Her eyes widen. "Your fever is worse."

I want to lean against her hand. Maybe it's the fever or something else but my pulse is racing. My thoughts are jumbled and words spring out of my mouth: "When was the first time you experienced beauty?"

"That..." She pulls away. "I think we should break the curse and get you home."

I catch her hand. "Humor me."

She thinks before she answers, a crease between her eyebrows. "I suppose when I was eight. There was a meteor shower and I ran through the fields chasing the stars. I thought I could catch them."

"I was five," I tell her. "My mother brought a lantern from her homeland. The panes of glass were dyed—purples and blues and greens and yellows—and when she put a candle inside, it would cover the room in colored light."

Confusion still masks her expression. "That sounds lovely, but I don't understand why—"

"Don't you miss the person you were when you felt beauty first?" I ask. "Don't you miss your old body?"

She stares at me, her cheeks paling.

"I only mean, don't you want to go back?" My head swims and the only way I can find my own reasoning is to speak aloud. "When I leave my body during the dances, I feel void. But you bring me back and I find beauty. Wholeness."

"It's different for me." She lowers her gaze and seems to shrink in front of me. "My old body was not all delight."

"Mine isn't either." I shift on my aching feet. "But it isn't all pain, is it? You were in that body when the stars fell. And when you stood in the fog on the dock. And a thousand other moments that you haven't shared with me."

She winces and I fall silent. I don't know what she remembers, but I feel the darkness of it between us.

Carefully, trying to find what I'm feeling as I go, I say, "Use the wand for yourself. Break your own curse."

"That's foolish." She jerks away from me as if I've struck her. "Catharine and I are only inconvenienced—you are *dying*."

"I don't want to break this curse at your expense," I counter. "I don't want a cure. Not like this."

She crosses her arms over her stomach, the wand still in one hand. "Why in the world not?"

"Because I would have you be yourself," I blurt. "Whole and happy. Your own person. Radiant."

"I can be myself like this." She gestures to her face. "There was *nothing* 'radiant' about what I was before."

I remember our brief interactions, back when she was herself. Her stubborn grace when she was hurt. Her ready smile and laugh. The vastness contained in her when she stared over the loch. "On the contrary."

She shakes her head fervently, refusing to look at me. "That's not true. You don't mean it—you only think that because I look like this now."

"I thought you were amazing even back at the ball." I reach for her hand, but she draws back. "It's not what you *look* like, it's *you.* Your spirit. Your laugh. I am mesmerized by *you.*"

She waves this aside as if batting off a fly. My heart twists, raw from the confession, but I keep pressing. I can't seem to stop. "I want you to be yourself, and safe, and all right."

"And what if I'm meant to remain this way? What if *this* is my healing?"

"Who you are is body and soul. Can you heal one without the other? When I danced—"

"We are not the same!"

"I just mean that if you were back in your own body—"

"You do not—You cannot *order* me to go back! You cannot…dictate how I choose!"

I blink, surprised. Had I been doing that?

"I'm sorry," I whisper. "It… I do not seek to command you, one way or the other. Only to offer you my sincere feelings."

"I do not want them!" she cries, flinging her hands over her face. "You would not…if you knew…"

I open my mouth to insist but force the words back. I have said too much, and at the wrong time, and I've hurt her. I can't seem to stop hurting people, even when all I want is to spare them. A dark corner of me whispers: *Everyone around you will hurt, as long as you are with them.*

"Keep the wand," I say as gently as I can. "Do what you will with it, but let me make my own choice. I'll find another way free. If I cannot find the selkie skin, perhaps I can at least remove the iron boots."

She does not answer, turning away from me with her face still covered.

But perhaps that voice in me is right.

As long as I am here, there will be pain.

So I leave.

SEVENTEEN

Kit

I realize too late that he's gone.

My emotions are at war, too torn and splintered for anything to be clear. I cannot move from my spot at the cliff edge. Far below, a boat has set out from the bay. Idris. Idris, who likes my laugh and is amazed by my spirit. Idris, who thinks I'm *mesmerizing*.

Does he really? asks a voice that sounds like my stepfather's. *He couldn't have meant it.*

From what I know of Idris, he is kind and noble and good. A bit of a martyr and too impulsive, but someone so totally different from Byrne. A tiny, naive sliver of me brightens at the thought.

Do you know that? asks another voice, this one like my mother. *Is any man truly* not *like Byrne?*

Waves of shame and regret choke me. Guilt. In any story shouldn't this be a moment of triumph? I like Idris. I don't know if I love him—though just the thought of the possibility of it sends giddy warmth, followed by a streak of terror, down my spine—but I *like* him a very great deal. If

I were any other person, I would be happy now. I would be warm and giggling and blushing. I would have stopped him before he left and declared myself with sparkling words, maybe even with a kiss. I wouldn't have raged.

What is wrong with me?

The boat, a speck against the shimmering blue of the ocean, shifts southward toward Stromwell. I should have accompanied him to the manor house, should have insisted he take his horse. He isn't well—anyone could see that. He shouldn't be alone.

And yet, I'm grateful he left. I don't want to see him—not now, maybe not ever. I never want to feel this excruciating chaos again.

But he didn't mean to cause this. He doesn't know what he's asking, what he's said. Would he ask if he knew? Would he ever think any part of me is radiant if he knew?

I grip my fists against my forehead, turning from the view. My breath comes in gulps and I can't get enough air. My body shakes and I sink onto the plush grass. Deep in the core of me, there is a jittery instability that I recognize, though I've never felt it so strongly in Catharine's body before.

Unsafe.

I force myself to sit straight. I'm not allowed to feel this way anymore. I'm in a perfect body, a healthy body. The turmoil in me radiates out from my fingers into the earth. I choke, squeeze my eyes shut.

A faint *thrum* answers me.

I draw another shuddering breath and open my eyes. It comes again, a distant *thrum* through the ground. A murmuring wail that matches the one inside me.

Still shaking, I run my hands across the grass. The *thrum* morphs into a painful buzz, like an open burn that has been grazed by cloth. I crawl across the lumpy ground, following the rising hurt, searching it out among the ruins. When the feeling centers at a point below me, I claw through the grass and moss. I dig with my fingernails, scraping away clay and rock. My nails chip and skin breaks, but it doesn't matter. I am all instinct. Somewhere in this mess is a wound that feels like mine and I urgently have to find it.

Perhaps one foot down, my fingers knock against something that is not soil or stone. A cluster of small roots? But as I begin to pull it aside, the thin threads tug. It is some kind of wider material. The hurt sings from it.

I dig around, carefully freeing the thing until I can lift it without tugging. It comes up from the ground covered in red and brown. I brush my palm against it to wipe it clean. Velvety bristles rise and smooth depending on the direction I move. Fur. Fur that is softer than the richest silk and moves just as fluidly. I pinch a bit between my fingers, trying to feel resistance in the hide, but there is none.

The fur is short, like a seal's, and under the stain of the dirt it is still silver as raindrops in the sun. I spread it out in front of me, wincing at the places it has been folded roughly, the places the skin puckers.

My heart nearly stops.

I recognize this. And I understand why it called to me.

"What did he do to you?" I whisper, tears blurring my vision.

I have found the selkie skin that Mervyn stole. Fury quivers under my grief, under the grief that radiates between me and it. He took something beautiful, something sacred, and he stuffed it in the ground like it was rubbish. He didn't even place it in a sack to protect it. He left it here to rot.

I gather the skin gently into my arms and hold it to my chest. The wind dies around me and suddenly the world is still. The air is comfortable and almost warm. Far away, the sea murmurs. The wild hurt quiets into a kind of calm.

I've found what Idris was looking for. I should spring up and ride after him, but I need a moment to just breathe.

Perhaps I should have just struck him with the wand, taken the decision out of both of our hands. I could still do it.

Frustration rises in me. He had no right to tell me how to use the wand—and I *want* to use it on him. I want to do the right thing. And going back to what I was—to my old body—can't be the right thing. Can it?

Clinging to my growing, stony certainty, I gingerly place the wand in my reticule and fold the skin against my chest. I climb back to the main island and find Idris's gelding. He's a mild horse, with delicate features and beautiful brown eyes. His ears swivel as I approach and he lifts his head curiously. An empty saddlebag is attached to his gear and I slide the selkie skin into it. That taken care of, I take the reins and lead him to one of the nearby rocks so I can mount. The horse isn't trained for sidesaddle, so I awkwardly position myself with my skirt bunched up on either side. I turn toward the west and begin my way back, alternating between a trot and a canter. During the journey, I do my best to steel myself. I'll walk right up to

Idris and smack him with the wand. The curse will break and that will be that. We can decide how to return the skin afterward.

Then I won't have the wand burning a hole in my reticule, whispering that I could use it on Catharine to cure the wasting and keep everything the way it is.

If I give up the cure to Idris, it means I am not being selfish in keeping Catharine's body—at least for now. Right?

I take the back route the servants pointed out to me earlier to avoid parading through Stromwell on their prince's horse. The manor house is ahead. The sun is nearly set, though it's not even late enough for the evening meal. Red and gold streak the sky, and everything below sinks into violet shadows.

I ride into the courtyard and dismount with a little difficulty. A stablehand takes the reins and holds the horse steady while I unhook the saddlebag.

"Thank you." I put the bag's leather strap over my shoulder and use my newly free hands to tug my skirts into place. "Is Prince Idris back?"

"No, miss."

I frown. I didn't think it would take him longer by sea than it took me by land. But before I can decide the right course of action, the servant speaks again.

"Your stepmother—the queen—has arrived."

My heart stutters. "What?"

The stablehand glances toward the house uncertainly. "We're not meant to, um, know who you are, Princess Catharine, but…servants talk. The queen arrived this afternoon and I thought you'd want to know."

"What about King Byrne?" I ask, a rushing building in my ears.

"I believe he is at the Guildhall," he says.

I exhale. But my relief is short-lived. I may not be in immediate danger of running into my stepfather, but I need to get Catharine and myself off Skyare as quickly as possible. Perhaps I can give Abram the wand—get it as far from me as possible—and ask for his assistance to travel to one of the more remote islands.

The stablehand is still standing in front of me, waiting for a dismissal.

"Where is Prince Abram?" I ask quickly. "King Hugh?"

"Prince Abram is at the Guildhall too. The king left this morning for one of the islands and we haven't had word of his return."

I want to swear. My stomach clenches at the thought of leaving Idris to his fate, despite all my fury with him for choosing it. But if I linger here—if we are caught—I don't know what Byrne will do to us. And I can't very well just leave the wand on Idris's doorstep and hope he'll use it.

"Daughter!" calls a voice behind me.

I freeze. My mother. There is a moment when I could run—just outright flee—but I hesitate. I don't have time to know why. Then she has grabbed my arm and wrapped me in a hug.

My throat tightens and my eyes burn. I bring my arms loosely round her to return the hug, wanting to pretend for a moment that we are as we were: just a mother and daughter reunited. But in Catharine's body I am too tall and I cannot tuck myself under her chin like I used to. I am the wrong size, and she did this to me, and I am longing and anger, betrayal and sadness all together. I pull away from her.

"You're well?" Mother asks, brushing back my hair and looking me over head to toe. "I was so worried."

My gaze catches on her stomach. The gown she wears bulges and when she sees me look she rests her hand on the bump.

"You—you're with child?" I say, bewildered. I haven't been gone long enough for her to have grown this much.

"This isn't a conversation for such a public place," Mother says with a glance at the stablehand, who bows his head quickly. "Let us walk."

I need to get to Catharine. But, I reason, Abram and the king know that we are hiding from Byrne, even if they don't know why. The king gave his word he would not give us away. Catharine has never even come into the city, so the chances of her and Byrne meeting are slim to none. And this might be the last time I see my mother. Ever.

I let her lead me to the garden round the back of the manor. Dusk has fallen, but light lingers enough that I can see her face. Her eyes gleam with concern when she turns to me again.

"Why did you run away, Kit?" she asks when we are alone. "You shouldn't have taken off. You could have been hurt."

"I couldn't let Catharine come to harm."

Mother sniffs. "She would not have come to any if her father had behaved himself."

I shake my head. This conversation will go nowhere and I don't want to hear my mother say these things again. Instead, I ask, "How long have you been pregnant?"

"Four months, nearly five," she answers. "Don't look so hurt. After I lost Byrne's first baby, I wanted to be sure before I made it known."

I remember the first, only a few months after their wedding. My little brother had been so small, though the maids had whispered that he was too big for his supposed time. I always pretended not to know. He came out silent and blue, and it wasn't his fault if he came about on the wrong side of wedding vows.

Byrne has wanted a son for as long as he has known my mother and a new thought occurs to me.

"You knew you were pregnant when you had us cursed," I say out loud. "You knew he wouldn't dare harm you, even if he found out what truly happened."

She dips her head. "And, should it become a problem, I could always disappear after the birth."

"You would leave your child with him?" I ask, surprised.

"The child is already promised elsewhere."

Another memory rises to the surface: Speir saying to my mother, "The price is still acceptable?" And her answer: "Yes. Come in five months."

"You didn't—" I can hardly speak it. "Tell me you didn't promise Speir—?"

Mother lifts her chin. "Magic always has a price."

"How could you?!" I exclaim. "It's just a baby! How could you promise it away to *them*?"

"Why would I keep his spawn?" she hisses. Her pride melts into fury. "Why would I give him an heir after all he's done? It would serve him right."

"But you aren't only punishing Byrne! You would punish an innocent!"

"How innocent can his child really be?" She shakes her head. "Fate gave me this child so that I could secure your safety. What happens to the babe is beyond my control. And do you understand? I don't *want* it."

I stare at my mother, dismayed—not only by what she is, what she's done, but because I *understand.* A part of me understands carrying an unwanted burden, being so desperate to be rid of it that you would allow anyone else to be hurt if you could just be free. Pain pricks my heart. I always thought my mother was different. Better. I want the mother I thought I had, but I'm not sure she ever existed.

"You aren't escaping what he's done," I say out loud. "You're only passing the punishment on to someone who doesn't deserve it."

"Let me be concerned with this," Mother says. "Tell me—what are you doing here? Prince Abram acted as if he had not seen you, but you came in riding one of their horses."

I pause, unsure if Idris would appreciate me spilling his family's secrets. But there is too much in common between Idris's circumstances and the fate that awaits my mother's baby. So I tell her, hoping she'll see the dangers of it and change her mind. "Ours isn't the only family cursed."

I keep secret the details of the cause of the Hidden Queen's curse, trying to preserve what privacy I can, but emphasize the results—that Idris is now dying for something that isn't his fault.

"Except he wouldn't have to die," I blurt, my frustration overcoming my caution, "if he would just let me *help*."

"What do you mean by that?" Mother asks.

"I've found a way to break his curse, but he won't take it because he wants me to use it to undo the curse *you* caused."

"The royal family knows about that?" Mother asks, eyebrows lifting. For the first time in our conversation, she looks surprised.

"They figured it out," I answer. "Most of it."

"Hmm. And still he's rejected your offer of breaking his curse?"

I clench my hands, angry with him all over again. "He's so fixed on being noble about it that I can't get him to see reason. He claims…fondness for me. Wants me to use it to break my own curse."

My mother watches me, her eyes sharp. "This cure—it works on any curse?"

"Speir said so. He said I could use it on Idris or Catharine or—"

I snap my mouth shut. My stomach sinks. I've said too much. I've exposed my weakness, put a drop of blood before a hound. And my mother is not the mother I wished for— she is all the darkest parts of me.

"Or you could fix your old body," Mother finishes for me.

I don't answer.

“Darling, why do you even hesitate? The prince doesn’t want your help.” She waves her hand dismissively. “He is a fool, but let him be one.”

“But he’s doing it because he…because of reasons that aren’t right.”

“Because he thinks he’s in love? Because he’s too proud to accept help?” Mother shrugs. “Let him. What does it matter to you?”

“I never said *love*!” A flood of embarrassment heats my face.

“It is inconvenient that he won’t be able to marry you,” Mother muses. “But if you look like this, it will not be much trouble to find someone else to take you in. And perhaps it would be better to seek someone farther abroad—someone who knows less of your history.”

“I’m not going to keep Catharine’s body,” I say, though my voice sounds too firm, too confident. Like a child who knows she is lying.

Mother fixes me with a gentle smile. “Why not? You told me you did not like my methods because Catharine would be trapped in your body, at risk from her father. So cure the wasting and keep her away from Byrne. Would it be such a punishment for her to continue to look like you used to? You were not so very plain.”

I wince. My mother has never called me plain outright before, but I’ve always known it to be true. And it never bothered me—I don’t think—beyond the occasional, fleeting moment of regret. My mother is right, though. Were it not for the wasting, mine would not be such a horrible body to have. What’s worse is, I think Catharine might even agree to it.

But even if the wasting stopped, there would still be the damage to her hands. And even if the damage was minimal…would it be right to keep her body from her just because it might make my life easier? Just because I'd like to be admired and strong and graceful? My body is mine, for all its faults, and Idris wasn't entirely wrong—it has carried pain, but it has also been a vessel of delight. And isn't Catharine's the same for her?

I tighten my hands on the straps of my reticule. Darkness has fully come over the garden now and the wind rises. My head feels clearer than it has all day.

"No, my body isn't so very plain," I agree. "And even with the wasting, maybe it isn't so bad. It is mine, either way."

Mother frowns. I begin to walk back toward the manor house.

"Do not use the cure to undo my spell." Mother places a hand lightly on my arm. "Whatever you may think now, I gave you a gift. You shouldn't squander it."

"It wasn't a gift," I say, stopping in the courtyard. Torchlight illuminates us now, the wind whipping at the flames and making the light dance. "It was an escape. And…maybe I needed it. But I don't anymore."

"You would go back to what you were?" Her expression is part disappointment, part disgust. "You will be crushed by the wasting, make no mistake."

"You underestimate me, Mother." I lift my chin. "I can carry this. And when I can't carry it—I have friends who will help me. And I'm not too stubborn to ask."

"King Byrne won't let you slip away the next time he catches you," Mother warns. "You have hardly begun to feel what it is to be imprisoned by that man."

"He won't catch me again." I am mapping my way to the Westness house in my head. I'll need to find Abram before I go, give him the wand and selkie skin. Then I'll collect my sister. We can sail from a different port than Stromwell. Abram will save Idris and I will save Catharine. I will just have to find another way to break the other curse.

"Are you sure?" Mother tilts her head, her expression innocent. "Byrne has a way of claiming what he wants."

Cold runs through me that has nothing to do with the wind. "What did you do?"

She shrugs. "Servants talk, my dear. I found out where the two of you have been staying. I merely sent word. I meant to warn you—but it seems I've just told Catharine that her father is in town looking for her."

All the blood drains from my face.

"Don't tell me you haven't told her the truth of it all?" My mother almost preens. "After all, she's the one you chose."

"When did you send that message?"

"Oh, near two hours ago now."

I turn and run for the town before she has finished the sentence.

✦

My pulse roars in my ears by the time I make it to the market. I do not spare a thought for my mother or unborn sibling, though I feel the war in the back of my mind. Maybe she didn't intend for Catharine to go to her father in my body. Maybe she thought that I would have told Catharine the truth by now and that Catharine would stay away. But I haven't. And Catharine thinks her father is safe.

I shove open the doors to the Guildhall and stumble to a stop, breathing fast and strained. A few servants pause to look at me in surprise. Abram leans out of the door of a side room and hurries over once he sees me. "Kit—"

"Is my sister here?" I ask, the barb in my throat stopping me before I can say her name. It stabs as I stutter, "Is my st—my—the king?"

Abram nods, looking confused. "She arrived a quarter hour ago. King Byrne asked to speak with her in private."

Surely he wouldn't dare. Not here. Not mere steps from so many people.

"Where?" I demand.

Abram straightens at my urgency. "The audience room."

I push past Abram to take the servants' stairs to the archive, as Idris showed me. Abram starts to follow but I hold out a hand to stop him. "Let me handle this—stay here unless I call."

I don't look back to see if he's listened. I dive through the darkness of the hall and grab the door to the archive. As I emerge into the room, the smell of old papers and dust surrounds me. My entire attention, my entire being, focuses on the door at the far side. My hand, searching for something to use as a weapon, closes round the wand in my reticule.

Even as I run, I hear him speaking.

"I knew you would come back," he says, and his voice is the silky gloating I remember. "You only had to get used to the idea."

My other hand closes on the latch.

Catharine, in my voice, stutters, "I—I don't understand—"

I pull the door open. It doesn't so much as squeak. My stepfather has cornered Catharine near the curtained window and he is closing the distance between them. He is so intent, he has not heard me.

Catharine stares with wide eyes. The moment before he's close enough to block me from her view, her gaze darts to me in the doorway. Horror and fear and confusion are written across her face—across my face—and I am suddenly looking at myself. The first time. I am fourteen, and I am alone, and I am trapped. Then he steps forward again, and I can't see her—I can't see myself—beyond his broad back.

He bends to kiss her neck. And I know with a searing clarity *exactly* what I have to do.

Fury and revulsion rise in me so violently that the wand almost snaps in my hand. I cannot spare Catharine the knowing—but I will spare her the touch.

I strike my wrist with the wand. My body lurches forward and I squeeze my eyes shut against an unbridled nausea. My soul seems to tumble free of my skin, and for a moment I fall and fall and fall. Then, with a painful *snap*, I am in a body again. Just in time to feel a kiss land on my neck.

Wild anger cuts through me like a tempest and a scream tears from my throat as I ram my head against his. "Get the hell off me!"

King Byrne stumbles to one side with a cry and raises a hand to his nose. I shove away from the wall, twisting into open space. I am little again, in my own body, with aches and fatigue murmuring for my attention. I shove that aside, only focused on him. On his surprise turning to fury.

He lunges and I grab a book to smack his hand away. He shouts an oath, grappling for me, trying to get a hold of my arms and pin me back.

But someone moves between us, shoving me back and raising her arms like a shield. "Stop it!" Catharine shouts.

King Byrne reels back, face red. I straighten behind Catharine, my chest heaving.

"Don't *touch* her," Catharine hisses.

"Catharine!" King Byrne says, schooling his expression into something benevolent. He even smiles. "I'm afraid you misunderstand—"

"How could you?" she says, voice ragged now. "How *could* you?"

King Byrne opens and closes his mouth, his expression becoming guarded and eyes calculating. The floorboards groan behind me and I look over my shoulder.

Abram stands in the archive doorway. He glances from Catharine to me uncertainly. "I heard someone cry out—"

"I want my father escorted from this building," Catharine says, lifting her chin. She looks every bit a queen. "I do not want him in my sight."

"I'm not sure what you think was happening, Catharine," her father protests. "But—"

"Do not speak to me!" Catharine snaps. "Do not say anything. Just leave."

With Abram here, King Byrne hesitates. Finally, his jaw tightens. "We'll talk later. But don't be so quick to believe everything that chit—" he nods toward me—"tells you."

Still gripping my hand, Catharine points to the door. Abram holds it open for King Byrne. Face red with anger, the king leaves. Abram glances at us, but then steps out after him.

For a moment, neither Catharine nor I move, frozen with her hand gripped in mine. I'm suddenly aware of myself—of my shallow breathing and the ache in my fingers and the tightness in my shoulders. I don't know what to say or do.

Catharine turns to me, her eyes shining with tears. She starts to speak, then closes her mouth. I meet her gaze and watch her expression crumple as she reads the truth in my face.

"Yes." The word is so soft, I almost don't hear myself speak. "He hurt me."

With a whimper, she begins to pull away, to bow her head.

Before she can, I wrap my arms round her and hug her as tightly as I can. Her arms close just as fiercely across my back and suddenly I am the one crying. I am raw and exposed and for the first time someone else knows—someone else is with me in my loneliest, ugliest moment. Once I thought my mother's anger on my behalf was the most I could hope for. I thought that she had seen me and felt for me, but in Catharine's embrace I realize that wasn't true. My mother only saw the shame of me—Catharine stands in the shame with me and holds me, turns the shame from darkness to a searing, bittersweet love.

"I'm so sorry," Catharine babbles, her voice broken. "I didn't know—I never thought—"

I squeeze her tighter. "It isn't your fault."

Catharine leans back, wiping her eyes with her palms. "I… Kit…"

I swallow on my raw throat. It is strange to see the distress on her face and I want to soothe it away, but at the same time I feel it burning through me. Leaving behind something purer, someone stronger. I clasp her hands between my broken, misshapen ones and try to focus on this moment. On my heart, so full of pain and delight and empathy and sadness that it seems to break and mend at once.

"I should have told you," I whisper.

"I should have seen it," she replies. Her gaze goes distant. "How could I not see it?"

"Almost no one else has." I pause, thinking of Idris and the ball. "I think sometimes it's harder to spot when it's right in front of you."

Remembering Idris brings me back to the wand. I search the floor and find it cracked in two. Spell didn't lie, it seems. It only worked on one curse and I've chosen the curse to break. I look down at my hands. I don't know how I'll stop my wasting, or how I'll save Idris from dancing to death—but in this moment I'm glad I'm in my own body.

I look back at Catharine. "Are you all right?"

"Not exactly," she says with a fragile laugh. "What about you?"

"I'm all right." I look in the direction her father left. "What will you do about King Byrne?" Though it pains me, I add, "I understand if you…if it's important for you to… make peace…"

"With him?" she finishes, incredulous. She shakes her head. "I don't know exactly what is next, but whatever it is—I stand with you. What else would I do?"

Gratitude swells in my chest and my vision blurs. I lean my forehead against my sister's shoulder; she strokes my hair, and I breathe.

EIGHTEEN

Idris

I dock by the pier in Stromwell but remain in my yole. I don't seem up to standing, much less hauling the yole onto the noust. My thoughts keep circling back to Kit on that cliff, and her offer to cure me, and my blundering half-baked confession. And then there's her adamant rejection. A lot of not-so-pleasant memories to haunt however many days I have left.

The boat rocks as True moves closer to me. He puts his large head on my knee and lifts his eyes. It's dark now, but somehow his eyes still shine with doggy adoration. I feel a laugh tickle my chest, but only manage a small smile.

"You've chosen the wrong human, True," I say.

True wags his tail, recognizing his name if nothing else.

My quest to find the Hidden One's selkie skin has gone exactly nowhere. And in a few hours I'll be sailing out again—this time without Kit. Perhaps it's the fever or our conversation or something else, but a cloud of finality has settled over me. I feel like maybe I won't come back this time.

What is the point of returning, anyway? I am only prolonging the inevitable and hurting everyone in the process. If I just left, and stayed away, I could fade somewhere where the people who love me won't have to see it. Maybe the most I can hope for is to minimize their pain while seeking some sort of redemption for my family.

It's too late to avoid hurting everyone on this side of the Hidden Lands with my choice, but there's still something I can do to help redeem my family there. The Hidden Folk can't touch the iron shoes, but I can. And perhaps I can get them off. That's one thing I can do to take away some pain, instead of causing it.

With a deep breath, I push myself to my feet and clamber onto the dock. True springs up behind me. I turn toward the city and the forge. With the sun down, my body seems to know that these are the only hours I have for sleep, and I fight the impulse to lie on the flagstones and close my eyes. I'm not sure I'll even bother going home tonight—I'm not sure I could make it up the hill in this state.

Outside the smithy, the confounded noise starts again: *Clink, clink, bang.*

But this time it's not in my head. It's the sound of the smith working.

The blacksmith hands over the tools I ask for with a confused look. I wonder whether the whole city—the whole island—knows that I'm cursed at this point. It does seem that people's gazes skirt away from mine when I step back into the street. Like there's something uncanny about me. I want to give them a pat on the shoulder and say, *Not much longer now.*

I'm on my way back to my yole when I notice a boat has docked near mine. It's a bit bigger, with the word *Suraya* painted in white on the bow. My mother's name; my father's vessel. I'm tempted to duck back into the dark streets and wait until he's cleared the harbor. But if I don't return home, I will never see him again, and there is a small, young part of me that wants to speak. To say goodbye, even if I don't use those words.

As I approach, my father disembarks. He calls back to the captain, "Mind the rudder is repaired before we sail again."

I slow to a stop. "Did the ship take damage?"

Father glances at me in surprise. "We ran too close to a rock." His gaze gets more concerned as he comes within reach of me. "You look terrible. Why aren't you sleeping at the manor?"

I shrug. The world tilts under my feet and my father catches my arm to steady me. The tools in my pockets weigh me down. I feel heavier than a barrel of cannon balls.

"Come, sit a minute." Father directs me toward Mr. Muir and his bench. He raises his voice to call, "Mind if we borrow this, Merlin?"

"Was just about to retreat to the pub anyway," Mr. Muir says, rising. "There's a storm on the wind tonight."

Father nods his thanks and tugs me to the bench. I sink without resistance. The night must be cold, and the wind tangles in my hair, but I feverishly think I could close my eyes and sleep right here.

Father frowns. "I'll have someone bring a horse round. You need to go home."

"No," I say, rousing myself. "I'm fine."

Father makes a frustrated sound in the back of his throat. "You only have a few hours before you'll be enchanted out to sea. You should be spending them in peace, not wandering around the docks."

I rub my face. "I don't want to go all the way up."

"Then we'll get you a room at the Stromwall Hotel." Father turns away.

"Just leave it alone," I snap, my ire rising. "Stop trying to command me!"

"I'm not trying to *command* you. I'm trying to help you."

"I can do this on my own." I try to push myself off the bench. "I chose this. And I'll finish it."

Father plants his hands on my shoulders. "The point is, you don't have to." When my strength gives out under the slightest pressure from his arms, he sighs sharply. "Damn it, Idris, why do you have to be like this?"

Something tugs in my chest, the deep hollow between my ribs. A despair that doesn't begin here. I close my eyes and concentrate. There is a memory, far back and faded.

"Did you ever hold me?" I ask. Not an accusation—just an idle curiosity. "As a child, I mean. I don't remember you ever holding me."

Father looks startled. "What are you talking about?"

"It was that way with your father," I continue, almost to myself. "Wasn't it?"

I see through the eyes of a small child. Mother, in bed, her face drawn as the injury in her leg slowly drains her life away. I am snuggled against her, listening to every rattling heartbeat with my ear to her chest. Grandfather, my father's father, is reading aloud from the Psalms. Father sits nearby and, as he watches me, his eyes begin to fill with tears.

Grandfather suddenly cuts short his reading. "Stop that, Hugh. Control yourself." I shrink closer to Mother and he gestures to me. "Look at your son—if you aren't stronger, he'll turn out as soft as Erik. Do you hear that, boy? Do you want to be like Mervyn's useless brother?"

My mother rouses herself and says other things, kinder things—and I want to hear these other things, I want to remember them. But I don't.

I am too tender when she is hurt. Too wild when she is gone. Too much.

"What does this have to do with anything?" Father asks.

"You asked why I'm the way I am." I lift my gaze to his and the effort even of that small movement is enough to make my head swim. "I am what Mervyn made, what Great-grandfather and Grandfather made, what *you* made."

For me, it wasn't one dramatic moment. It wasn't a violent confrontation, a ferocious flash of lightning, a sharp word that went straight to the marrow.

For me, it was a thousand small seconds. A glimmer of disappointment. A reprimand edged with annoyance. A quiet thrum of *not enough* and *too much* that whispered in silences until it seemed to shout.

Father puts his cold hand against my forehead. "You are delirious."

"Maybe you were right," I mumble.

He looks at me with wary surprise. "About what?"

"Maybe I didn't do any of this out of noble intentions. I only chose the hardest path because I felt I…needed to.

That I deserved it. Not because it was the right thing for the family but because it was the cruelest thing for me." I stare at my lap. "I inherited all the empathy and guilt that you postponed."

"Don't talk like this," Father says. "Of course you don't deserve this."

"Mother held me, didn't she?" I ask, mild and calm. "Until the fever's end. And I suppose she held no one after that."

Father opens and closes his mouth.

"King Hugh!" calls a man's voice from down the street. There's something familiar about it, but my mind is too exhausted to place the name, to identify the prick of unease that stirs in my heart.

Father turns toward the man—he's still some distance from us—and I take the opportunity to stand. Father reaches to stop me, but the voice is saying something else, and I slip away while his attention is divided. True follows beside me as I duck onto the nearest street toward the stable beside the hotel. It's cozy and warm, lit by a single lantern, and presently empty of stablehands.

I find a rope in the tack room and loop it round True's collar, my stomach tight. The sense that I must be going, must leave before Father or anyone else can stop me, thrums with urgency. I linger, resting my hand on True's head. He wags his tail and looks at me in confusion.

"Sorry," I say. "But if I'm not coming back, you have to stay here. You'll be safe. Abram will look after you."

True licks my palm, not understanding. I swallow on a dry throat and make myself step away. I grab a hold of the stable doors and step through. Behind me, True whines, then yelps. I glance back. He's pulling against the rope, straining to get to me, and barking frantically now. I want to cry, but I pull the doors shut. The noise dulls behind the thick wood.

I return to my yole, raise the sails, and turn to leave the harbor.

It isn't yet time for the curse to guide me to the Hidden Lands, so I settle for a cove about ten miles down the coast. I anchor my boat, then lie down against the hull and pull an oilskin over me. It's not comfortable, but I am asleep as soon as my head comes to rest against the wood.

✦

It scarcely seems seconds later when the curse stirs in my chest. I'm too far out to hear the cathedral bells, but it must be midnight. My body buzzes with energy, though my head feels too heavy to hold up. I raise the anchor and hoist the sails.

The wind has risen and I find myself sinking into the half conscious state I used to be in when enchanted. Without Kit, my senses fade in and out—one moment, the sway of the boat and the texture of the wood fill my attention, the next all is mist and dark. A storm is coming in, and the rain is mixed with snow and ice. But even the sting of the cold can't keep me from falling into a daze. I cannot tell if an hour has passed or only a few minutes when, by the sharp rocks and whirlpools, I realize I've come to the cliff.

My voice rips out of me. "Open, black cliff, and let the young prince in and out with his boat!"

And out. The words escape before I think to stop them, though I don't intend to leave. I feel the emptiness at my feet, where True would normally sit. Ahead, in the dark, the rocks cleave in a blast of thunder and I know the passageway is opening.

A bout of dizziness rocks me to one side and my hand slips, jerking the tiller. I duck just in time to avoid the swinging boom as it whooshes inches above my head. But before I can correct the course, wood crunches on stone and I'm tossed over the side onto sharp rocks.

A surface as jagged as daggers cuts my palms and salt water burns into the wounds. I cough, digging my fingers into the rock as a wave sloshes over me, dragging at my heavy greatcoat. I shake hair out of my face, looking for my yole. Without my weight to hold the boat down the sea has pulled it free of the breech. It's already nearly five feet away.

I lunge for the gunwale. But another wave hits me from the side and I'm plunged into the freezing water. I kick for the surface, fighting the weight of the blacksmith tools, but the current twists and drags and I can't find air. My shoulder rams into another rock and pain splinters down my arm. I scramble for a purchase and manage to haul myself up enough for one breath. Then I'm under again.

The curse tightens over my limbs, and my senses go dull and then sharp again. I kick, propelling myself toward the Hidden Lands, even though I have no idea what direction is up. A compass inside of me points directly toward my destination. A moment ago, I was too tired to do anything beyond sit in my boat, but now I swim harder than ever in my life. The current propels me forward and I gasp a lungful of air when I crest a wave. Then I'm down again.

I lose track of how many times it happens—half a lungful of air, half a lungful of water, and the turbulent sea everywhere. My skin goes from burning with cold to numb. Even when my arms and legs feel too heavy to move, I'm pulled forward, more by the curse than my own will.

My foot hits something submerged, but it isn't the cutting rocks. It's soft and gives way. I push myself off from it and find air again. Warm air. The water ripples around me, calmly, and I blink the haze out of my eyes. The cove. I'm in the cove.

I settle my feet on the sand, surprised to find I can touch the bottom. But no sooner do I put weight on my legs than my knees give out. I can't tell if I'm injured or just too exhausted to stand. I swim until I can crawl, then drag myself up onto the beach. Digging my fingers into the hot, pale sand, I close my eyes and sink into darkness.

NINETEEN

Kit

Catharine and I emerge from the room once we are composed, long after Byrne must have left. Abram lingers in the main hall. He gives us a concerned look and I muster a small smile.

"We're all right." I answer his unspoken question. "And… back to normal."

Catharine dips her head. "Thank you for your assistance."

"Of course." Abram straightens. "King Byrne stormed out. I'm not sure where he's gone."

"Has Idris returned yet?" I ask.

Abram shakes his head. "I haven't seen him."

I glance at the clock on the mantel. It is only seven, though the night feels much longer. We still have a few hours before the curse will pull Idris away.

"I don't think Idris should go alone," I tell Abram. "I spoke with him earlier, and he seemed… I fear he might do something rash."

Abram frowns. "I'll look for him."

"I have something for him." I touch the bag at my hip. But it doesn't feel right to just pass the skin along like a parcel. "Can you make sure I see him before midnight?"

"Yes. In the meantime, you should both get some food." He glances at Catharine again. "Do you need passage off Skyare?"

"Will your father allow us to stay longer?" she asks. "If he can provide refuge for us, I think we would be safer here."

"I'm sure something can be arranged." Abram steps toward the door. "The hotel serves a good meal. Let me get you both settled, and then I'll go and find my father and explain the situation."

I'm not sure that Abram himself fully understands the situation, but my heart warms with gratitude. He is willing to take our word that something is wrong and act on it without the details.

As I walk with Abram and Catharine out onto the street, I let myself run through the possibilities. To expose Byrne would cost my own reputation. Any prospects I had—such as they were—would dry up immediately and forever. If Byrne could so casually do what he did, why would any other man consider me worthy of more? A familiar question echoes in my mind: What about me is so broken that it attracted Byrne's attention?

I shake my head, trying to banish the thoughts. Catharine accepted me and puts the blame squarely on her father. If she can do it, perhaps others would too.

Perhaps I can.

But even if my reputation were miraculously intact after we made the accusation, there is still little chance Byrne would be punished. He is charismatic, known as a good ruler, seen publicly as a kind father. He would twist our words and, somehow, come out the victim. I don't know what kind of retribution I want, but justice doesn't seem like a possibility.

My joints are less swollen than I remember and though making a fist is not easy, it is *easier.* I wonder if, just as Byrne's attacks woke a "curse" in me, Catharine's kindness has woken something else. I weave a new future in my mind, the threads made from moments I've collected today—Catharine's tight embrace, Idris's earnest gaze. In this future, I am not alone.

The street narrows to only allow two together comfortably. I slow, letting Abram and Catharine ahead of me. As I follow, I catch Abram asking softly, "How are you?"

"A bit shaken," Catharine answers.

His hand moves as if to take hers, but he lets it fall back to his side. Before his hand comes to rest, Catharine extends her fingers and brushes them against his. As I glance away, a tiny glow of happiness grows in my chest.

Abram finds us a private table in the hotel and excuses himself to search for his father and Idris. He promises to bring them back so we can all make a plan together. I hold my bag with its precious skin on my lap, waiting for the chance to tell them the news. While Catharine and I eat, I listen to the murmur of voices and snatches of song in the main room. I wonder whether Idris has eaten, wherever he is. Somewhere outside, a dog barks.

"Shouldn't Abram be back by now?" I ask, my leg bouncing as I watch the clock tick toward eleven. "He's been gone a long time."

"Maybe..."

The dog has been barking for several minutes now with an increasingly frantic edge to it. I wait for someone to go out and calm him, but as the seconds crawl by the howling continues.

Finally, I can't stand to listen anymore and I rise. "I'm going to go make sure that dog's all right."

"All right." Catharine begins to get up too.

"It's fine. I'll be right back." I slip out of the door, leaving her by the warm fire.

The hotel has grown crowded, with enough noise in the main room that the dog's barks are lost amidst the talk. I slip out into the cold dark, pulling my pelisse closer round me. I follow the sound of the barking round the side of the hotel to the stables, where the door sits closed. Beyond it, the dog has worked himself into a frenzy.

"Just a moment," I call, raising the latch. "I'm coming."

At the sound of my voice the barks split into whines. I push the door aside and True flings himself in my direction. A rope at his neck jerks him back before he can reach me, and he paws the ground and whimpers.

"True!" I hurry to him and work at the knot on his collar. "What in the world...?"

True licks my wrist frantically, wagging his tail so hard it whips me. The knot only grows tighter as he pulls and with my stiff fingers it takes me a minute to get it loose. The moment he is free, True bolts for the door.

"True!" I run after him. He makes straight for the harbor and as soon as he reaches the water's edge he paces the shoreline, whining. I look to the boats pulled up on their nousts and then out at the ones moored near the pier. Though it is still an hour till midnight, Idris's yole is missing.

My blood goes cold. Idris has left True. I am not sure exactly what that means, but I know it's bad. I turn away from the harbor and scan the surrounding streets. Three men are speaking in one of the nearby squares and I recognize Abram's glasses. I take a step forward and check myself. Across from Abram stands Byrne, gesturing to emphasize whatever he is saying.

I can't risk being seen by Byrne. But Abram needs to know something is very wrong.

I grab True's collar and haul him round to face the men.

"Look!" I command, pointing. "Look, True! It's Abram!"

True tries to twist toward the water and my fingers pinch as the joints strain. It takes all my strength to keep him facing the right direction.

"Look!" I point again.

Abram steps away from the other two, preparing to depart. At last, True fixes on him. With a wild wiggle, he wrenches out of my hands and flies down the street. I follow in the shadows, though I can't get close enough to hear clearly without stepping into the light of the square. The wind whips the men's voices away from me.

True barrels into Abram, nearly knocking him flat. With an exclamation, Abram drops into a squat, saying something to the dog. I can see the third man clearly now—King Hugh. He speaks quickly, looking around.

The wind stills long enough for me to make out a word. "Idris?"

I press into the alcove of a doorway. When Idris does not emerge, his father walks swiftly toward the harbor. The others hurry to keep up, and the three men pass close by me. As Byrne moves upwind, I catch the faintest hint of his evergreen scent. My stomach twists.

"He's gone," King Hugh says. He swears and turns to Abram. "That settles it. I'm getting the yole ready. We'll need your help to navigate."

"Of course," Abram replies, "if you're really sure…"

"I am." King Hugh hurries toward the docks, Byrne on his heels.

Abram stays where he is, looking down at True as if considering whether he should bring Idris's dog. True whines.

"What are they doing?" I ask, stepping out of my hiding place.

Abram jumps. "Kit!"

"I found True tied up at the hotel," I tell him. "Idris left him there, I think. What's going on?"

"Father is determined to go after him this time," Abram says. "I didn't have a chance to explain about King Byrne—they were already in conversation when I got there and I didn't wish to…"

"Upset him?" I can't keep the disappointment out of my voice.

Abram flushes. "I'm sorry. I should have spoken up."

I can't really blame him, considering *I* have barely spoken against my stepfather. I tuck away my annoyance for later. "What does Byrne have to do with your father sailing after Idris?"

"I don't know. Father was upset about an argument he had with Idris. He wants to go after him and evidently King Byrne is determined to help." Abram rubs his arms against the cold. "I'll have to navigate—no one else knows the way."

I touch the folded selkie skin inside my bag. It thrums with longing. I wonder if it senses the door to the Hidden Lands will soon open. "I'm coming too."

Abram opens his mouth as if to protest, then seems to reconsider. "It will be dangerous, but I could use your help. If Idris is fully enchanted again, you're better at bringing him round than I am."

Warmth spreads over my cheeks and I hope the dark will disguise it.

"But a yole won't leave you any place to hide," Abram continues. He turns toward the harbor and adjusts his glasses, examining the boat the two kings are now preparing. "Will you be all right with Byrne?"

A long, dark journey sitting across from my stepfather sounds like the stuff of nightmares. Even if there are two men with me to act as a buffer, I would do almost anything to avoid it. "If there was a way we could postpone him realizing I am with you, I would be grateful."

Abram nods, thoughtful. "If we took two yoles, I could tell them Jay has come with me."

I hadn't thought of Jay in some time. "Where has Mr. Berd been?"

"Home." Abram looks pained. "He wanted to stay out of your way in case he inadvertently caused more trouble."

I nod, not sure how to feel about someone who thought I would kidnap Catharine.

In my head I trace the watery journey to the Hidden Lands. We will travel without the aid of the calm enchantment. Sailing one yole there safely seems risky—two seems impossible.

At the harbor's edge Byrne steps away from the yole and King Hugh. He calls orders to another, larger ship—one that's being unloaded by various men.

"What are all those trunks?" I ask.

"Your father apparently brought Catharine's dowry with him," Abram says, sounding embarrassed. "I think he was hoping to avoid any further scandal by playing it off that she'd come here to get married."

I'm no longer surprised by the lengths—delusional though they might be—Byrne will go to in his attempts to secure what he wants. His daughters have run away and of course he turns this into an opportunity to force the marriage he needs. I straighten my shoulders. "Hide me in one of those. We'll go on one boat."

Abram nods and starts forward, catching the attention of the two sailors as they set the trunk down. He speaks to them quickly and they open it. Abram waves me over. I check that Byrne and King Hugh are distracted, then dart to Abram's side. The trunk is filled with various silks and fabrics, but the lid has a generous arch to it. When I step in, the fabrics sink low enough that it can be closed over me without much effort. I'm grateful for my own body and its small size. Catharine would not have been able to squeeze into this trunk without holding her knees to her front for the entire journey. I curl to find a comfortable position. Then I am being lifted.

Holding my breath, I listen as the sailors carry me toward the kings.

"Hold on, what are you doing?" comes the voice of Byrne.

King Hugh's voice follows, "Abram, we need to keep the yole light."

"We're going to the Hidden Lands," Abram says, "and we're trying to enter without Idris's aid, assuming he beats us there. We might need gifts and it would take an extra hour to get anything from the manor." A pause. "I'm sure King Byrne would not mind if we use some of the dowry that will soon belong to both families to secure our means to save the bridegroom."

"Of course," Byrne says, with only a flicker of doubt in his voice.

The servants place my chest in the hull. I exhale into the pile of silks. Abram manages to open the lid just a crack, enough to give me some fresh air and a tiny glimmer of light from their lanterns. The sliver of view rests right at my eye level so I can follow their progress without moving more than my gaze. True stations himself in front of the opening like a guard on watch.

King Hugh dismisses the sailors.

"Don't you need the hands?" Byrne asks.

"I won't risk my men," King Hugh replies. "It's enough to take Abram. And I have to emphasize, again, that there's no need for you to put yourself in danger by coming with us."

"Nonsense," Byrne says. "Your family's troubles are mine."

I frown. Byrne must be more desperate for the marriage—and the connections it would bring—than I thought. But though he doesn't know it, Byrne isn't wrong that this involves his family as well—Mother has promised his babe to the Hidden Folk, after all. Another curse I will have to untangle. If he knew his own family's connection with these magic folk, would Byrne so readily venture into their midst? I find it difficult to believe he would involve himself were he not certain that he could skirt any real risk while still benefiting from the outcome.

The yole glides so smoothly from its mooring, I don't realize we've begun to move until we pass the breakwater into the ocean. With a jerk and lurch, the waves rock the boat in long rises and swift falls. The sea is far rougher than during the enchanted journey with Idris, and rougher even than it had been when Catharine and I made our crossing. I swallow, waiting for the nausea to rise up my throat.

But I am in my own body and my own body is apparently seaworthy.

I cannot tell the passage of time from within the trunk. Bursts of rain and ice occasionally splatter the wooden slats of my chest, but I am protected from the elements. True remains steadfast in front of me. I listen to Abram and King Hugh calling instructions to each other. They're both clearly familiar with the water and the yole. These men seem born to ride the seas. Idris's expert maneuvering under enchantment might have had less to do with magic than I suspected.

I hope he hasn't done something foolish.

My mind circles to the cliffside and his words. *I am mesmerized by* you.

A vivid warmth tingles through me. I brace, waiting for the panic or anxiety that often follows. But the fizzy feeling in my gut stays…pleasant.

He was right that this body has held delight. Maybe not as much as it—as I—deserve. But there's still time. I want more. More delight, more joy, more *everything.*

Catharine accepted me with all my complications. Can I trust Idris to do the same?

After lying in the same position for so long, the shoulder bearing my weight aches. Carefully, I begin to dig my arm between layers of fabric, trying to find a way to adjust it enough to ease the pressure. The journey seems to be taking longer than it did when the enchantment spirited Idris along. My fingers brush embroidered cloth and thick wool, seeking gaps between folds to bury my arm deeper.

A shout rises from the deck. Abram. The wind shifts, carrying his words—along with tiny pellets of ice—to me.

"—cliff, just there! It's still open!"

I wonder if, without Idris to speak the words that will let us enter and leave, we will be able to depart come dawn. The spell or password or whatever it is that opens the way has already been uttered and there was no one to add *his lady*, or *his hound*, or *his brother*, or *his father*. Or Byrne's name, I suppose, if someone wanted him to leave again.

Abram calls directions from the bow, and the yole weaves left and right. Round the rocks, I imagine. I try not to think of the razor edges slicing through the water. Idris was guided by magic, in gentler weather and on a smooth tide. I close my eyes and move my free hand into my bag. The velvety fur has a comforting warmth to it. I hold on, praying for safe passage.

Outside, the roar of waves suddenly cuts off. I look through the crack into absolute darkness. We have entered the cave. True's tail thumps against the side of the wooden chest.

Thank you, I think as a follow-up for my prayer.

"We're here," Abram says.

My view lightens, barely, but I can see the shadows of the men as they disembark, which is more than I could make out before. I wait until I hear three pairs of boots splash in the water, and then I carefully lift the lid of the trunk. The men are beyond my sight here. I tilt it back until it rests, fully open, and climb out quietly. True squints his brown eyes at me in a doggy smile, his tail wagging double time.

"Good boy," I whisper.

My hand is still resting on my bag and I move the flap to check the skin. The starlight makes the delicate silvery fur shimmer gently.

"Idris!"

King Hugh's voice jerks me back to the present. Quickly, I close my bag and go to the other side of the yole, True against my leg. Idris is collapsed in the sand at one end of the cove, nearly hidden against the rocky wall. There is no sign of his yole. My chest tightens and I clamber over the gunwale into the shallow water.

King Hugh drops down beside Idris and turns him over, Byrne and Abram just behind. Idris doesn't respond, his head lolling against his father's chest.

My throat tightens and I hurry unsteadily across the shore, my gaze fixed on the men clustered round the body. True pins his ears back but remains beside me.

"Is he alive?" Abram asks.

The cold in my heart steals my breath away.

The pause seems to stretch out and out before King Hugh exhales. "Yes. Yes, he's breathing."

As I reach them, my gaze snags on Byrne. But there's no point in me remaining hidden now. I push in front of my stepfather and kneel in the warm sand.

"Kit!" Byrne exclaims.

I pay him no attention.

"Here." I put a hand on Abram's shoulder and carefully move him aside. Abram did say I was better at bringing Idris back—hopefully I can do it even if he's unconscious.

King Hugh casts me a surprised look, but immediately his attention is back on Idris, propped in his arms. Idris's hands are twitching in a rhythm. I realize there is a faint beat thrumming through the sand. The music from within the Hidden Lands.

"True," I command, patting Idris's chest. True eagerly flops down over Idris, whining and wagging his tail. I fold back the collar of Idris's shirt and place all five fingers of my left hand on his bare collarbone. My face burns, but I ignore the men watching.

I brace for that crack to open in my mind—that war between what I want and what the feral part of me considers safe—as it did last time I touched him like this. But my heart continues steadily. Breathing doesn't hurt. Something in me has changed and I feel…all right. Beautifully, miraculously all right.

I adjust my fingers, taking in the cool feel of his skin, and close my eyes. I imagine a clearing in a forest and I tap my own rhythm in defiance of the Hidden Folk's music. A march like the woodpecker's beat.

"You'll be all right, Idris," I whisper as I tap, tap, tap. "It's safe to come back."

It takes a moment. Then he blinks, eyes unfocused.

My breath whooshes free in relief. At the sound his gaze flicks to me. Before memory or reason has cleared the fog in his eyes, he smiles—natural and nearly sleepy, as if I were the very thing he most wanted to see. I smile back, my hand resting on his chest.

"Idris?" King Hugh asks.

As I shift back to give them space, a hand clamps on my shoulder. And I know it without looking—know its shape and heaviness and grip.

Byrne tugs me away and I struggle to my feet. Abram glances from Idris to me, clearly unsure where to place his worry. King Hugh is speaking softly, his gaze fixed on his son, but I cannot make out the words.

"I'm glad you're here, Kit," Byrne tells me. I steel myself and face him. His nose is swollen where I rammed my head into it earlier, and given a little more time I think he might develop a black eye. He has the nerve to smile, gently as if we were two friends in on a secret. "I wanted to speak with you."

"What could you possibly have to say to me?" My voice comes out hoarse. I wonder, fleetingly, whether he might apologize. Whether I could forgive him, even in a hundred years, much less in this moment.

"Catharine obviously thinks she saw something misleading," he says, dropping his volume.

I almost snort. I had no need to worry about the ethics of forgiveness—he will never ask.

"I want you to assure her that everything is well between us," he goes on. "Nothing must get in the way of these arrangements, you see. No…unpleasant rumors."

"Catharine knows the truth, Your Majesty," I say coldly. "I cannot make her unknow it."

Byrne frowns. "Catharine would believe what you tell her. If you've said something to make her think the worst…"

"Catharine believes what she *saw*," I hiss. "Though I should have told her a long, long time ago."

Byrne's gaze hardens.

"You've hidden in my silence long enough." I pull myself up straight and am surprised to find courage rising as I do. "I won't take ownership for what you've done. It isn't my fault."

"If people hear *stories* from you, it will ruin your family." He steps closer to me. "Your mother, your sister, and even me—your father."

"Oh?" I tilt my head. "I believe you told me you do not want me as a daughter."

With an oath, Byrne lunges for me. But before he can strike, Abram has caught him by one arm—and Idris has caught the other. I stumble back, surprised by the violence in Byrne's expression—and equally surprised that he has been stopped. True jumps in front of me, hackles raised.

Idris hardly seems well enough to stand, but he glances at me with bright awareness.

Byrne relaxes back, giving the princes an apologetic look. "Sorry, lads—not sure what you think is happening, but there is no need to restrain me."

King Hugh steps to my side. "Are you all right, Kit?"

"Yes, thank you," I say, glancing from the king to his sons.

"Tell them that there's no need for this," Byrne says, trying to shake Abram off. "Tell them it's only a family matter."

"You and I are not family. We are *nothing* to each other." I lift my chin. "And as far as I am concerned, after tonight we will never speak again. But I will tell you I am here partially for the sake of your child. The babe my mother bears has been promised to the Hidden Folk. I mean to dissolve that deal. I won't let your sins—or my mother's—steal another life."

Byrne blinks in surprise. Idris passes a hand over his face, the wan exhaustion leaching him of color again.

King Hugh's expression hardens. "This is ridiculous," he snaps. He turns and walks toward the tunnel that connects the cove to the Hidden Lands. "I am done letting children pay for our mistakes."

"Father?" Idris lets go of Byrne and stumbles after him.

Abram hesitates but releases my stepfather at my signal. I hold my bag close to my side, feeling the weight of the skin within. True joins me and we walk with Abram toward the entrance.

"You will ruin everything," Byrne hisses after me.

"Look to your own house," I reply over my shoulder. "I will look to mine."

TWENTY

Idris

The light of the dancing hall stings my eyes as I hurry after Father. I am not sure how he came to be here—I don't remember anything between the heat of the sand on my cheek and waking: Kit's hand on my collarbone, father's arm round me, True lying on my chest. All I know is that my attempt to remove myself from everyone forever has ended up with even more people following me.

Abram comes to my side and Kit to my other. For a moment, I study Kit. She's back in her own body. With the direct, transparent honesty of her expression, I never mistook her for Catharine.

"The wand worked?" I ask, my voice ragged from salt water.

She nods, then her eyes harden with determination. "And I think I've found another way to help you."

"So has Father," Abram says, his tone grave.

I open my mouth to ask what he means, but before I can, Father steps into the dancing chamber and the music abruptly dies.

The dancers turn as one to face us. Tonight, bright crystal glows across the ceiling, large stalactites and stalagmites forming columns that don't quite meet in the middle. The ground is covered in a few inches of water, just enough to turn it into a mirror.

Beyond the throng, the queen sits on her throne—straight and regal, black eyes burning as she regards my father. He pauses a moment on the threshold, then marches forward. The Hidden Folk part to make a path from him to the queen. I follow after. Other than our steps, which splash loudly, the hall is eerily quiet. When my feet falter, Kit slips her callused hand into mine. I glance down, surprised. Her touch, I know, is not easily given, and I feel humbler and stronger for it.

Father stops before the queen and bows. "Hidden One."

"Hugh." She watches him icily. A crown of delicate seashells adorns her white-blonde hair and a gown of green silk flares out around her knees. "I did not invite you to my ball."

"You did once," he replies.

"And if I recall—" she lifts her chin—"you declined that invitation."

"I have come to beg your lenience." Father stands straight as a mast. "I understand that our family harmed you and that a price must be paid to atone for it. I have tried to find other ways of sparing my sons from this price, but Idris has helped me see we cannot escape our legacy by running or hiding. So I have come to pay it."

I start forward. "Father, no—"

"Let me do this, son." He turns toward me and his gaze sharpens, fierce, before it suddenly changes. Softer. Sad.

"You have done all you could and I should have stepped in sooner. I should never have let this pass to you. I won't see you die for something that should never have been offered to you as a choice in the first place."

I open and close my mouth, desperate for a way to make him see reason. For a way to show him that the old crime isn't his fault any more than it was mine. But the irony of finding myself on this side of the argument steals my words away.

"You were right," Father adds. "I made you the man who would take this on, who would cling to it alone. And I'm sorry, but you are *not* alone. I will not let you do this alone."

I take an unsteady step forward, with Abram and Kit still supporting me.

"Id," Abram murmurs. "Let us help you. There's no need to carry it by yourself."

"You can't be serious," I say to my brother. All of my attempts to protect my family have shattered around me. "You can't let him do this!"

Abram meets my eyes. "We love you, Idris. Let us fight for you."

Father turns to face the Hidden Queen again. "I claim the rest of Idris's dancing days. Look at him—you won't have another week at this rate and you'll get at least a few months out of me."

The Hidden Queen inclines her head, considering.

"Wait, wait," I protest, stumbling forward and fishing in my pockets. The blacksmith's tools are still inside, miraculously. "I came tonight to try to remove the iron shoes. I know it's the least we can do. I didn't—I *don't*—mean it to be a bargaining chip. But maybe, if I can do it, you might extend mercy to my father and brother?"

The Hidden Folk nearest us move back another few paces at the sight of the iron in my hands and whispers spread across the crowd. I watch the Hidden Queen. Her serene mask slips, revealing something young and vulnerable in her pale face. Fear—and *hope*.

She takes a shallow breath and pulls her long skirt to one side. "You may try."

I move forward and sink down in front of her feet. The iron shoes are crude, little more than blocks of metal. Where they touch her skin, livid blue lines flare up her legs. I set the tools beside me and select the nail puller. When I tentatively prop her right foot up, she hisses in pain. It is a strangely human sound and my grip weakens as uncertainty flares through me. I don't want to hurt her even more.

The Hidden Folk still stand at a distance, murmuring but apparently unwilling or unable to come closer to the iron. Instead, Kit steps to the left of the Hidden Queen. She tucks something under her arm, then takes the Hidden Queen's hand and holds it tightly.

Kit gives me an encouraging nod.

I try to slide the nail puller's notch under the old nail head at the bottom of the shoe, but the nail head is almost welded to the metal round it. I angle the puller in a different direction and push. My strength is even weaker than before—I can't get enough force to wedge the puller into place.

Someone kneels beside me and Abram takes the nail puller.

“Hold her foot,” he says, repositioning the tool. He glances up at the Hidden Queen. “This will hurt, I’m sure.”

“It has never stopped hurting,” she murmurs.

I close my hands round her foot, trying to keep it steady. Abram takes a deep breath, then shoves the puller under the nail head. With a scraping and a sickeningly fleshy sound, he maneuvers the nail until it’s loose enough to grab. He takes hold of the head and eases the nail free. It clatters to the ground beside us, coated in sea-foam.

The Hidden Queen shudders but lets no noise escape. I adjust my hands over the shoe, glancing at Abram. His face is a little green, but he turns to the next nail. Together, we extract four more from this foot. When they are scattered around us, Father moves beside Abram and helps us ease the shoe off her foot. The skin that’s revealed is raw and burned as if the hot metal had been poured over her mere minutes ago. When the last of the shoe slides free of her toes, the Hidden Queen lets out a cry, leaning to one side on her throne. Kit wraps her spare arm round the Hidden Queen’s shoulders.

We move to the other foot and the process begins again. It is slow and sweat stands out on my forehead even though I am not the one doing the most labor. The only sound in the hall is the scrape and clang of metal, along with the rare, almost inaudible whimpers of the Hidden Queen.

At last, the second shoe comes free. We set it down beside the first. Father and Abram help me stand, and we retreat to give the Hidden Queen space. Kit makes to do the same, but the Hidden Queen's hand tightens on hers, keeping her there.

"I have something for you as well," Kit whispers. She pulls the bundle from under her arm—a silky fur of some kind. A selkie skin. "Is this yours?"

The Hidden Queen stares. Slowly, she reaches out and touches the fur. Her fingers tremble.

Kit leans forward and spreads the skin across the Hidden Queen's lap. It drapes over her elegantly, shimmering in the light of the walls.

"It *is* mine," the Hidden Queen says, her black eyes shining.

Kit smiles in a wavering way. She steps back and I go to her side. A tear slips down her cheek when she raises her gaze to mine, and my heart twists. I reach for her and to my surprise she gulps a breath and wraps her arms round me. My chin rests on her hair and I tighten my hold on her.

"Are you all right?" I ask, close to her ear.

"I will be," she says into my shoulder.

A moment later, she pulls back. Her smile is steadier now. She slips her hand into mine and we turn again to the Hidden Queen.

"Thank you," says the queen. Her voice is low. "I have longed for this."

Father shakes his head. "We have only undone what Mervyn did, if even that."

"True. And no retribution will restore the years he took from me." She considers us, clustered together, and I cannot read the expression on her face. "You would still serve out the dancing days?"

"For the sake of the ones I love," Father says. "I am prepared."

The Hidden Queen's gaze falls to my hand, clasped round Kit's. "And you, sister, trust these Skyare men?"

Kit looks at Father, Abram, and finally me. She nods, once.

"If you can trust, perhaps so can I." She pauses a long time, then her shoulders relax as if relieved of a weight. "Hugh, I will not hold you or your kin to the price. Your offer and your sons' actions have proven that your line has grown very different from Mervyn. May it continue to be so. You are free to leave."

The itching in my legs, the beat that pounded in the back of my head, recedes. I am suddenly light. I am free. Father and Abram are stumbling through thanks, but their words blur in my head.

Kit studies me, searching for a sign. As shock and relief chase each other through my mind, I take the chance to look at her—really *look* at her, Kit, in her own body—the way I should have the night of the ball. Her eyes swim between green and a golden brown like a shallow creek in sunlight. Freckles spread vivid and small across her cheeks, then bigger and fainter on her forehead and chin. I envy the sun that kissed her skin and made them. Her lips are pink and full, pressed together in concern.

I keep my attention on her lips as I say, "The curse has broken."

Her smile starts in the left corner of her mouth. Then it spreads quickly—wide and reckless across her face, shining from her eyes. She clasps her hands round the back of my neck and I feel her smile even there—in the pressure of her fingertips under my hair and the gentle confidence in her touch.

She presses her face against my chest. I close my arms round her, reeling in the perfect way she fits against me. My surprise melts into something giddy and bubbling. I laugh into her hair and feel her smile even wider, the crinkle of her cheeks against my shirt.

Kit lets me go and someone else grabs my shoulder. I turn to find Father standing beside me. Before I can say a word, he closes me in an embrace. A warm glow spreads right through me. This time, I really feel it.

I am not alone.

TWENTY-ONE

Kit

While Idris and his father collect themselves, I glance around the hall. Speir has come to the edge of the crowd, his gaze fixed on the Hidden Queen's face in astonished joy. A rare smile flashes across her mouth and Speir returns it.

I take a step toward them. I still need to rescue my unborn sibling from any curses, deals, or trades. A hand catches my arm and Byrne firmly pulls me toward him. I had never really forgotten he was there, but the suddenness of his touch makes me flinch.

"Which of these creatures did your mother speak with?" he asks in my ear. "We will certainly see the magical side of that settled here and now. And once your mother has the babe, I'll make sure the matter is settled at home too."

I tighten my jaw and nod toward Speir. I have no intention of letting Byrne harm any of us ever again, but if he wants to try to save his child—it is the least he can do.

"You," the Hidden Queen says, her gaze fixing on Byrne's hand on my arm. "I did not give you leave to enter and I do not see how you are connected with these events." She tilts her head. "You would have committed violence on my land."

I feel the phantom sting of the blow he hadn't landed.

Byrne pauses, then straightens. "My judgment lapsed for only a few seconds. But my true purpose in being here is to beg for the freedom of my unborn child."

"Your son and heir," Speir adds with a trouble-making smile.

So it is a boy.

"Yes." Byrne's eyes gleam with eagerness. He glances back to King Hugh, now standing between his two sons. "I, too, wish to offer myself in my son's place."

A silence falls for several breaths. Byrne's sudden selflessness tastes false and sour in my mouth. I glance toward Speir, wondering if I should point out that his curse has already been undone—I have been restored to my body. The deal my mother made has been broken, with no need for any further sacrifice.

"I would accept this exchange," Speir says. He adds, looking straight at me, "Magic always comes at a cost and the magic was spent even if the curse has ended."

The queen leans back in her throne. Without pain holding her rigid, she almost lounges there. Relaxed. Comfortable. She props her chin on her hand, considering Byrne with cool interest. There are two kings, two princes, and a princess in this room, but power radiates from *her.*

It makes the air weighty as the fate of my unborn sibling dangles between us.

At last, she says, “Very well. I accept these terms.”

My heart lifts a fraction. The babe spared and Byrne trapped. Can it be?

Byrne watches the Hidden Queen expectantly. Then he shifts his weight back and forth. Finally, he says, “Is that all?”

“What more do you want?” the queen asks, lifting one pale eyebrow. “Your babe will be free to live his human life. And you will remain here, as our servant. Exactly as you have requested.”

“B-but—” Byrne sputters. He points to King Hugh. “You spared him. How is my offer any less noble?”

The queen’s black eyes crinkle at the corners. Her silence grows through the room, its own presence. She does not answer because she does not care to. Because Byrne is not worth the words.

He seems to shrink. I watch him feel it—watch him feel small, perhaps for the first time in his life—and a slow *rightness* grows in my chest. He glances around the chamber wildly, a fox in a snare. The room is full of more and more silence. The Hidden Folk exude absolute indifference and I watch in mild fascination as his panic rises under it.

“This is ridiculous!” he shouts. He makes for the exit, toward the cove.

The Hidden Folk do not move to stop him.

Byrne hesitates as if unnerved, then marches forward again.

I check the faces around me. Surely they won't just let him walk out? That isn't how a deal with the Hidden Folk works.

At the opening of the tunnel, Byrne stops again—this time abruptly as if he's run into something. He mutters to himself and then puts a hand to the air and pushes.

"I wouldn't—" Abram calls.

My stepfather does not heed him. He shoves harder. Suddenly, a cry rips out of him, and he stumbles back, turning toward us in the process. His hand has blackened and as I watch it disintegrates to ash.

"Enough," the Hidden Queen says, almost bored. She motions to an attendant. "Put him to work."

Byrne babbles, looking between his blackened wrist and the Folk and me. When the attendants grab him, he tries to jerk away—but they pull him deeper into the cave, toward one of the tunnels without any effort. He roars curses, but his words are all bluster and no sense. I stand where I am.

When Byrne disappears—when his voice suddenly cuts off—I breathe.

It feels like the first real, deep breath I've taken in two years.

"Come, sister." The Hidden Queen beckons me to her. "Let me see you."

I step to her and she holds out her hands palm up on her lap. Uncertainly, I set my warped hands on top of her perfect, pale ones.

The Hidden Queen studies my fingers—bloated, crooked, and broken—and says, "You chose well."

"What?"

"You chose well not to use the wand on this." She traces one swollen joint. Her touch is feather-soft. "It is more ordinary and terrible than magic. The wand would have done nothing to help it."

I shoot a glare at Speir, still standing near the throne. I clearly remember him asking, *"Didn't your mother tell you the wasting is a curse?"*

He shrugs. "I only reminded you what your mother said. *I* never told you it was magic."

The Hidden Queen's words settle, and my annoyance sinks into something colder and deeper.

"So…it isn't a curse?" I whisper. "King Byrne isn't to blame?"

It is only my own fault, I think. *My own body.*

"I did not say that." The Hidden Queen tucks a strand of hair behind my ear like my grandmother used to do. "Your world is complex. Many circumstances met to create you as you stand before me. Blame and chance, inheritance and circumstance. I cannot read the threads."

My throat tightens.

"But…" The Hidden Queen's voice softens, more like Catharine when she's uncertain than the unshakable wisdom of a grandmother. "Is there not something to be said for the fact that you are here—you, *yourself*, wholly as you are?"

We both look down at her feet, still inflamed and streaked with sea-foam. We are both ourselves, wholly, in a way we would never have been without our pasts. Is there something redemptive in that—something that makes who we are worth what we've suffered?

"I don't know," I whisper.

The Hidden Queen smiles and leans her forehead against mine. She smells of the north wind, of changing tides and far-off storms.

Quietly, she says, "Neither do I."

✦

I join Idris and his family as they give formal farewells. True walks beside Idris and me to the exit tunnel. At the far end, in sight of the cove, a sudden pressure rises before us like an unseen wall. I hesitate, visions of ash in my mind, but the next moment the force has dissipated. I move forward again, uninhibited.

"She's really let us go," Abram says, looking around with relief.

King Hugh continues to the water without stopping. "Idris, why don't you rest while we check the yole? We came near some of the rocks and I want to make sure we're seaworthy before we try that again."

Idris glances at me.

"I'll stay," I tell him. "I wouldn't be much help, anyway."

We find a spot on the warm sand and sink down. True tucks himself against Idris's side. I arrange my skirt round my legs, then lean back, digging my hands into the soothing heat and tilting my head back. The sky above us, framed by the black edges of the cliffs, is filled with stars scattered in strange constellations. As I watch, green and blue light drifts across them like a sheer shawl.

Idris leans back, mimicking my pose, but his fingers in the sand aren't quite close enough to touch mine. I let myself study him while he studies the stars. Dark hollows under his eyes speak to his sleeplessness, and in the dim light I cannot tell if color has returned to his skin. But his eyes are clear and focused. I hope that, with his lively spirit, his recovery will only be the work of a few months.

I curl my fingers in the sand, feeling the joints aching already from leaning on them. My stomach tightens. Not a curse. Just wasting without a cure.

"How are you?" Idris asks. "That...with Byrne..."

"I'm fine." I dig my fingers deeper in the sand. "There was never any... That is, I never thought of him as a father. I won't miss him."

Idris doesn't answer, and I wonder if I've been too harsh. If perhaps I should, at least, pretend some sadness that a man has been trapped in the Hidden Lands forever.

"I didn't mean that," Idris says hesitantly. "Or—I wasn't thinking of him being taken away. He almost hit you, Kit."

"Oh," I say without thinking, "that was nothing."

I bite my lip, wanting to swallow the words back but also feeling—strangely—lighter now that they're out. Out of the corner of my eye, I can see Idris looking at me. Studying me. A weight settles in my chest and I search for words. But I'm not sure now is the right time. We only have a few minutes before we're called to the boat and even many hours would not be nearly enough time.

"It... He..." My breath trembles down my throat. "He's done worse."

I can't seem to find the sounds I need. Frustration and shame begin coiling in my stomach and I'm sinking into a spiral when Idris's voice pulls me back to the present.

"All right," he says. He moves his hand closer to mine, so that just our fingertips touch. "We will face the worst of it, then, together. Whenever you are ready."

I raise my gaze to his face, surprised to find my vision blurred. His eyes are kind.

"Whatever has happened," he says, "I am with you."

A wild relief sears through me. Two tears drop down my cheeks, but they're full of something pure and vivid. Not sadness. Hope, maybe.

"I think," he says, brushing away my tears with his knuckles, "the point maybe isn't so much...who is hurt and how long and how badly, but who stands by us before and through and after. The secret is to not try to do it alone."

"You've grown wise in the past hour," I say, gently teasing.

He nods toward Abram and King Hugh. "I had good teachers."

But though he nods toward the yole, his gaze remains fixed on me. I feel my cheeks heating and look away.

"Kit," he says, soft as a whisper, "I—If it would help, if you wanted—I wish I could be with you in the *after*."

My heart pounds. I stare at the sand, braced for nausea to follow.

But it doesn't.

He pauses, then adds, "Which will probably turn into the *before* and the *through* and the *after* all over again, given the way life seems to work. But...would you let me? Be with you, I mean?"

The wounded part of me clamors, *Curl up, hide, flee!* If I encourage him, I'll enter uncertain ground. I would be safer alone.

But I am not my wounds. Taking a deep breath, I make myself look him in the face, make myself meet his eyes. His mouth quirks in an uncertain smile, but his eyes shine with sincerity. And a new feeling burns through my fear and my ghosts. It steals my breath, painful but good.

My fate isn't set by Byrne. It isn't even set by my own warped bones.

I can claim the future I want. And I want a bright one.

Joy bubbles in my stomach. Catharine is going to love this part of the story.

I open my mouth to answer, but King Hugh's voice cuts across my thoughts.

"We're ready!" he calls. "Just needed some minor repairs. Let's go."

Startled, I scramble to my feet. I'd nearly forgotten we weren't alone. When Idris struggles to rise, I give him my hand. He takes my arm instead, to avoid putting pressure on my fingers, and gets to his feet. Even after he does, he doesn't let me go.

I guide him toward the water. Every step lessens my doubt and a new, shining certainty bubbles up inside me. *I can claim the future I want.*

King Hugh leans over the yole's gunwale to help Idris board. "Kit, it occurs to me you haven't asked for a reward for this third trip to the Hidden Lands."

I blink at him. "What?"

"You asked for silver the first night, gold the next." He passes Idris to Abram as Idris makes his way to the bow of the yole. "But this time you've helped save my son's life. What can I give you for that?"

I consider his question, my skirt in my hand as I climb over the side. My pulse turns to fire. Suddenly, I know exactly what I want.

Abram and Hugh help me in, but before I can follow Idris to a seat, I gulp a breath and turn to the king.

"I would ask for Idris."

Behind King Hugh, I see Idris break into a wide grin.

King Hugh lifts his eyebrows, clearly surprised.

"I mean," I blurt, my face hot, "I would ask you don't engage him to Catharine, and perhaps you'll allow us to court, and maybe in a little while we—I mean, it would be up to him and we'd have to see how it goes—but...I suppose I'm asking for the chance to try."

King Hugh takes one look at Idris and then dips his head. "Very well. Take him, with my blessing, and whenever you are both ready."

While Abram and King Hugh bring the yole about, I join Idris near the bow. I'm almost shaking with giddiness and embarrassment.

"Well, then," he says with a grin. "I suppose that answers my question."

I can't help but grin back. Idris takes my hand and lightly kisses my fingers. I tighten my grip on him. We emerge from the cave. A rush of cold wind brings color to our cheeks, and we watch as the sun rises with the gale. Together.

✦

The sky is still pink-tinged when we come to Stromwell harbor. Men rush to help secure the boat, questions radiating from their glances at King Hugh, Idris, Abram, and me.

"I think the word is out, Father," Idris says. He and I are standing shoulder to shoulder, but I edge back a little to make some distance between myself and the men's hungry curiosity.

King Hugh huffs a sigh and steps onto the dock. He announces, "Yes, we have been to the Hidden Lands and, yes, you'll all get to hear the tale. But you'll hear it faster if there's a warm breakfast waiting for us at the hotel." Singling out a boy, he says, "Could you please go and let the cook know we are coming and we are hungry."

The boy races toward the Stromwell Hotel. The crowd keeps growing, their murmurs getting louder. Abram disembarks and joins his father in conversation with a uniformed man—the dockmaster, I think.

Watching the king, I ask Idris, "What version do you think he'll tell?"

Idris rests a hand on True's head, thoughtful. "I'm not sure, but I hope he'll tell the truth."

In the distance, where even more people are gathering in the city square, a young woman catches my attention. Catharine. She had been sitting on the bench beside Mr. Muir, but now she rises. She waves to me, a relieved smile breaking across her face.

My heart lifts at the sight of her. And then swoops down all at once.

King Byrne has not returned.

I chart her gaze as she takes us all in: King Hugh, Idris, Abram. Me.

The word is out, Idris had said. Word that included her father boarding this boat.

Her smile fades and her eyes widen. We are across the crowd from each other. There are too many people, and more and more arriving. Their words buzz and rise and already I hear snatches of the stories they're telling each other. The way they're already weaving the last few minutes into something new.

"Can you get me to Catharine?" I ask Idris, grabbing his sleeve and pointing.

Idris nods and pushes ahead of me. The people make way reluctantly, some trying to stop him to talk, but he waves them aside with jokes about breakfast. True stays close by me, forcing the crowd back a little more.

My chest squeezes as I try to think through what to say, how to tell her. Byrne was a monster, but he wasn't a monster to her. I know what it is to lose a father. And soon the tale will be everywhere—the king of Aberloche, trapped in the Hidden Lands as a servant. Everyone will be adding their own slant, their own twist. It will be their retelling, but I am the original. It is my story, at least to begin with.

Do I tell her my version—about a man cowardly and cruel, who tricked himself into his fate? Or do I tell her another version—about a man who traded himself for his child?

At last, we reach Catharine where she stands by the bench. Mr. Muir has vanished, and in the sea of movement and noise she is a lone, still island. But when I come in reach, she grabs my hands and studies me.

"None of that, Kit," she says before I can find the right words. "I can see you thinking. You don't need to shield me anymore."

I'm caught off guard and simply blink at her. I'm vaguely aware of Idris turning away from us, engaging nearby people in conversation to give at least the illusion of privacy.

"My father went with you and he has not come back?" Catharine reads the answer in my face and nods to herself. Her lip trembles, just for a moment, and then she schools her expression into brave determination. "Don't hide it from me, please. I want to know."

I exhale, relieved and grateful. I have been so used to protecting her, I did not realize I was already twisting my words to find the kindest ones. "It might be painful," I warn her.

"You've carried the pain long enough." She presses her thumb against my palm. "Let me take a turn."

"Very well," I say, closing my fingers round Catharine's. "Let me tell you my story."

ACKNOWLEDGMENTS

The kernels of this book began with Margaret Mayo's *Magical Tales from Many Lands*, which is where I first read the folk fairy tale "Kate Crackernuts." The story stuck in my head, and a few years later, in the early stages of my PhD study, I came across it again in Donald Smith's *The Anthology of Scottish Folk Tales*—a version of the tale written by Orkney folklorist Tom Muir. The magic, relationship between the stepsisters, and romance with the princes immediately caught my attention. I knew then that this was a story I wanted to retell.

I owe a great thanks to my support system throughout my studies. Thank you to Lucy Christopher, Steve Voake, and CJ Skuse for being a consistent source of challenge and encouragement. Thank you to Sabrin Hasbun—your calming words and straightforward solutions have saved me so much angst. And thank you to the rest of my Bath Spa University gang. I was blessed to walk this path with you, if only for a while.

Thank you to my lion-hearted agent Amber Caravéo, as well as my lovely editors Tamara Grasty (Page Street

Publishing) and Katie Jennings (Rock the Boat), who all worked their magic to make this story shine. Also Celia Tang and Christin Engelberth for their gorgeous cover art! And Hayley Gundlach, Meg Palmer, Emma Hardy, Rosie Stewart, Rowan Jackson, Rob Wilding, Mark Rusher, Paul Nash, Laura McFarlane, Francesca Dawes, Julian Ball, Kobe Grant, and Hayley Warnham, who all had a hand in sending this book into the world.

Hats off to Megan, my niece, who joined me in my research by reading an extensive number of retellings, discussing her opinion as a fourteen-year-old (and then when she was fifteen, sixteen, seventeen, and so on). She even went so far as to travel to Orkney with me one stormy autumn.

Visiting Orkney (first in a gloriously sunny June, then an atmospheric October) left an imprint on my heart that remains. I stepped out of lockdown, where I had been alone for many months as an immunocompromised woman, and the great endless skies of these islands woke something I thought had died in me. Wonder.

An enormous thank you to Tom Muir and Lynn Barbour, as well as the staff at Kirbuster Farm Museum and at Skaill House. Your collective expertise was immensely helpful. Tom, I hope you don't mind I've used you for inspiration in my retelling.

Thank you also to Rebecca Harris, whose expert skills in driving on tiny lanes is only to be topped by her enthusiasm for folktales and history. And thank you to Mary Cate Miller for quickly answering some horse-related queries when I was on a frantic deadline. Thank you to Lisa M., Hannah R., and Louise G.—you know why.

Thank you to Mom, who did everything she could to make sure I had the resources I needed for my quests abroad. Thank you to Dad, who in addition to being a rock also used his sailing knowledge to help the scenes with yoles. (Any mistakes that remain are mine.) The two of you are my resilience.

I must also thank Maeve, whose mischief and snuggles and doggy-snoring kept me laughing through the darkest parts of my journey. I would not have stayed in the UK without you, pup, and my life would have been the worse for it.

Gareth, thank you for encouraging my neuropathways to connect in new patterns…which is really just another way of saying, "I love you."

Finally, I want to acknowledge the crafter of all stories and all wondrous islands. You are the God who sees me through my trauma, my illness, my everything. Keep the plot twists coming.

© Claire Roige

ALYSSA HOLLINGSWORTH was born in small-town Milton, Florida, but life as a roving military kid soon mellowed her (unintelligibly strong) Southern accent. Wanderlust is in her blood, and she's always waiting for the wind to change. Stories remain her constant.